My
Not So
Functional
Family

Bridie Jabour is a writer who has worked as a journalist for News Corp, Fairfax and Guardian Australia. *My Not So Functional Family* is her first novel.

My Not So Functional Family

Bridie Jabour

ZAFFRE

First published in Australia as *The Way Things Should Be* in 2018 by Echo
First published in Great Britain in 2019 by
ZAFFRE
80–81 Wimpole St, London W1G 9RE

A CIP catalogue record for this book is
available from the British Library.

ISBN: 978-1-78576-928-3

Also available as an ebook

1 3 5 7 9 10 8 6 4 2

Typeset by IDSUK (Data Connection) Ltd
Printed and bound in Great Britain by Clays Ltd, Elcograf S.p.A.

Zaffre is an imprint of Bonnier Books UK
www.bonnierbooks.co.uk

For Poor Matt

Chapter 1

Winston was like every other home town in our collective history in that it was incredibly dull but had the power to both enchant and provoke regression in its former inhabitants. It was the beginning of spring so it was a particularly dangerous time to return – the bitumen was warm enough to give off the smell of your childhood when the rain hit and every flower seemed to be in technicolour.

If that was not enough to give a 28-year-old woman whiplash from the nostalgia, Claudia Carter had returned that September to get married. Despite being the perfectly average age to do such a perfectly average thing, Claudia was feeling radical. The idea of marriage still seemed so foreign to her that it was almost subversive.

This was just one of the many ridiculous things that crossed her mind as she sat on a kitchen island in her mother's house, listening to her mother cataloguing her younger sister's flaws.

'And you know, out of all of you, Poppy was the one I breastfed the longest,' Rachel told Claudia, 'so it's bullshit that it fosters a bond.' Rachel stabbed viciously at the sausages browning in the pan in front of her as she spoke. Rachel subscribed to the idea that cooking dinner was some form of martyrdom.

Rachel's list of grievances was familiar. Her youngest daughter Poppy did not phone her 'Mother'. Poppy never said sorry. Poppy expected everyone to do the things she wanted to do, go to the places she wanted to go for dinner. Poppy always said exactly what she thought. ('That skirt is ugly. Why don't you cut your hair? Your best friend is a monster.')

The truth being that Poppy was – in fact – just like her mother.

At the core of Rachel's gripes, although she would be insulted if it was ever actually suggested to her, was that Poppy did not ask permission to do anything, and even though they were all adults, her children were all expected to ask permission. Claudia did a good job of pretending to ask permission. Poppy, on the other hand, never bothered pretending anything.

'How long did you breastfeed her for?' Claudia asked abruptly.

Her mother looked at her blankly. 'What? Oh, eighteen months.'

Claudia snorted. 'So she could say words and you were still putting your tit in her mouth?' She knew it was somehow wrong to be grossed out, probably something to do with the patriarchy, but it was too juicy. So she filed it away for further mocking at a later date with a more receptive audience.

Poppy was due to arrive tomorrow; their brother was already here, upstairs, avoiding all women, and Claudia's best friend

Nora would arrive in just a few days. Claudia worried that this would be the spark to quickly engulf the bone-dry kindling of the family dynamics. Everything a woman feels for her sister – protectiveness, envy, passion, competition – is magnified twenty-fold when her best friend is around.

And the longer they all hung around Winston the more they would all regress. There would be screaming at each other. Last time they'd met up, Claudia had screamed at Poppy, telling her that (at twenty-five) she had fucked her life up and destroyed Mum and Dad. So Poppy had thrown a wine glass that had shattered all over Claudia's chest. The next morning Poppy had got up and left and they had not spoken since.

And now Claudia was getting married in a week.

Last to arrive would be lovely Dylan, a crucial element for the marriage. His presence would help diffuse any tension between the siblings. That was the kind of man he was: soothing, reassuringly sane.

Claudia was perched at a solid oak island, so close to the gas stove she could reach out and grab her mother if she wanted. The island was too big for the space, of course – it always had been – but Rachel had fallen in love with it, and when she fell in love with something, her steely determination to make it work could only be worn down over painful decades. The kitchen was old but all the utensils were brand new, bought on a glossy-magazine-abetted rampage. She had not bothered to replace the stove, although it was entirely possible it was older than her. But her knives, toaster and kettle all matched and all gleamed.

Claudia had spent her late teenage years living in the house, an inheritance from Rachel's mother, but today she was not

3

comfortable here. Why wasn't she comfortable here? When had this town stopped being her home?

'I thought you would be more excited.' Rachel glanced across the kitchen island and eyed Claudia, who kept her head down. She was fiddling with her ring.

'I am!' Claudia responded brightly.

'Your dress is beautiful. You're going to look beautiful, don't worry about that,' her mother said. 'And you look very slim, you've always been so slim,' Rachel continued, admiringly.

'Yes, well,' Claudia said, picking at her ring again, before looking up and smiling sweetly back at her mum. 'I've always had such motivation.'

Her mother let the comment blow past her: a piece of interloping dust, never to be thought of again. Rachel had endured a lifetime of commentary from her own mother about her weight, who had endured a lifetime of commentary from *her* mother. You might as well feel guilty about the sky being blue if you were going to feel guilty about teaching a girl her size mattered.

Despite being in her sixties, Rachel remained a very attractive woman. She was the only mother at the high school gates who had not conceded her femininity by cutting her hair short; she wore her silver-streaked hair carefully styled with three blow-dries a week. Sometimes, just looking at her mother's figure made Claudia want to sit down, contemplating the sheer amount of effort that went into maintaining it. The daily cycling, the aqua-aerobics classes, the pacing around the house with weights strapped to her ankles, the measuring out of portions. Rachel was the kind of thin that required an immense amount of time and effort; daily self-denials that ensured she remained under sixty kilograms when over sixty years of age. On top of all of that Rachel was just pretty – radiant, even. This hadn't quite been passed on to any of her daughters, who had been polluted by their father's genes, their eyes slightly too far apart and mouths too narrow. Even with youth on their side they did not feel they had a patch on their mother, something they had each made an uneasy peace with towards the end of their teenage years.

Rachel shifted from one bare and pedicured foot to the other. 'I'm still not sure about the bridesmaid dresses you know,' she said.

Claudia exhaled; she had not wanted a bridal party but her mother had called her sobbing about the prospect of her sisters being left out of the wedding. 'It will look so odd if you are standing at the front of the church with nobody around you,' she had wailed down the phone, so Claudia had acquiesced, just as she had by agreeing to a church venue – she had wanted a garden wedding – and to holding it in Winston. She and Dylan had originally wanted to marry in a coastal village halfway between the towns in which they'd grown up.

'If I'm going to have bridesmaids, I definitely do not want to go the full matchy-matchy,' Claudia told her mother firmly.

'Well, just in case you change your mind, I popped down to the dress shop and put a dress like Poppy's on hold in Zoe's size as well. I think when you see them standing next to each other at the dress shop you will see how funny it looks if they are in different dresses to each other.'

'You really shouldn't have done that.' Claudia emphasised the 'shouldn't'. 'I'm not worried about how their dresses are going to look.'

'Well, what are you worried about then?' her mother asked her.

'What do you mean?'

'If you're not worried about how the dresses are going to look, why are you so agitated?'

'I'm not agitated. I'm just sitting here.'

'Well, since you're not agitated and you're not doing anything useful, can you finish these sausages?'

Claudia took the tongs from her mother and watched her walk to the bathroom for what she knew would be the precise length of time it took for dinner to be finished. Rachel might have seen the martyrdom potential in cooking dinner, but that did not mitigate the tediousness of the task.

Claudia started turning the sausages with her left hand so she could see her glinting engagement ring, picked out and paid for by her at an antique fair, almost on a whim, when she was feeling particularly dreary about her job and prospects. It had been so long since she had felt excitement in her life, but the most drastic thing she could think of was getting engaged. She didn't even bother to hint to Dylan about what she wanted, she just gave the box to him and told him to produce it at a nice time in the next month. Dylan, who was always happy as long as Claudia was happy, obliged a few weeks later.

She did not know why she wore an engagement ring.

She tried to turn over how she felt about the marriage in her mind, as she had done so many times before in her own kitchen, her friends' kitchens (even on one occasion her boss's kitchen), in the shower almost every morning and anytime she was in a supermarket, a task so mundane it regularly sent her into a meditative state. When she had bought the engagement ring she had not really thought much past what time of the day she would announce it on Instagram for maximum likes. Claudia might have thought she and Dylan would just be engaged forever, or even that it was a bit of a joke, or that she would just feel more excited. But it had turned out that she didn't really think she would get married, and she had felt like a spectator through the past year. She loved Dylan, but when she wore the ring she felt like a traitor. Then she felt indulgent for feeling like a traitor. She had never actively wanted to get married. When she was a teenager she'd revelled in brazenly describing it as an 'empty constitution' after once mishearing a teacher who had been asked about its place as a traditional institution.

Claudia had always been the one for whom events just happened: always in the right place at the right time – a geospatial and temporal nook that never required more than a minimum expenditure of effort. She had fallen into a well-paid job for a boutique bank when she was nineteen, she had earned her degree in Economics while hardly showing up for class, and had been promoted almost as soon as the Dean-signed document was in her hands. She had met Dylan and had a blissed-out few years and now she was getting married, having barely made a decision along the way.

And now here she was in her mother's simultaneously posh and decrepit kitchen, dreading the arrival of her sisters and wondering if the next decade of her life was going to look exactly like it did now.

'Hi sweetie, hi doll-face, hi SNOOKUMS.'

Her brother Phinn was doing a pitch-perfect impersonation of their aunt Mary. The aunt who always hugged the girls a little too long and liked to look them up and down while telling them they were looking healthy. Phinn leaned over and bear-hugged Claudia, lifting her off her feet, as if to underline the point.

Once back on earth, she handed the tongs to him. 'Finish these.'

He took them good-naturedly.

'Settling in well? Ready for all your dumb girl craic?' he said cheerfully.

'What exactly do you think is so painfully girlish about this week? Both of us are getting married you know.'

'Yeah yeah, I'm sure the focus on Dylan in all of this has been entirely equal; nobody has made more of a big deal about it for you, I'm sure,' he said, mildly sarcastic.

'If you mock me I will cut myself,' said Claudia, reverting to a joke born years before in the disinfected halls of the local hospital, when she'd been having a particularly tough time. Their oldest sister Zoe had swept into town whispering to Phinn that she'd had great difficulty choosing a wardrobe that said 'concerned but effortlessly elegant sister'. That night she had refused to give Claudia the remote control and, without missing a beat, Claudia delivered the po-faced threat about cutting herself. After a moment of leaden silence, the trio collapsed into laughter. Since then it had become a running joke.

Phinn chose not to react this time and looked over the top of Claudia's head. 'Have you heard the latest?' he said, all the while looking at the doorway for interlopers.

'You finally got laid this year?'

'No. Well, not that, none of your business.'

'You know what you want to do with your life?'

'Unfortunately for you, no.'

'God has called you. You weren't in.'

'No ... Seriously ... Old mate is back at it again.'

Phinn did not need to explain any further. The recent reconciliation between their father and his girlfriend, Lisa, had always been fragile to say the least.

'This is none of our business,' Claudia finally said.

Phinn gave a grunt of assent. 'But you know who is making it their business.'

Claudia groaned. 'Rachel.'

'Yep, none other than our esteemed mother, and who else?'

Claudia stared at the ceiling, stretching out her arms so she could do a full body groan. 'Poppy.' She hadn't needed to guess; she'd known straight away which of her sisters it would be.

'Award yourself a PhD in Juvenile Behaviour and Failure to Thrive as an Adult and call yourself Doctor Carter because you just scored 100 per cent in the "could our family behave more idiotically?" exam!'

Phinn turned the stove off and moved the pan of slightly too-crisp sausages to the side.

'What are the briefing notes?' Claudia asked.

'Apparently shit-for-brain's car has been seen outside some local footy player's house – and may I put in an aside here, does this woman have any imagination? And Mum thought it wise to let Poppy know, so now Poppy's apparently preparing for the warpath upon arrival.'

'Hmmmm, that's odd. They're meant to be on the same team. Mum was gleefully going through Poppy's shortcomings earlier. She was even referring to me as the "good one".'

Phinn scowled. 'There's more.'

Claudia braced herself with a tight smile.

'Poppy is already here,' Phinn told her.

Claudia propped herself up on her elbows. 'What do you mean? Where?'

'She arrived this afternoon and has set up camp at Dad's house so they can have their crucial favourite parent–favourite child time while we pay our dues here.'

'I knew this was going to be a disaster. Why did I agree to this whole shitfight?'

'Hardly a shitfight, dear,' he responded, grinning. 'I would say this whole situation is utterly fucking predictable.'

∞

Phinn leaned against the doorframe, allowing his shoulders to fill the space in the way of someone who is sizeable enough to have thrown down a few people in his time but not so big that he invariably becomes the target of every dickhead with eight schooners under their belt at any given time. You never want to be the first, the best or the biggest. It's too much pressure.

He was comfortable in his skin. This was partly because of his medium size, which precluded him from having to prove too much in the schoolyard, and partly because of his three sisters. When your youth is spent playing the fourth Spice Girl, you shed anything resembling self-consciousness fairly quickly.

He thought about the week stretching in front of him and immediately felt weary. Not that it would ever show. He kept the same measured disposition whatever the turn of events. He could be relied upon never to lose his temper, but what swam beneath the surface, what was really going on under his dark eyes was never quite understood by the women around him. And there were a lot of women around him.

He gave his mother a kiss as she squeezed past him, and he lazily picked up the knives and forks before he was told. He was already exhausted but at least tonight was just his sister and his mother. Claudia would not fight with Rachel and Rachel knew better than to pick on her. Her excitement at having two children at home at the same time would be enough to make a pleasant evening. It would be another day or even two before Rachel would be driven mad by towels left in the wrong place and yoghurt tubs with missing lids in the fridge.

Phinn had laid down the third plate on the table next to the kitchen when his mother crossly peeked over his shoulder. 'Where's Mary's plate?' Phinn did not sigh. He rarely revealed his exasperation to his mother.

Claudia was not so circumspect. 'I thought it was just us.'

'Your aunt wants to see you – she might be coming around.' Rachel's tone stopped any complaining from Claudia. The ingredients for a successful evening were in place but it still turned on Rachel's whims.

'Well, these sausages are going cold and I have the salad so let's eat.'

The three sat down in the formation that had existed for almost thirty years. Rachel at the head of the table, Claudia at her left, with her brother sitting across from her. If the other two had been there they would have sat in the next seats down, the oldest, Zoe, next to Phinn, and Poppy next to Claudia. Phinn reflected on an article he had seen on how the Queen fed her waiting corgis by seniority, but, as always, thought better of mentioning it.

Rachel bowed her head for a quick prayer, more out of habit than any real devotion, and the three soon were enjoying an easy banter. The camaraderie was built upon an unofficial truce between mother and daughter, enacted years before when they had both decided to stop fighting one another. They had never discussed the reasons, but Rachel assumed that Claudia might have realised that her mother was actually not the most idiotic person she had ever met, and perhaps her mistakes were just as forgivable as anyone else's.

Tonight, unusually, Rachel privately indulged in what was for her a very risky thought: life was easier with just two children. Claudia and Phinn would not fight, almost could not fight. They were not rude to her; they didn't roll their eyes when they thought she wasn't looking. Sometimes she thought they actually liked her. Back when they were all hers, a bunch of still-random cells sitting in the bottom of her belly, causing her breasts and stomach to swell, Rachel had wondered a lot of things. She had wondered if they would be a boy or a girl, if they would have dark hair and light eyes, if they would be smart, if they would make friends easily. But it had never occurred to her that they might not like her. She had never wondered if they would like her. And she missed the bliss of being so naïve.

'Why didn't Dylan come home with you?' Rachel finally asked her daughter.

'Well, I thought it would be nice to hang around without him.'

'You thought it would be nice to hang around without your fiancé?'

Claudia snorted. 'Mum, it's fine to not want to be with someone all the time, to be your own self. You have to keep a bit of yourself for yourself.'

'Why?' Rachel seemed genuinely puzzled. She was one of eight children, she had married young, she'd had four children. Being a family member had always been full-time work for her; it was an alien concept to be by herself for any extended period of time, let alone to actively seek out seclusion.

'It's good for you. You can't be defined by your partner, you lose yourself a bit. You've always got to be able to survive by yourself.'

'Claudia Carter, are you already setting yourself up for divorce?'

Claudia started laughing. She knew her mother was not angry, but sometimes she could not believe how oblivious she was.

'Don't you think you learned that lesson?' asked Claudia. 'Don't you wish you'd held on to yourself a bit more?'

Rachel thought for a moment. 'I never felt like I lost myself. Certainly in the beginning I would've liked to have been with my husband in the week leading up to the wedding.'

Phinn sniffed. 'Claudia's problem is she wants to be adored and she wants to be left alone: it's profoundly inconsistent.'

Claudia had only a split second to decide whether she should take offence, but found herself laughing instead. 'He'll be here in a few days and you can all calm your farm.'

The tranquillity of the evening was shattered by the sound of the door swinging open. Claudia knew who it was from the rhythm of the footsteps. Poppy appeared in front of them, leaning across Rachel to take the rest of her sausage from her plate and waving hello with her mouth full.

She wore R.M. Williams boots and torn stockings potentially made specifically to annoy Rachel. She was taller than the rest of the women in her family, and wore her dirty-brown chin-length hair brushed out of any real shape. Despite her cowlick she had a fringe and the overall effect was a bush framing a face that always seemed to be tinged pink. Her eyes widened as she stopped chewing, momentarily enjoying the suspense.

'Hello fellow fuckheads!'

'Hello,' Phinn responded, deadpan, but Rachel was already standing up to hug her and deliver the habitual lecture.

'Why do you talk like that? You didn't learn it here.'

Claudia didn't say anything. If there was an upper hand to keep it was importantly maintained by refusing to give her younger sister anything to react to. But then she noticed her bright pink socks dotted with teddy bears.

'Are those my socks?' she asked as Poppy grinned at her over their mother's shoulder.

∞

Rachel's house was old but solid and had been subjected to more than one harebrained renovation. Spread over three storeys, it had rooms that led into other rooms which led into bathrooms which led into dead ends, and there were odd built-in cupboards all over the place, with knobs too high and hidden doors. The siblings had given up on any notion of having their own rooms years before, and now on trips home they slept in whichever

14

room they came across that was still free, sometimes still forced into beds together when Rachel was too enthusiastic with her guest list.

Claudia dragged her feet up one stair at a time, the slow steps a way of bracing herself. Earlier she had staked out a room for her visit, but now when she opened the sliding door she was confronted with Poppy, sprawled across the bed, her boots still on each foot as she lay on top of the doona flipping through Claudia's diary.

Claudia snatched it from her hands, but not with enough righteous vigour: after all, she was well aware that Poppy read the dog-eared notebook she used as a diary every time she saw her.

'You know, if someone read your diary without knowing you, they would think you were single, did not have a brother and completely hated your sisters. It's borderline obsessive about Zoe and me in there.'

'The only thing I care more about than myself and the only thing I hate enough to write about is you two; it is a classic Rachel move to go straight for this you know,' Claudia said, putting the diary back at the bottom of her now empty duffel bag, its other contents spread across the floor following Poppy's arrival.

'Some interesting stuff in there about your wedding.'

'Yeah.'

'Do you have a cigarette?'

'Yeah.'

The sisters changed into bed socks and Claudia stuffed two cigarettes into her bra before they crept downstairs in tandem.

Poppy peeked around the corner. 'Clear, Mum's watching *The X Factor*,' she whispered out of the side of her mouth.

In coordinated movements honed over many years in another house when they were much smaller, they silently crept past the living-room doorway and didn't speak again until they had unlatched the back door, closed it behind them and were standing beside the two wheelie bins in the part of the garden that was hidden from sight of either the kitchen or verandah.

Claudia lit each cigarette in her mouth and handed one to her little sister.

'We are the last twenty-somethings in the world still smoking.'

'We are also the last twenty-somethings in the world still scared of our mother.'

'We're not scared of her, we respect her! I've told you!'

Claudia smirked.

'So what's wrong with you?' Poppy finally asked, breathing a steady column of smoke in the general direction of a frangipani tree.

Claudia shrugged. 'I don't know if I want to get married.'

Poppy shuddered with the visible effort of keeping her laughter silent. 'And this is the week you've finally thought you can do something about it?'

'I can't quite put my finger on it. I love Dylan. Well, I am pretty sure I do. But is this it? What if I broke up with him and met a minor royal, some cousin of Wills and Harry, and he was my next boyfriend?'

'Well, you couldn't marry him either.'

'Catholics are allowed to marry into the royal family now,' Claudia told her sister.

'But back to your actual country town wedding, where, at the very least, there will still be a very nice picture of the Queen near the pokies of the pub everyone goes to afterwards.'

'Hmmmmmm. Yes. Classic first-world problem here. I love Dylan. Sometimes I adore him. I like my job. I like feeling powerful.'

'You're not powerful – your boss runs the bank, not you.'

'Thanks for the reminder. I like all of this. Nineteen-year-old Claudia would look at this life and just be fucking ecstatic. I pulled it off, I really did. I shook off the dirt of where I came from, I made a life for myself where this town doesn't matter, our parents do not matter, even you don't matter. I fell in love, and it was all going well until I decided to get married.'

'What? Why?'

'I have become such a magnificent class traitor I can now dwell on this lovely life and really indulge in the superfluous question of whether I am happy. It's triggered a really weird mind-frame for me. Or maybe my crisis triggered my decision to marry Dylan. I keep wondering if this is it; if this is the right path for me or if I am giving up other opportunities, places to travel, even maybe a better relationship. It's like the clichéd Aesop's fable about the dog, who is running off with a stolen bone, who stops and sees his reflection. I have a great, juicy bone – say, marry Dylan – but then what? Is there another bone? So I take the bone that is marrying Dylan and miss out on the bone that is a dream job somewhere because now I have to consider someone else. In the fable, believing that the dog in the reflection has a better bone, he opens his mouth to bark at it and the dumb dog loses his own bone and is left with nothing. The story's moral in Olde English is that "the one who all coveteth, oft he loses all".'

'You mean like in the Devo song?'

'What? "Whip It"? Isn't that about leaving out cream?'

'No, no. "Freedom of Choice",' Poppy started humming. 'You know, about the dog finding two bones in ancient Rome and dropping dead after going in circles between the two.'

Claudia stubbed out her cigarette and turned to creep back into the house. 'So freedom of choice means I drop dead?' she whispered over her shoulder.

Poppy smirked and thrust her hips aggressively. 'Maybe. Or just maybe you're the one who needs a bone.'

Chapter 2

Poppy stirred and squinted to find the morning light was hitting her directly in the eyes, at an odd and blinding angle. 'Shit motherfucker bastard,' she muttered. Instead of the old sarongs she usually arranged as a sad ode to curtains she was confronted with lace and blinds. Where was she?

She realised as she turned over. Her mother's house. In her old bedroom. With another body next to her.

She studied her sleeping sister. Her Claudia. She was lying on her side, breathing shallowly, so close that Poppy had copped a mouthful of her cropped hair when she'd rolled over. Claudia murmured and rolled onto her back and Poppy noticed with satisfaction her eyes were smudged with liner she hadn't bothered to wash off last night. So Zoe, their oldest sister, had not completely infiltrated Claudia. Zoe swore by a skincare regime that was complex, rigorous and seemingly 80 per cent unnecessary, and which she was forever trying to foist upon her sisters. She double-cleansed at night, before applying a serum then a night cream, or maybe a night cream and then a serum, Poppy did not quite know or care. Zoe double-cleansed rain, hail or the temporary inner shine caused by sixteen vodkas, and Claudia, when she was on one of her self-improvement kicks would take what Zoe said as gospel before discarding it within a few weeks or months from boredom.

She was joined to their older sister by some invisible, pulsing cord, and when not resisting her, she would try to impress her.

Poppy dug her phone out of the sheets. She physically braced herself and opened her email app.

Dear Ms Carter,
Thank you for your interest in interning at the *Mail*. We regret to inform you our program is full for the year but encourage you to gain some experience writing for us and apply again next year.

Dear Ms Carter,
We have reached the capacity for this year's intern program at LOTL but thank you for your enthusiasm in the interview. Feel free to send us pitches; in addition to the intern program, we are willing to take three articles a month for the exposure they provide participants.

Dear Ms Carter,
We are pleased to offer you a four-week placement in our September intern program of forty-two hours a week at Them Apples.

Poppy lay back in the bed and practised her conscious breathing exercises. She focused on her breath and tried to quieten all around her. Namely, her thumping chest caused by the email and her thumping head courtesy of the night before.

Forty-two hours a week in September. That was the middle of her university semester. She needed to work at least sixteen hours a week at the chain store to make sure she made her $500 a fortnight rent for her room in a six-person share house, and then more hours in one of the mid-market restaurants in the city to buy some groceries. Could she do fifty-eight hours a week and her minimum contact hours? She felt her head slipping beneath the waves. She had been paddling so furiously, paddling so hard for so long, and where had she reached in the seven years since school?

She had a bachelor's degree and was earning $3 more an hour than she had when she was nineteen years old and scanning groceries at the checkout. She was slightly comforted that none of her high-school mates was doing much better than her. Everyone had a shitty job. Some people had a nice husband, some people had a kid. Nobody was a raging success yet. Not so for her first-year university mates. Her market socialist mates – who got nine hours' sleep a night in a bed they did not have to pay for – raged against the privileged at parties filled with Downtown Boys' first album *Full Communism*, never once seeming to notice how rich they were.

Their parents' houses were in the same city as the university.

They only needed spending money.

They didn't need rent money, they didn't need food money, they barely needed transport money. After all, what parental monster would charge their twenty-one year old for their childhood bedroom?

Those freed up from fretting over their bank accounts used the time to cultivate the connections their parents established through friends of friends on the fringes of the industry. That's all you needed.

Poppy allowed herself a moment to reflect on what she was eternally fending off, and let the thought wash over her: Am I going to fail?

When was the time to pack it in and come home? When was the time to accept not everything you had in life was something that you earned, that pretty much none of it was earned, no matter how much or how little work you did, or what your university marks were or how many times you had been published? No matter how much you tried. Poppy longed to be one of the mass oblivious; she longed to be born on third base but still convinced she had hit that home run.

She visually tried to move what she carried around on her chest to her shoulders, to shift it, to make her constant dread wearable for the day. Was she going to work as a typist her entire life; how was she going to pay the rent when she was fifty; where was she going to live when she was too old to work; who was going to look after her parents when they completed their rapid descent into old age; how was her mother going to afford to live; could she die and not be discovered for days? Would Poppy eventually get the phone call that her mother had lain alone quietly for four days? Or worse, had been screaming with nobody to hear her?

Was Poppy going to meet somebody? Did she even want a girlfriend? What if the woman she met was the same as her? What if they both struggled along in crappy jobs and at the end of twenty years had $1300 in savings and a credit card to show for it? Would it be worse if her girlfriend were more successful? Did they want to struggle together, or could she handle being supported? Of course she could handle being supported; she could be pious about it, though: pretend she was conflicted about someone else paying the bills while she wrote but really she wouldn't give a shit. Did some of her family still think she was a freak? Should she listen to Zoe? Now she was getting into ridiculous territory. Of course she shouldn't listen to Zoe.

Poppy steeled herself for kitchen combat and swung her legs out of bed. She wasn't going to spend this week freaking out; she wasn't going to think beyond the next hour for a week, then she could go back to the constant low-level hum of anxiety as the soundtrack to her life.

Downstairs in the kitchen, to her immense relief, she found no sign of her mother. Just her brother rinsing plates at the kitchen sink.

'Mornin'' she said.

'Eat a dick.'

Despite herself, Poppy laughed.

'And what the shit is this?' he continued. 'A man doing the dishes?'

Poppy rolled her eyes and picked up a banana from the counter.

'What are the plans for today?' asked Poppy. 'Is She Who Must Be riding into town?'

Phinn raised an eyebrow.

'Our lovely sister, held in high esteem by many, not just by me her humble sidekick, does indeed arrive today, and you know nobody is going to deduct cool points or Marxist points or whatever points you value on this day of the week if you are nice to her.'

'I'm always nice to her,' Poppy assured her brother. 'I've never been not nice to her,' she went on more adamantly. 'Why would I not be nice to her when there is a ridiculously priced wardrobe and an endless stream of advice on how to better myself without me even having to ask?'

Phinn sighed deeply. 'Just be nice. Or, how about this, be nice to Mum – just be nice to one of them.' He turned to face his sister. 'Zoe's flying here so I'm going to pick her up after lunch, if you can bear it.'

'There was room on the train yesterday,' Poppy replied cheerfully. 'But that wouldn't befit the duchess's image and nine and a half hours rolling through the country with patchy reception may offer too many opportunities for self-reflection.'

'Eat a dick.'

Claudia tried to feign anger but instead let out a giggle that she almost choked on.

'Speaking of self-reflection, how have you found Claudia? She seems, what's the word, pensive? Slightly neurotic? Completely allergic to the idea of getting married in five days?'

Before Poppy could reply there was an almighty crash in the exhibition room.

While their mother referred to it as the dining room, her children gave it its more grandiose moniker due to it being fitted out with what could be best described as an homage to their mother's bloodline: every piece of giant, ornately carved, dark cedar furniture was bestrewn with photos. Photos of their mother, their mother's mother, her sisters; long-forgotten uncles, whose stern faces helped drive out anyone who wandered into the room for a quiet drink. And photos upon photos upon photos of the children: the children as babies, newborns wrapped in blue or pink blankets depending on the assigned gender; toddlers with mud on their faces and gumboots, backs straight in crisp uniforms for the first day of school; eyes glazed as teenagers. There was a deep green couch, luxurious rugs, two dining tables with lace settings and ornaments. So many ornaments. Bronze ballerinas, music boxes, vials of holy water, vases and porcelain children dressed like shabby aristocrats from eighteenth-century England. Sitting in the middle of the floor was Mary, clutching her hand and howling, with shoeboxes of photos not good enough to be framed spread around her.

'Hello Mary,' Phinn and Poppy said in monotone unison.

Mary held up her hand and howled, 'Who puts a mousetrap on top of a shoebox on her shelf?'

'Probably Mum, as this is her house you are snooping around,' Poppy said unsympathetically.

'I thought your mother might have a photo of Mummy that I've been looking for and have lost.'

'And you thought you would take it?'

'I was going to ask.' Mary scowled.

'Why aren't you in your own home? Where's Mum?' Phinn asked.

'Oh I don't know, I let myself in. She is my sister, you know.'

'So you can come in and take photos as you please? I suppose you always do what you like when it comes to Mum,' Poppy said.

Mary stared straight ahead. 'My hand got caught in the mousetrap.'

'Maybe it's not for mice; maybe it's for unwelcome snoopers.'

'You shouldn't talk to your aunt that way,' Mary said, looking Poppy in the eyes.

'You shouldn't go through Mum's things. Offer up the pain to the babies in purgatory,' Poppy replied, refusing to break eye contact.

Mary stood up and made a show of brushing her red dress off. It was ill-fitting and made Mary look slightly witchy with her corkscrew black hair, but everything made Mary seem witchy, including her personality.

Just then Claudia appeared, rubbing her eyes and wearing a striped blue shirt with 'Eat The Rich' written on it.

'Is that my nightdress?' Poppy said automatically.

'She's your sister, she can wear it if she needs,' Mary said gleefully. 'That's what sisters are for.'

'Ah, to take your stuff without asking,' Poppy said as Claudia ignored them both.

'What happened to your hand?' Claudia asked, giving Mary exactly what she wanted, as she dramatically nursed it.

'I got it caught in a mousetrap.'

'You should offer the pain up to the babies in purgatory,' Claudia said as she walked away.

Poppy bent down and began picking up the photos. Mary made louder and louder sighs and sat down on one of the velvet chairs. Most of the photos were black and white and featured an array of sullen children and stoic teenagers. Poppy used to love looking at the photos of her cranky aunts and uncles as children; it had been years since she had seen the pictures.

When two people marry, half of the couple usually find themselves colonised by the other's family. In this case it was Rachel's that demanded complete subjugation. There were weekly dinners with her siblings, her aunts, her uncles, her cousins. Their father's family obligingly faded into the background, only seeking acknowledgement in early December when the Christmas cards began to arrive.

But as the children grew older they began to distance themselves from the drama and grievances that followed Rachel's family wherever they were. The pleas for recognition of their suffering – and by extension their existence – went unanswered. On their myriad feuds the kids remained silent, hoping to snuff out their manufactured needs with lack of oxygen.

The drama continued without them, but the kids slowly learned the lesson guilt-ridden lapsed Catholics can take decades to settle into – if you do not acknowledge it, it may as well not exist.

Their mother, over her sixty-two consecutive years of being part of the family, still had not learned that lesson. It's not that Rachel had an addiction to conflict – the emotional brawls took their toll on her, ignited by bored and unhappy cousins or siblings, pointing their fingers at everyone but themselves for the miserable ways their lives had turned out. If Rachel had an addiction, it was to providing genuine emotional support.

And so she found herself dragged to the middle of whichever tiny opera had been concocted by the various members of her family and, just as they had between the American Civil War and the Second World War, the techniques had evolved with technology.

The favoured strategy at the moment was for whoever was feuding (over slights that happened in 1985, or who had taken a salad bowl the week before, or who Rachel was not showing enough affection to) to play it out through email. Their uncle Peter would email whoever had wronged him and list everything that was wrong with them, calling them idiotic misers or Chelsea Clinton imitators, under the cover of the latest argument. But he would not just send it to the villain of his hour, he would copy in those two or three siblings who he perceived to be his allies. And when they responded, which they always did (to *not* respond was unthinkable), the other sibling would copy in another sister, whoever they thought would be sympathetic to their plight. Eventually the creation would be a chain letter of familial dissent.

Rachel was always one of the first to be put in these rage missives and would find herself on the phone that night for hours, reassuring whoever she happened to pick up the phone to first. Once Poppy and Zoe (in a brief interlude during their teens when they could stand the sight of each other) logged on as their mother and sent a group response: 'You are all behaving like the bastard children you are. I want no part of this pathetic charade of a family'. But they were found out in less than an hour when their mother, upon picking up her mobile during her lunchbreak, saw she had eighty-seven missed calls and thought an aunt had died.

'Did Claudia invite them to the wedding?' Mary asked.

'Who?' Phinn responded as he took each photo from Poppy to take a look himself.

'My brothers and sisters.'

'I think Claudie was generous enough inviting her own brothers and sisters; I don't know that Mum asked about her family,' Poppy said, gently correcting Mary's declaration of ownership over her and Rachel's brothers and sisters.

'Well, she should've,' Mary said petulantly.

'How about you have your own wedding and you can invite whoever you want?' Poppy said, immediately regretting her words.

Mary was not married. She was supposed to be, everyone knew. In Mary's vision of how her life turned out, she was married. Preferably to a man who would pay the bills. The kids were vaguely aware of a couple of men, shadows in their lives when they were young. Mary was really and genuinely supposed to marry one of them, but then one Sunday night he was not at roast dinner and somehow they knew never to ask why or what had happened to him.

The kids intuited that there were reasons but knew not to ask what they were, reasons their mother put up with Mary, her demands, her constant incursions on their lives, her petty tantrums over perceived slights. The explanations were something deeper than 'she is my sister'. But Rachel's children did not want a reason to feel pity, or even kindness, towards their unbearable aunt.

By now Phinn and Poppy had packed away the photos, with Phinn taking care to put them on an even higher shelf, out of

Mary's reach. Mary, noting the new hiding place and seeing the purpose behind its selection, abruptly got up and stalked out of the room without saying anything.

Phinn watched her walk out and then retrieved the box of photos and walked to the other end of the room. He pulled a couch away from the wall and opened a small door behind it, long ago used to stash all of his teenage contraband. A faint whiff of marijuana came from it as he stuffed the box inside and quickly closed the door, pushing the couch back into position.

He turned to his sister and grinned. 'I'm going to pick up Zoe.'

'Ding dong,' Poppy responded gravely.

∽

In the kitchen Phinn found Claudia sitting cross-legged on the bench scrolling through her phone while she waited for the kettle to boil.

'Do you follow Rihanna's Insta?' she asked without looking up.

'Do I ever, it's the freshest thing on there; those tits, man, every shot. I think my favourite sports bra of hers is the fluoro pink one. Have you seen she posts Bible verses as well?'

'You know my position on Fitspo, it's a Pentecostal front. First you are devoted to the squats and soon the motivational posts turn to God; 123 years from now there will be PhD theses on how Christianity captured the next generations through burpees and destroyed their knees in the process.'

Claudia didn't look up, still scrolling.

Phinn shifted from one foot to the other.

'So, uh, how are you feeling?' He had always been terrible at broaching emotional terrain and could already tell his timid attempt at wedding inquisition was going to fall flat. Between his mother and sisters he felt there was enough emotional prodding going on, and so was loath to get involved as well as inexperienced at any strategy.

'How am I feeling? I am feeling like I can't even have my morning ritual of coffee and Instagram without some trespass.'

'Ah.'

At least Phinn was good at knowing when to shut up.

The kettle whistled and he picked it up, pouring it into the plunger, which already had two and a quarter tablespoons sitting in it. As he stirred it with the wooden spoon, Claudia grumbled about the brand of coffee their mother kept in the house.

'And she keeps it in the freezer. That doesn't do shit; it should just be in an airtight jar.'

Every return home was a series of shocks for each former member of the Carter household. Their parents almost affronted that their children had grown into adults with their own tastes and habits. The children taking each change in the household, from the brand of cereal to where the bread was kept, as a personal insult, an attack on the way things should be. Claudia had a theory that their mother kept so many photos of them as children because it kept them frozen in an idealised time when they could be told what their preferences were.

Every home visit was an onslaught of commentary on personal choices. Rachel shocked that Poppy now ate multigrain bread only. Their father becoming paralysed by what brand of beer he should be buying. Claudia now expected personal space, something she had seemed able to do without for her first eighteen years, and which now offended everyone else.

Every member of the family secretly thought that – apart from themselves – nobody should change.

Phinn pushed the plunger down and poured Claudia a cup, handing it to her. Her head was still down, offering the occasional comment, for which Phinn had no context without being able to see the photos.

'I can't believe somebody agreed to marry him,' she said finally, looking up.

'Who?' Phinn responded, biting his tongue before he named Dylan.

'Joe Gelder. He was always such a dick; nothing between his ears but the web address for RedTube. He hasn't even realised you don't need to know it anymore, just write the title in the browser search bar and it comes up. You think he knows that? I don't think he does. And someone agreed to marry him, in Fiji; obviously she has no imagination either, but still. So young too.'

'Didn't you go to school with him?'

'Uh-huh.'

'Then isn't he your age?'

'What's your point?'

'You're getting married.'

Claudia sighed and stretched out her legs on the bench in precisely the manner their mother hated in the kitchen.

'I am very young to be getting married,' she said solemnly. 'It's kind of radical.'

'Radical in a Joe Gelder kind of way, I guess,' Phinn said, attempting to sip his coffee.

'Oh, fuck off.'

Phinn quickly changed the subject. Life was too long to take such easy pot shots at his sister.

'I'm going to get Zoe,' he said.

'Good, that'll be fun ...' She paused. 'Don't tell Poppy I said that.'

'I don't know how long you can keep writing in both Poppy and Zoe's birthday cards that each is your favourite without them eventually reading the other's.'

'I also write in the card not to show the other.'

'Creating even more motivation for them to show each other.'

Claudia thought for a moment. 'Well, the first four hours with Zoe here will be great. I am glad she's coming. She doesn't agitate Rachel like the rest of us can. Are you going to take her to see Dad or just coming straight here?'

Phinn let the question, fat with implication, sit in the air.

'Whatever she wants to do. Pub tonight?'

'I think so.'

Zoe would be a visitor in their galaxy. She had long wrenched herself from the family grip and somehow managed to keep everyone happy without ever revealing much about herself or her life. They knew she worked as a florist in the city. Maybe managed the shop; it was a possibility. From her social media posts they gleaned that she enjoyed going out to dinner and had developed a taste for expensive leather bags. They knew of at least two friends because they would tag her in Instagram photos and, unlike on Facebook, they didn't think Zoe realised that people could see the tagged photos.

None of them was quite sure which suburb Zoe lived in, and she visited their cities frequently enough not to warrant them spending actual money on flying to her and finding any of this out.

Her arrival would be grand, it would take some of the sting out of Rachel's and Poppy's arguments, but beyond that Zoe did not offer much.

Claudia and Phinn knew they were thinking along the same lines but they didn't bother raising any of it.

'Do you want to come to the airport with me?' Phinn asked.

'No, I want to walk around in circles by myself for ninety minutes before I have to spend the rest of the week, which seems like the rest of my life, engaged in conversation and conflict with the rest of you.'

'Fair enough.'

Phinn went over to the drawer next to the pantry and fished through it before pulling out the BMW keys.

'Mum left the Falcon keys on the bench for you,' Claudia said, eyeing her brother.

'Well, if she really didn't want me to take the car I want to drive, she would have slept with these under her pillow.'

Before Claudia could issue any predictions of unnecessary doom he was out the door.

∞

Claudia looked around the empty kitchen and picked up her headphones and phone, slipping her wallet into her pocket. She walked slowly to the front door, a practised, silent movement that signalled to nobody she was about to leave so nobody could ask her where she was going.

She tipped her head to the photo of her mother as she stepped over the threshold, and leaned on the door handle as she closed it so it made no click that could give her away. She bounded down the narrow paved path and, without stopping, shoved her earbuds in her ears for company on the walk. She briefly checked her work email; she had her out-of-office on but she liked to stay in the loop. Of course there was nothing of interest there, there never was. Claudia had not set out to become an economic consultant at a boutique bank; when she'd embarked on her Economics degree she had not really set out to become anything. She was interested in economics and had some inexact ideas about helping developing countries through an NGO, maybe, but instead she had found herself on a very pleasant salary, moving steadily up the ranks of a business which prided itself on the oxymoronic label of being a 'good corporate citizen'. She could build an actual fun life around the hours and her colleagues were decent, and Claudia eventually let go of the fantasy that work was supposed to be meaningful. That was a lofty ambition only the children of the upper-middle class and beyond got to indulge. The rest had to actually earn some money. For most, a job was just a job, and she was thankful that hers was permanent full-time.

There was nowhere in particular she wanted to be or had to go. She just needed to be away from the house and, more importantly, anyone in it. She thought about ringing Nora but what was there to say? 'Hurry up and get here. I don't know if I can do this.'

Claudia took a breath and glanced either side of her at an intersection before crossing the road, a Spotify daily playlist delivering comfort songs from her teenage years. Killing Heidi. Tegan and Sara. Placebo. She giggled as she thought about who she had pined after during that supposedly wretched time. Ryan from *The OC*, mainly. For years she had swung wildly between wanting a boy to save or a boy to save her. She was such an earnest teenager – gullible, too. She believed in the potential thrill of relationships, that they would be tumultuous and take courage and overcome any storm. It had not occurred to her that a relationship could be easy; that it is supposed to be easy.

There was no Ryan carrying her out of Mexico after she passed out in an alleyway. Mostly because when she and Dylan met she could not afford to party for a week on the Gold Coast, let alone Mexico. But also because there was nothing she ever really needed saving from. She was no more tragic or complicated than the next comfortable country girl.

Still.

She thought life could have been a little bit thrilling. That the man she would marry would at least excite her. Nora still jumped out of her seat with glee every time Tom showed up at a restaurant. Claudia could not remember the last time she felt delighted with Dylan. Content, sure. But not delighted. She tried to square this with how she felt about seeing him in a few days. Was there excitement? She did feel a yearning for him, to feel his body close to hers, to be reassured she was not the one being difficult in the face of any family spectacles. But what if he got here and she felt nothing? What if it was confirmation she had only been tolerating him?

She turned into the street that housed her old gym and realised she was inadvertently on the same route she had walked

36

three mornings a year for three years towards the end of high school. There was a quicker way to the gym – where she'd done aerobics – but she had walked these paths regularly because they took her past Charlie Bryson's house. She thought she would become physically ill from the ache of wanting him when she was a teenager, but he had never noticed her, and she'd survived. Claudia smiled and shook her head. The minuscule stakes had seemed so monumental back then.

The first strains of a Verve song filled her ears and Claudia stopped walking. She was going to walk down the aisle to this. She looked down the street, lined with lilly-pilly trees, and waited for an old four-wheel drive to pass her. With the street empty it was time for some visualisation exercises. She pictured herself in the sleeveless sheath dress she had long coveted and wrapped her hands around her imaginary bouquet of Australian native flowers. Her mother had demanded she wear sleeves in the church and somehow her intention to have an A-line skirt had morphed into three petticoats at the bridal shop, but this was Claudia's visualisation and she could wear the dress she wanted. She thought of her sweet Dylan and saw him 15 metres in front of her. This visualisation stuff was a piece of cake. She took a step forward in time to the music, and then another.

And then she saw Rachel leaning forward in the pew, frowning at the crown of flowers Claudia wore on her head instead of a veil. She could see only ugliness reflected in her eyes. She saw her father sitting four pews back instead of at the front, refusing at the last moment to sit anywhere near Mary, who had demanded she be next to Rachel.

Claudia narrowed her focus to the Dylan of her imagination at the end of the aisle. His hair was cut too short. She had told him to get it cut before he came to Winston but she knew he was going to arrive with shaggy hair and end up under the scissors of a 65-year-old woman who had never once done anything but short back and sides.

Everything was off.

Her phone buzzed, snapping her out of the walk down the aisle before she turned and ran in her pretend green heels out of the pretend church.

It was an email confirming an upgrade at the hotel she had booked as a treat for when they went back to the city after the wedding. She had gone into a raffle for the penthouse, but she knew she would get it. Things always turned out fine for her in that enchanted kind of way.

Chapter 3

Phinn carefully reversed out of the driveway, keeping watch on the garish pink bougainvillea that grew more like a weed than a hedge at the end. One of his many recurring daily fears was that eventually a child was going to run out from behind one when it was too late to brake. He held his breath for a second as the back tyres went over the footpath. Today he was in the street without having run over a kid. Small achievements and small mercies.

He switched on the radio to hear the first strains of Amy Shark's 'Adore'. He breathed out through his teeth. 'Just five more nights,' he muttered. Just five nights where they didn't have to completely devastate each other.

He raised his finger to Mrs Dowd as she walked down the street, probably towards the newsagent to collect the five newspapers she read each day. Only one newspaper was from this actual town, another was national and the other four were from three different cities, although Phinn had not been able to figure out the connection between them.

Phinn turned left, taking the longer way to avoid the main street where he might as well, publicly check in on Facebook, for how quickly the news would spread he was back in town. He was keeping a low profile. He knew he wanted to delay his old friends and elder cousins from knowing he was back. It would be the same as it was every time.

A flurry of excited text messages, and then he would find himself sitting at the same pub they had been going to since they were eighteen, for one beer at two p.m. The next stop would be twelve hours and twenty-one shouts later and, most likely, smoking his first joint since he had last been back in town. It would be a brief but familiar stumble through what the boys knew as the glory years – trying to recapture how they felt from ages sixteen to twenty-two. Invincible but still open to the possibility their lives could change.

He would see them, just not quite yet.

He followed the road until the houses dropped off and it was just rolling yellowed fields with half-hearted attempts at fences. In another twenty-five minutes he pulled up at the airport and let out a little laugh to himself. There was no designated short-term pick-up; there wasn't even a gate on the car park, let alone anywhere to charge money. Just twenty parks outside of a corrugated iron shed.

Inside was the 'check-in', where a maximum of twenty-eight people would have their bags weighed and tagged before they walked across the tarmac to get on the propeller-driven plane. In a roundabout way it was probably more like how people travelled on private jets than in big airports. No security pat-downs, no racial profiling through random explosive tests, no fluorescently lit food courts selling burgers at a 47 per cent mark-up. Just a pleasant man to take your bag before you boarded the terrifying small plane a 35-metre walk away.

Phinn settled into one of the plastic moulded chairs to wait for Zoe's plane. He thought the younger girls were harsh on Zoe for daring not to be the same person at thirty years old that she had been at seventeen. Poppy, in particular, resented the way Zoe spoke, how she did her hair, how she dressed, the bags she carried. Poppy even felt it as some kind of betrayal that Zoe wore lipstick now. That she was smarter than their parents.

The longer Poppy and Zoe had to spend time together, the angrier Poppy got and the stiffer Zoe became. The last time they had to spend four days together over Easter, Zoe had become so quietly defensive she would eat breakfast in high heels and carry her Chanel bag to the table, a quilted burgundy leather and gold-chained 'fuck you' to greet Poppy first thing in the morning.

Phinn liked Zoe. He liked all his family members but he especially liked Zoe. He didn't care that she had pretentious tendencies, or that she spent stupid amounts of money on getting her hair coiffed. Really, she was just the same as when they had been ten and eight years old and she would smuggle him the Bob Dylan tapes he wasn't allowed to listen to because of a line about the president being naked that Phinn had ruined for their mother by repeating it again and again and again while giggling.

In the distance he spotted the plane, a slightly alarming rusted colour white, coasting towards the airstrip from the west. As he raised his hand to his forehead against the glare, out of the corner of his eye he caught a glance from someone sitting down, just two seats away.

Discreetly, he nodded.

Damn. He knew that he would know them. It was that girl who used to work the checkout with Claudia; she was always too excited to see him. He focused on pretending not to see her.

'Lord, Allah or David Foster Wallace, spare me the small talk,' he muttered under his breath, automatically evoking the structure of the same prayer he had been using since he was a teenager, whose childhood religious curiosity had predictably started shifting to minor rebellion on the literary scale.

The plane dropped closer to the ground so that, satisfyingly, hearing anything else was impossible in the old shed as it landed. Even the overexcited kids who gathered at the fence to be as close as possible to the action resembled mime artists, their squeals of delight lost in the tiny roar of the small plane engines. The propellers slowed down as the engines sporadically coughed into silence, and the stairs to the plane unfolded cautiously, just kissing the tarmac as they were extended out.

Phinn half expected Zoe to step off the plane first, to have her hair blowing just-so and big sunglasses on her face, wearing a crisp white shirt and with leather luggage slung over her shoulder. He didn't know why he expected that image; the reality was that Zoe rarely lived up to what she was trying to project.

Instead an older lady, maybe in her eighties, emerged, and was helped down the stairs, taking them one by one and having

42

a little rest in between each exertion. She truly was a lady, not a woman; she had on a linen skirt suit with beige stockings and a purple silk scarf knotted at her throat. Phinn laughed to himself. This would drive Zoe, the least patient person he knew, nuts. She had been known to interrupt children at McDonald's if she felt they were taking too long to choose between nuggets and a cheeseburger.

Then a man appeared, whose florid, sunstruck face, expanding gut under a pressed chambray shirt and unblemished 'town' R.M.s denoted him as a farmer, who most likely had been down in the city for the day on business. An older woman followed, then a teenage girl, looking surly towards her home town in general, and finally Zoe.

The illusion of easy glamour she was trying for was, as usual, slightly skew-whiff. Her sunglasses fell down her nose and her hair blew into her mouth. Her flared white shirt (Phinn had at least envisioned that detail correctly) was crumpled and her navy skinny cigarette-style pants slightly clashed with her black leather boots and the red carry-all she had slung over her shoulder. She descended the stairs looking down the entire time and began walking towards the shed. Phinn waved through the window and, as she looked up, Zoe grinned. She was happy to see her brother.

The two embraced with the easy joy of siblings who have not seen each other in months and who have all the cross words of a visit ahead of them, but the shared delusion that perhaps it could be different this time.

∞

'Does Mum know you have the BMW?' Zoe asked as they walked into the car park and she eyed the red trophy parked lazily across two spaces.

'Hey, she said I should take the car.' Phinn grinned, dramatically opening the passenger seat door to allow his sister in.

'Hmmm.' Zoe threw her bag in the back seat as she slid in and looked back at the airport. 'If I was a terrorist, this is definitely where I would come. Shave off your beard for Allah, put on a flanno and you'll have control of that plane with enough petrol to get to the nearest tower in no time.'

'Good to see you are still analysing the best ways to kill the maximum number of people with minimum effort.'

'I'm not going to do it myself, I was just observing.'

'Observing how to commit a terrorist act. Yep, uh-huh.'

Phinn slid the car into gear and revved the engine in a display of showmanship before meekly easing the car out of the car park.

'So, how's the first night been? How's my most adored human being? How are our venerated and sane parents?' Zoe settled into the leather seats.

'In a shock to nobody, Mary has been hanging around the house, but Poppy still managed to get her hackles up about it. We found Mary this morning going through Mum's photos in the exhibition room. Poppy really gave it to her.' Phinn chuckled to himself. 'If by adored human being,' he continued, 'you are talking about Poppy, then she is looking forward to seeing you as much as you are looking forward to seeing her. If you are talking about the sister you actually like, then she is fine, but I think maybe having second thoughts about the wedding. Mum is the usual, Dad is fine – from all accounts and text messages.'

'Second thoughts about the wedding? You mean the wedding that is on Saturday? The wedding I am here to perform maid-of-honour duties at?'

'Claudia doesn't have a maid of honour,' Phinn quickly corrected. He had heard Claudia herself say – about 172 times in the past year – that, while there would be a wedding party, there would be no rankings.

'That's just what she tells Poppy; I know I'm her maid of honour,' Zoe said breezily. 'Anyway, second thoughts?'

'Yeah, she just seems, uh, nervous, I guess is how I would put it. She hasn't actually said she doesn't want to get married, but it very much seems that she doesn't want to get married.'

'What do you mean it doesn't seem she wants to get married? And she hasn't said that?'

'Well, not in those exact terms to me, but she seems kind of listless. Like we're talking to her through a glass pane.'

'Talking to Claudia has been like talking through a glass pane since she was four. You still haven't given me any reason you think she might want to call the wedding off.'

'Well, isn't that in the maid-of-honour contract?' Phinn replied, watching Zoe out of the corner of his eye. Checkmate. 'Don't tell her I told you that, by the way; I'm not supposed to be talking about it.'

Zoe glared at him and looked out of the window at the cows in the paddocks with the shoddy fences. She watched a kangaroo bound too close to a cow and then realised there were about

45

fifteen other kangaroos standing very still in the next paddock sniffing the air. The colour of the grass, the smell of eucalyptus and something slightly burnt in the air, of the sun on bitumen for too long, was unconsciously familiar to her, much in the way of one's own limbs. She looked into the distance, realising it had probably been more than half a year since she had seen a proper horizon: one that wasn't the end of a street, or the stars.

'I hate coming home.'

∞

Without having to discuss it, Phinn pulled into their mother's driveway. It was where the girls – only referred to as that between brother and sister – were, and the days of emotional wretchedness would not be worth it if they dared to call in on their father first.

Zoe got out of the car, without bothering to glance back to make sure Phinn would fetch her bag from the seat. She knew he would. As she passed under the kitchen she looked up and saw her aunt's judgemental face peering down at her over the antique kettle, framed by the dark green borders of the window. Zoe thought to herself, Mary could be held up as evidence of Roald Dahl's theory that if you think ugly thoughts they begin to show on your face. She allowed herself an unenthusiastic wave but knew that Mary wouldn't bother coming to the door to greet her, so she was safe if she circumvented the kitchen – Mary's preferred domain – once inside. She entered through the back door in the long tradition of anybody who comes home again, whether it was against their will or with joy in their heart. The front door was for visitors.

Her mother also left the back door unlocked and Zoe could not be bothered knocking. She paused to breathe in her mother's smell – a mixture of shampoo, body oils and, inexplicably, freshly cut hair – before calling out.

'Muuum.'

'Zoe!'

She listened for the sound of her mother's light step practically running through the house. And then Rachel appeared, hair slicked down with dye underneath cling wrap and wearing a shirt of Claudia's from high school – meaning the shirt itself was probably in its teens – emblazoned with the words 'The Good Times Are Killing Me'. Paired with her knee-length bright orange shorts, the overall effect was unhinged but, Zoe knew, Rachel being Rachel still looked about six times more attractive than Zoe on a good day.

'You're home!'

'Am I?' Zoe said automatically. Her query was more an instinctive response to her mother's factual declaration than deliberate insouciance. However, she forgot that homecomings to insecure maternal figures are no time for flippancy.

'What does that mean?' Rachel said, pulling away sharply. 'Have you seen your father?'

Zoe groaned.

'Nothing, Mum, just a joke … How are you? What's happening?'

That was enough for Zoe to spend the next fifteen minutes quietly with her thoughts while Rachel rounded off in great detail her friends' latest marital and health ailments, her latest grudge at work, despite being on a three-week break from the cleaning company, as well as something about the garden that nobody had been able to make sense of yet. Zoe made sounds at intervals of sympathy, interest and agreement before finding a gap in the conversation.

'Where's the bride?' she asked brightly, treading carefully so as not to flick the unpredictable switch on her mother's virtual mood settings – from nervously excited to overwrought. The genius had been in using Claudia's role for the week and not the name of Rachel's least favourite child, Poppy. Well, least favourite was probably a bit harsh. Perhaps 'the name of the child she has the most agitated relationship with'.

Rachel waved to the stairs, 'Oh, she's in her room,' allowing herself the language that pretended her children still lived with her, that they still needed her, and only ever resided in their rooms in her house.

'Okay, I have to say hello, you know, as maid of honour.'

'I thought Claudia didn't have a maid of honour; she didn't tell me you were the maid of honour.'

'Well I am,' Zoe said, bounding up the stairs.

'Mary's here by the way,' Rachel called after her.

~~~

At the top of the stairs, Zoe turned left and stopped for a moment to survey her sister. Claudia had headphones in and was lying diagonally across a bed that she certainly had not made herself that morning. She was engrossed in whatever she was listening to and had not heard Zoe's steps, despite Zoe being the kind of average-sized woman who still sounded like an elephant in the house. Claudia had her cropped hair pulled off her face by two bright green clips and was wearing what looked like bike pants with a faded green oversized sweatshirt. It was all wrong, but sartorially Claudia was always wrong. Zoe pulled on Claudia's foot, almost copping a kick to the chest for her efforts.

'Don't touch my fucking foot,' Claudia said, swinging around, the fierce arrangement of her facial features completely changing once she saw it was Zoe. 'Hey!'

'Hey yourself; man, could you be more like Rachel with your touchiness about feet?' Zoe grinned back and lay down on the bed next to her sister. 'Are those my socks?' Zoe asked, pointing her head towards Claudia's feet, which were clad in anklets with drawings of pigs flying all over them.

Claudia shrugged.

'I hear you don't want to get married,' Zoe continued.

Claudia shrugged again. 'It's not that – I don't think ...'

'Well, whatever's going on, your maid of honour should be able to help.'

'You're not my maid of honour.'

Zoe nudged her with her elbow. 'Why is Phinn saying you don't want to get married?'

'I told him not to tell anyone I told him that,' Claudia replied.

'Yeah, he told me not to tell you that he was the one who told me. Don't tell anyone, but.'

Claudia began giggling.

'Don't tell anyone, but' was an old shorthand between them. In their family, any news spread more quickly than syphilis during King Henry VIII's reign, and Zoe and Claudia had long mocked it after the quick observation that the most common greeting between relatives was, 'Don't tell anyone, but …'

'Well don't tell anyone, but I don't know what I think. I can't tell if I am having misgivings about marrying Dylan or if I am having misgivings about spending this entire week with our family.'

'Well, I would rather marry Dylan than spend the week with our family if I had to choose.'

'Hmmmmmm.'

Zoe decided to drop it. There was no use being too direct with Claudia. Whatever she was feeling would come out at an odd moment, such as when they were discussing what happened to their childhood trampoline, or trying to decide if their favourite colour was purple or blue. It wouldn't be revealed through direct questioning.

'Where's the light of my life, the eternal joy of my soul?' asked Zoe.

'I don't know what yours and Poppy's problem is.'

'I don't have a problem with my baby sister. She's great; I really enjoy her particular brand of petulance mixed with self-righteousness. I find it invigorating.'

'Zoe, not this week,' Claudia pleaded. 'Poppy has actually been looking forward to seeing you.'

'I can't believe my own sister can look me in the eye and lie as if I am a calorie counter in your phone, as if I am a doctor asking if you've ever taken drugs, as if I am our mother.'

'Just be nice.'

'I'm always nice.'

'Don't lie to me – I'm your sister.'

The Imperial was one of the oldest surviving pubs in Winston. It had originally been opened by a Spaniard who sailed to Australia on a promise to his bride-to-be he was going to find a better life for them. He had reached Winston in the middle of summer, a small town high in the tablelands beneath Sydney that had to him the perfect climate. The days reached 28 degrees without ever getting humid. Today's one-hour trip to the beach was back then a day's journey, but the Spaniard was happy enough with that – he had arrived in Australia by boat from Europe, after all. By the time he was shocked by the sub-zero temperatures of winter he had already won some land in a complicated bet with a fellow penniless European.

He worked as a farmhand for five years to save enough money to open the pub in a simple wooden structure to which, over the years, he added a second level, wide verandahs, a heavy oak bar and elaborate doors carved from a eucalypt native to the area. His vision for the pub was a mosaic of influences: from his home town, to the bush surrounding him and the sea he had travelled on, as well as the Indigenous stories he had heard on Gundungurra land. Inspired by their name for a nearby area, Winge Karrabee Karrabee – a place of many wildfires – he painted the bar in flames. Images of mermaids adorned the walls and carved corbels supported the ceiling beams. His mother, weeping for three months after he had announced his intention to come to Australia, had made him two pots that he had carried in a bag on his back and had sat on a shelf near a painting of a heartbroken matador taunting a bull. The Spaniard had done the painting himself, with little to no talent or technical skill, and hung it on the wall in the ancient tradition of doing as you like when you're the boss. After thirteen years he had travelled home to fetch his bride and found she had married his brother and had three daughters.

Brotherhood is like an illness.

Now, all that survived of his lopsided vision were the carved doors. The Imperial had borne witness to the changing fortunes of the town as the bush was bulldozed for farms, small businesses boomed, factories were built and emptied; it had found its niche as a quaint destination for the city bourgeoisie wanting to pretend to escape to the country for the weekend. As agriculture and manufacturing waned, the Imperial had hosted hundreds of leaving parties as the smartest kids fled for larger towns or cities, desperate to be closer to what they thought was the action. Those left behind, the defiant stragglers, soldiered on as the population dwindled, the supermarket and clothing chains replaced their local markets and boutiques. It was the Great Australian Story. The Great American Story. The Great *insert any developed country with a rapidly shrinking middle class* Story.

None of this was on the minds of the Carter kids. A war was brewing. They walked through the doors of the Imperial in the pairs they had established long before they had any concept of battle lines.

Phinn and Zoe entered in lockstep, with Zoe purposefully not making any eye contact with her fellow patrons until she had found a table she liked, beside a window, with four stools scattered around it. She wore a short purple dress with a hot pink cashmere sweater over the top and a denim jacket. Around her neck was a black choker, such a flashpoint trend that it would cause noses to wrinkle in embarrassment in just a month. Pinned to her denim jacket was a small brooch of a koala holding a bunch of roses, and on her feet were Adidas Stan Smiths. If she could have she would've kissed the feet of Victoria Beckham for making the comfortable sneaker okay sartorially, and she was considering asking if she could wear them with her bridesmaid dress but had not quite got the timing right yet. She put her small leather Gucci handbag on the table and dug through her wallet, handing Phinn her credit card. He did not even bother with the pretence of reaching for his own wallet.

'I'll just have a riesling.' Zoe glanced around the bar, taking in the grimy pool table of her teenage years, a few men her age in their tradie gear leaning against the bar with their beers, and the jukebox playing U2. 'Actually, just get me a schooner of whatever you're having,' she said quickly.

'Safest bet.' Phinn nodded.

As he sloped towards the bar, Zoe saw Claudia and Poppy emerge from the bathroom and she stiffened involuntarily. Claudia had parted her cropped blonde hair on the left in a style that should have looked dorky but managed to seem chic on her, offset by a black turtleneck, high-waisted black jeans and shiny pink leather brogues.

What Zoe noticed were her little pink and blue diamanté earrings.

'Are those my earrings?' she asked by way of greeting.

'Is that my brooch?' Poppy said.

'What's everyone drinking?' Claudia said purposefully.

'Hmmmm, white wine?' Poppy responded.

'Really?' Zoe said, turning to Poppy.

'Don't tell me what fucking drink to order, Zoe.'

'I'm not. I just don't think the wine here is going to be very good.'

'I'll have the chardonnay, Claudie,' Poppy said, not moving her eyes from Zoe.

Claudia sighed and turned back to the bar. Zoe looked around desperately for Phinn and saw him leaning casually across the bar, chatting to Steve, who had just poured the drinks.

She scanned the room and her eyes widened as they settled on a man sitting in the corner in a tight black shirt, his chin-length blond hair twisted into miniature dreadlocks. She started laughing and, despite herself, elbowed Poppy in the ribs. Poppy had been working hard on not breaking the silence between them and was almost pushed off her chair for her efforts.

'It's Roy,' Zoe whispered out of the side of her mouth.

Poppy's face stayed completely still but a pinkness began creeping from her shirt collar across her chest and up her throat towards her face. A sight familiar to those intimate with her and barely perceptible to anyone else.

'Has he seen us?' she whispered, refusing to look in the direction in which Zoe was so blatantly staring.

Zoe started giggling. 'No,' she said, shaking her head for emphasis as Claudia arrived back at the table with Phinn, two chardonnays and two beers in tow, carefully setting Poppy's wine down in front of her as she put her head in her hands, groaning.

'Roy's here!' Zoe said joyfully.

'Aw, no way, where is the champ?' Phinn responded, looking around excitedly as Poppy tried to sink lower on her chair.

'Guys, why are we so thrilled about seeing Poppy's boyfriend from a million years ago?' Claudia asked wearily.

'This is a very significant man,' Zoe said between giggles. 'The man she lost her virginity to. The heavy-metal-listening, Being-a-Blairite-is-the-same-as-being-a-Tory, won't-stop-playing-Guitar-Hero wonder boy of Year Twelve for her.'

Poppy carefully raised her wine to her lips and Zoe pretended not to notice when she spat her first mouthful back into the glass. Claudia didn't even bother touching hers; she had wanted a beer all along but sacrificed her preference for diplomatic reasons.

'Heyyyy,' Zoe said, perking up. 'Does he know you're gay?'

Poppy shrugged.

'Imagine if he tries to hit you up for old times' sake. Remember when he wrote that piece for the school newsletter about why all men should be feminists and it got published instead of a piece by an actual girl for International Women's Day? Jesus, what did you see in him?'

'Well, cover, obviously.'

Phinn and Claudia exchanged looks: an almost undetectable raising of their eyebrows. Zoe shut up. Satisfied, Poppy began to loosen up and took a quick sip of her wine, surreptitiously trying to hold her breath at the same time so she didn't have to actually taste it.

Zoe maintained her silence as Poppy finally addressed the table. 'The funny thing about being gay is that there is this perception that you come out and the hard part is over. You wrestle with your sexuality for a few years, you come to terms with it, you come out, it's hard and then it's over. You're eventually in the warm embrace of affection and no secrets. When, actually, you never stop coming out. You have to come out maybe hundreds of times in your life. Does Roy know I'm gay? I don't know. Maybe someone told him, or maybe he will come over and talk to us, and he is a nice guy despite your delightful snobbishness, Zoe; but if he comes over, instead of just chatting I will have to ascertain if he knows I am gay and then find a way of letting him know. Maybe I will reference an ex-girlfriend, an imaginary current girlfriend, or maybe I will find a way to say "actually I am gay", but whatever happens I'll have to think about it and probably come out. Every time I start a new job, see an old friend, make a new friend, I have to come out again. It's funny – nobody really talks about it, and you don't get taught that part in lesbian college.'

Her siblings paused.

'You mean the inner west soccer team,' Zoe said before she could help herself.

Claudia and Phinn waited for Poppy's reaction. Poppy started laughing.

'You're a real bitch.'

'Are you allowed to say that? I thought that wasn't cool anymore. Aren't you gendering me?'

'Oh, shut up.'

Now on a roll, Zoe held up the credit card that Phinn had put on the table.

'Hey Poppy, is this credit card queer? Is it a feminist ally? Don't you have to make sure everything is these days?'

Claudia tensed up; the Sibling Agitator was in precarious territory. But Poppy just kept laughing.

'Not all of us can be satisfied with just being a petty consumer, Zo. Can't all be basics with money.'

'Just let me get you a beer with my mountain of money, dickhead. I told you that wine would be awful.'

Poppy nodded and smiled widely as she pushed her wine away from her; the glass was half full after all.

'Me too please,' Claudia said.

The night was going to be okay.

Chapter 4

Claudia: Poppy, where are you?

Zoe: Did you mean to send this to the group chat? Isn't Poppy in bed with you?

Claudia: Shit, ignore me

Phinn: Why. Why must we have a group message? It's just a lot of blundering

Zoe: CLAUDIA, WHERE IS POPPY?

Claudia: If I knew I wouldn't be sending her a message

Phinn: I hate my life

Zoe: Did Poppy come back last night?

Phinn: Lol

Zoe: I don't care! I'm sure she's fine, I'm just asking where she is too

Phinn: OK

Zoe: Did she come home last night; please tell me you didn't leave her at the pub with Leah

Phinn: ROY'S SISTER HAHAHAHAHAHAHA HAHAHAHAHA

Claudia: I'm sure she's fine

Poppy: I am fine. None of you are my real mum. I don't need you checking up on me. What did it take this time? 48 hours and I'm being treated like a fucking baby

Claudia: OK

Zoe: OK

Zoe: If you are a disaster this morning, Poppy, it's not for ever

Phinn: I hate our group chat

Chapter 5

Claudia put her phone down and rolled over in bed, looking out the window to the street below. It was not a view she had thought about very much while living here, but since her increasingly longer periods of time away from home, it now appeared ridiculously picturesque.

Massive fig trees, their roots slowly destroying the footpath from below and strangling any native tree that attempted to grow nearby, overlooked groups of unsupervised neighbourhood children as they rode their bikes down the street. Nobody ever had an overgrown lawn. Instead the air seemed to alternate between the constant smell of either freshly mown grass or baking.

Claudia thought of the studio apartment she shared back in the city with Dylan. Of its one bookcase. Of the rack next to the front door so his bike didn't get in the way too much and instead could look kind of decorative as it hung on the wall. Could she come home again? Kanye had rapped more than once about always being able to go back home.

But Kanye didn't have any siblings and his mother was dead.

She sighed and kicked her blankets off. Last night had not been so bad. They had got along, tolerated each other, chosen not to take offence whenever some could have been scraped together – like kindling for a larger blaze to come. It had been fun.

Three more days until the wedding. Dylan arrived tomorrow. Nora arrived today. Claudia wondered how the delicate balance of last night was going to be thrown off by each of them. The good mood Poppy had bestowed upon them last night was an anomaly. It wouldn't last with Zoe, and it certainly wouldn't last with her best friend – Poppy's eternal threat – around either.

Why hadn't Claudia let Dylan come earlier? It had been an act of complicated benevolence. Whatever happened, whoever was there, someone was going to tear someone else to pieces this week – Dylan might as well stay out of it for as long as he could. Claudia had also wanted some time to herself, a thought that made her chuckle out loud involuntarily. She always pictured herself at home, going for runs, walking around the town by herself, calling in for lunch on doting aunts. The reality was that she was either feeling guilty for not being at her dad's while in her mother's kitchen, or wondering if her mother was upset while walking around her father's garden.

The few minutes in the morning were basically all the time she got alone, and that was only because Poppy had scored the night before. She hoped her mother wouldn't be asking too many questions.

∞

Downstairs she found Rachel bent over the counter with Mary by her side, whispering in her ear. Claudia tried to stay silent until she was almost on top of them to see what was in their hands. The floorboard creaked as she was two steps away and the two jumped up. Claudia glanced down at her mother who was quickly shoving her phone in her pocket.

'Hello!' Mary greeted her.

Phinn came into the kitchen yawning. 'What are my favourite witches of the west doing this morning?' he said cheerfully.

'Don't talk to your mother like that,' Claudia said automatically, waiting for Rachel's scolding.

But she just walked over to the kettle and switched it on with all the concentration of a first-time neurosurgeon. Claudia eyed Mary.

'What were you two looking at?'

'Just Facebook, old friends, funny stories. Everyone is ageing but us. It does make one feel better about one's looks, seeing how classmates from forty years ago look today.'

Mary always tried to make her language embarrassingly proper when she was nervous. Embarrassing because it showed what she thought proper language was, her impressions mostly having been picked up from mini-series involving the royal family as soap-opera characters. Phinn suddenly started paying attention.

'Anyone specific you were looking at?'

'Of course not … Anyway, bride-to-be! Three more sleeps! Have you done the tables? I've completely forgotten to give you the name of my plus one.'

'I didn't give you a plus one.'

'Of course you did, you wouldn't be so bad mannered.'

'I didn't even give friends in relationships plus ones, unless Dylan has met them.'

'Those are friends, I am family.'

'What's the saying about which you get to choose again?' Claudia muttered under her breath as the kettle whistled. Claudia thought about the names cut from her guest list, as Rachel had asked then demanded more and more people be added. In place of thirteen of Dylan and Claudia's friends were Rachel's colleagues, schoolfriends, her cycling buddies and, inexplicably, her yoga instructor.

'Tea?' Rachel said cheerfully. She was dressed in her usual morning attire, which was a dressing-gown with absolutely nothing underneath. She thought she was appropriately and discreetly covered up but the thought of their pants-less mother often left the children stiff with mortification. Claudia never mentioned to Dylan that her mother was basically naked and Dylan hadn't seemed to notice. Claudia pushed the thoughts away as she accepted a mug from her. Nowadays she liked her tea black with no sugar, but when she was a teenager she'd had it milky and sweet, so that was how her mother still made it.

'Your aunt has a plus one now, Claudia,' Rachel said as she handed Phinn a green tea, something he had drunk for four months when he was sixteen when he was briefly in love with a girl named after a star constellation. Now he would consume it forever under his mother's roof instead of revealing he had long ago moved on.

'What?' Claudia said, nose crinkled mid-sip.

'It's manners! Of course your aunt gets a plus one. She is family, she helped raise you.'

Phinn spat his tea back in his cup at this delusional statement, but there was no point arguing with their mother about her awful, awful sister. Where they saw a lifetime of selflessness and generosity from their mother to Mary, all they had witnessed in return from their aunt was her brazen willingness to have her younger sister take care of life's difficulties while she herself sat around moping. But right now Mary's grim visage betrayed a self-satisfied expression from her spot in the corner.

The glance between Phinn and Claudia contained a simple, acknowledged message: 'Thank Christ Poppy isn't here.'

'I've done the invitations, I've given the restaurant the numbers, I've done the tables. This is the first time I am hearing about a plus one.'

'I had assumed I had raised my daughter correctly and I didn't have to ask about Mary's plus one.'

'But you're not even bringing a plus one!'

'Well, only because I don't have one.'

Phinn and Claudia turned to Mary and expressed almost in unison the thought that up until now hadn't occurred to either of them.

'You have someone to bring to the wedding?'

Mary just smiled. 'Maybe. Just put him down anyway, Claudia sweetie.'

Claudia sighed. 'Well, it is Rachel's big day, I guess,' she finally said.

❧

Claudia checked the upstairs bedrooms and found Zoe's bed already made with a note left on it 'Sorry. Not sorry.' Claudia sighed and asked the empty bedroom, 'Why leave tormenting notes when I have a phone?' She could hear Phinn's gait in the hallway, almost loping towards his bedroom, and she stepped out to cut him off.

'Why are you in Zoe's room?' he asked.

'I was just seeing where she was.'

'You don't need to go inside the room to see she is not in there.'

'Jesus Christ, Phinn, I'm not leafing through her diary. You don't need to be on permanent privacy patrol.'

'Well, hashtag just sayin'.'

'How can this millennial family be so bad at millennial mannerisms?' Claudia sighed. 'Anyway, I'm heading out to see Dad – are you coming?'

'If Zoe is gone, and you're going, and Poppy is content somewhere else, then I am definitely going somewhere by myself for seventeen hours. Or maybe two. I'll go kick the footy.'

'You don't want to see Dad?'

'Mate, unlike you I have a clear conscience, zero hang-ups – I don't feel the need to split my time down the middle and divide it completely evenly despite nobody, in particular Mum and Dad, noticing.' Phinn began to walk away. 'I see Dad all the time. We're cool.'

'Thanks for the life advice, solid coming from someone who still holds hands with his mother when crossing the street.'

Phinn didn't turn around or change his trajectory. 'I'm just fucking nice.'

Claudia kind of regretted her jab, but what was a trip home if not a thorough excavation through layers of guilt? As with rock formations created over hundreds of thousands of years, there was a completely random yet effective formulation for each level, holding up the next layer and with the oddest bits of history preserved. The deeper she dug, the more likely she was to come across areas that were still soft. Claudia couldn't just feel guilty about not spending equal time with each parent, she had to also feel guilty about telling her sister she couldn't come to her birthday party when she was five; about the last family event she had not made it home for; about her underwhelming reaction to her brother's thrilling news nine years ago; about calling her sister stupid when she was seven; about whether her low-level mocking was actually hitting a particularly vulnerable spot.

Claudia knew Phinn still held Rachel's hand when crossing the road ('Don't tell anyone, but...' Rachel had confided), but he was just an affectionate boy. Once he had told Zoe that one of his most devastating memories was when Rachel was busy in the kitchen and wouldn't give him his fourth hug of the morning. He told her in a moment of confidence and it had now become a folklore, used at Phinn's expense, just like most of the kids' deepest and darkest insecurities. Nothing was protected from their mirth.

Claudia stood still and listened for any sounds that would signal Phinn's return before ducking back into Zoe's room.

She got out her phone and took a Snapchat of the note on Zoe's bed, typing over it, 'bitch has jumped ship already', and sent it to Poppy. Her phone dinged back straight away with a photo of Poppy lying in bed with her arm covering her eyes.

'I wish I was dead', she had written across the photo. Claudia craned her neck but couldn't see if there was someone in the bed with Poppy.

'You want to come out to Dad's for lunch?' she messaged back.

'Yep,' Poppy wrote back, infuriatingly.

Her message habit was one- to two-word answers, a full stop, and none of the necessary detail unless it was specifically asked for. Claudia bent down from her waist and cradled her arms by the elbows, making a type of frame for her head before gently rocking it back and forth. It was the one useful yoga pose she had learned from the three times she had gone. She waited, let out a breath and then stood back up.

'Great! Where should I pick you up from? Looking to leave in about 45 minutes.' She kept her messages nonchalant after yoga breaths. There was no point in blowing up at Poppy for the way her message was written. That was a good way to get no response at all.

∽

Claudia pulled up by the side of the road two houses down from the address Poppy had given her. She rested her chin on the steering wheel and listened to the last strains of 'I Luv the Valley OH!', humming along before singing in a faux-French accent.

She lifted her phone to let Poppy know she was here, but put it back down in the console and leaned against the seat. A rare moment alone. She had been harbouring the delusion that she would get quality time with her siblings. She wanted to test the waters before her friend or fiancé joined her, gauge the mood of the family, see how she went solo. By this point she knew that she missed him, which on the one hand was surely a good sign, but on the other should be a given. She missed having a reinforcement, someone permanently on her side no matter which family member she was squabbling with and in which circumstances. She missed having someone to do the driving and someone to hug at night. She missed his clarity when she was emotionally charged.

There would be no time with him, really. And, with Nora, she would be busy soothing her sisters' egos, while ensuring her mother felt involved and cherished.

She picked up her phone and messaged Poppy. 'Here.' She picked it up again and added a smiley face. She couldn't help herself.

She leaned back and looked at the house. Like every other one on the street it was two storeys, probably four bedrooms. It was weatherboard and had been painted a dusty pink. Claudia noticed the one next to it had been painted a powder blue. If she stood directly between them across the street, it would make a pretty good Instagram shot. She smiled despite herself. A nice little portrait of home for all the followers. Before she decided whether her little lame joke to herself would actually be a photograph that could garner more than fifty hits on a little heart icon, the car door opened and Poppy slid in next to her. She had on the same denim skirt from last night but over the top was a faded red flannelette top, carelessly buttoned and pushed up at the sleeves.

'Fun night?' Claudia asked.

'It was fine,' Poppy said, staring straight ahead. 'Are those my shorts you're wearing?' she said without even looking at her sister. Claudia glanced down at the loose teal denim shorts she had on with a white T-shirt and gold Birkenstocks.

'I thought they were Zoe's.'

'Hmmmm.'

Claudia started the car before saying, almost under her breath, 'Nice shirt.' Poppy sat perfectly still. Claudia did not bother trying to make any conversation with her on the drive to their father's.

They drove down avenues lined with Moreton Bay figs and soon the similar two-storey weatherboard houses painted in pastels and gloomy neutrals gave way to single-storey brick bungalows. Identical houses all in a row: the front door on the left and the bay-windowed living rooms on the right-hand side.

Claudia pulled into the driveway of one of them, distinct only in that it had pink geraniums planted next to the letterbox. The arrival at their father's house shifted something between the sisters, who – from being single, different entities, drifting apart – suddenly reverted to the unison of their childhood. A time when siblings do not so much copy each other as unconsciously act in tandem.

They opened the car doors at the same time and quickly ran to the house. Inside, their father was waiting by the table where a roast chicken from the supermarket had been cut up. He had never been much of a cook, but what he lacked in culinary skills he made up for in faux grandeur. George drew himself up to his full six feet four inches of height and hugged the sisters at the same time – one in each arm – as they tried to wrap themselves around his enormous stomach.

Claudia rubbed his bald head. 'Hello, Dad.'

'Hello Claudia, hello Poppy,' he said, letting each of them go. 'There's still another fifteen minutes until lunch. You the only ones?' he tried to ask innocently.

Claudia looked at Poppy but she seemed completely unruffled by the suggestion that seemed to be hidden in his question. Claudia was always looking to interpret something as hurt, or anger, or sadness.

'Zoe has gone AWOL and Phinn said he sees you enough and has gone to kick a football by himself.'

George stroked his grey moustache. 'Good for them.' He turned to walk towards the kitchen and automatically Poppy and Claudia fell into step behind him. A habit they must have picked up from when they were children, but whenever they were near him they would follow him around, from room to room, into the garden. Wherever he was, they would be.

'So, Claudia, you're having a little party on Saturday.'

'Hmmmm,' Claudia responded, while picking bits of feta cheese out of the salad he was trying to make.

George looked up from chopping the basil and narrowed his eyes. He seemed to do a quick mental calculation and landed on the side he always did: against pushing the issue. Perhaps for fear that he might actually have to have a conversation concerning emotions, Claudia observed.

'Claudia doesn't want to get married,' Poppy said, reaching across George in a way none of the other kids would have dared and taking a piece of cucumber from right next to his knife.

George responded slowly, forced into the conversation despite himself. He glanced at Claudia. 'Really?'

'No, not really. Poppy has convinced herself I don't want to get married, maybe from a conversation with Mum, or Zoe, or an equally reliable source—'

Poppy interrupted, 'Dylan isn't even here yet, Dad. Claudia does not seem excited at all. It's all very weird.'

Claudia set her jaw and then let it fall back into place, a relaxation trick she used when she couldn't do her odd yoga breaths.

'Dylan's coming in two days because I thought I could spare him some of the inevitable drama. I thought, as I always do when I am quite far away from you all, that I would like some quality time with you.'

'What a silly thought,' George said.

'Anyway, I do want to get married, that's why I am getting married, but I also want to get out of here as soon as possible. So.'

'Well, it's always nice when you pop by,' George said, an edge of sarcasm to his voice. Claudia winced and knew he was referring to the fact she was staying at Rachel's and not his house.

'Did you get the tie I sent you?' She tried to change the subject.

'Yes.' George waved his hand dismissively. 'Does it go with your mother's dress? I hear she is walking you down the aisle.'

Now he was being deliberately obtuse. Claudia made her tone even. 'You're both walking me down the aisle.'

'A special request from your mother?'

'No, actually, I didn't see why it shouldn't be both of you – you both raised me.'

'God forbid she would let you do anything just with me,' George muttered. He reached for the spring onion as Poppy took another piece of cucumber and put the rest in the bowl. 'How *is* your mother?'

'Same. Same same. Mary's still hanging around, draining her energies, probably her wallet as well. Thank God she didn't have any children. Can you imagine how many people Mum might have had to look after?'

Glad for the break in scrutiny on her upcoming nuptials, Claudia warmed to the much safer subject of their conniving aunt.

'Actually,' Claudia said, 'Mary wants to bring someone to the wedding.'

George's breezy query came as he picked up the salad bowl and walked to the table in the next room, where he had left the chicken: 'Who?'

'I don't know,' Claudia said. 'She didn't seem to know herself.'

She set the ancient pink-bordered plates in front of her father, Poppy and herself as they sat down with George at the head of the table and she and Poppy on either side.

'Oh, I know who,' Poppy said, reaching for the chicken first, even though it was closest to Claudia. She started laughing to herself. 'Mick.'

Claudia, almost dropping the salad bowl, drew in a sharp breath. George speared a piece of chicken breast aggressively with his fork and looked up.

'Mick?'

Poppy nonchalantly finished her mouthful. Nothing either of their parents ever did ruffled her.

'Mick, as in your favourite little brother, yep. How do you think they got together?'

'Mary's usual desire to cause as much wreckage as she can, I'd say,' George said, still holding his poultry-laden fork aloft. Claudia suffered a sudden, inexplicable pang of sympathy for the skewered bird.

'What's wrong with Mick again?' Poppy asked, completely unnecessarily. They all knew the story. Nobody came out of it covered in glory.

'That's enough. Claudia, you said no, didn't you?'

'Yes, Dad,' Claudia said, looking at her plate. 'But I said no before she even told me who the person was. Although I think that Mick would know by now he didn't get an invitation.'

'Good. I can't believe your mother would put you in that situation,' George said.

Claudia just stared at him while he shook his head.

❧

'You mad, bro? You seem mad. You can only be mad, you mad, bro?' Poppy was bouncing up and down in the car seat on the way home. The tenser her sister became, the more opportunities Poppy saw to poke. 'That was a loverrr-ly lunch,' she continued.

'Uh-huh.' Claudia nodded.

'You mad?'

'Nuh-uh.' Claudia shook her head, then turned left without bothering to indicate.

'Are you mad because you don't want to get married?'

Claudia laughed mirthlessly. 'I can't wait for Dylan to get here.'

76

Poppy stopped bouncing in her seat and studied her sister's profile. Her mouth was set in a grim line with her eyes looking directly ahead.

'What's up?'

Claudia tensed her shoulder muscles, lifting her shoulders up to her ears and then back down again.

'Just: never get married, and if you do, don't tell our family, and if you do that, then don't listen to our family, or be directed by them, or be guilted by them. Although,' she continued, glancing at Poppy, '*you're* never guilted by them. It just washes over you for some reason.'

'I thought they had been good. Mum and Dad seem super-helpful. I haven't heard them complaining.'

'Were we not just at the same lunch?'

'What did Dad complain about?'

Claudia shifted down a gear as she approached a stop sign, looked both ways, and coasted through the intersection. 'I totally paused,' she muttered to herself, smiling. 'Y'know, I actually wanted to invite Mick, but knew it just wasn't worth the hassle.'

'You wanted to give Mary a plus one?'

'No, I wanted to invite Mick before he was Mary's plus one. I've always liked him. He was a good and generous uncle. I don't think Dad has a good reason to hate him so much.'

'Well, he did cheat on Vicky.'

'So? How is that any of Dad's business? Yeah, it's bad, but I don't know why Dad had to get so involved in it. And it's his brother. Anyway, I knew how Dad would carry on so I didn't even bother trying to raise the subject. And then we're sitting at

Dad's and he's complaining about the position Mum has put me in, which yeah, is out of line too, but he does it without even a hint of self-awareness. The way those two carry on, no wonder I never want to come home.'

Poppy looked out of the window, suddenly intently focused on the identical freshly mown lawns and the bright day lilies that bloomed all over Winston at this time of year. They were painted on tea towels sold as mementos for stopping in the town and worn in the hair of teen girls who picked them from front yards on the way to school. This year they had bloomed later than usual, something nobody in the town would think to regard as ominous, except perhaps a farmer. Eventually they eased into Rachel's driveway in silence.

Chapter 6

Phinn tried to keep a bead on the rotating hexagons spinning rapidly out of sight as the shapes quickly merged into a shrinking white ball still on an upward trajectory as it passed over the grey metal crossbar.

'Dribbly dammit,' he murmured, hands on hips, head tilted. The mistimed kick would mean a walk into the unruly scrub behind the goal net.

He was already tired of walking before he got to the fields, which served as the final border between the town and the bush surrounding it.

Without the car it was a good forty-five minutes on hoof to the browning glorified paddocks, and that wasn't even taking in the 400-metre driveway that the European arrivals to the area were forced to lay down to get to the last decent-sized expanse of land unthreatened by the bushfires during the worryingly more frequent dry seasons.

Still, it gave Phinn time to think on things without the irritating volleys of perceived offences constantly arcing between his sisters, his mum and his aunt back at the house. At one point he had tried to tune out the chatter and petulant stomping up and down the hallway by reading one of the abandoned history books, before he realised that the background white noise had trapped him in one paragraph on the post-World War II origins of the CIA for forty-five minutes.

He looked back at the looping blue gravel track towards the highway. Phinn had a theory about driveways and the blokes he grew up with.

He noticed that with his invariably wilder mates in town, they would be out of the school gates in a flash and back to their local streets. He watched and waited as they sprinted up the slightly uneven concrete drives to their houses. Once inside they would quickly shed their navy school clothes for different uniforms of Kmart surf-branded T-shirts and hoodies and almost run back into town to yell their expletive-laden greetings to the same wayward schoolmates they had just spent the last eight hours with, in and out of detention. The only difference was that this time the disapproving scowls came from civilian adults outside of shops, not just the exhausted ones in the playground on the Department of Education's meagre payouts.

But when it came to his mates whose houses lay on the other side of the highway, it was a completely different equation. The battered silver bus would stop and drop them next to either a mounted keg or a white-painted stump with a number serving as a postbox. Beyond that, there would be another off-orange trail, sometimes winding a kilometre back to a homestead, usually bordered with barbed wire.

These guys didn't seem to be in any rush at all. They slung their bags over their shoulders and shuffled on, sometimes pausing to launch one of their scuffed sneakers at a fence post.

Phinn marvelled at it. With his pal Zeke, a ruddy-faced son of a dairy farmer, it had been a lazy twenty-four minutes before the pair saw the rusted rotary hoe, the first sign that they were approaching his fourteen-year-old mate's red-brick home. After banging open the screen door leading to the kitchen, Zeke had dumped his grey bag and rummaged in the fridge for the lime cordial as Phinn had watched on, curious. Zeke's movements betrayed no urgency.

'Aren't you going to change out of your uniform?' he'd finally asked.

'What for?' Zeke replied. 'To do what? Make more washing?' He'd lazily pointed at the two-metre-high squat rainwater tank outside. 'That's a flogging, Phineas.'

Embarrassed, Phinn had looked around at the lemon-yellow cabinets. 'Ah, so are we going back to town? To do stuff?'

Zeke turned back to his mate with a withering look. 'What for? We just got here.' He'd suddenly arched an eyebrow and delivered the first of what would eventually be many references to the family's undeclared cash crop. 'I've got to go check on the old man's ... ah, green patch, out near the pump, just down the road. You can come. If you're not scared of tearing your uniform.'

'Walking?'

'Walking.'

More driveways, Phinn thought now as he rubbed the mud off the Barça-branded sphere and walked back to the bag of other soccer balls in the net. Zeke and all those other blokes outside town. Always shuffling on a driveway to another driveway just to get back in time to another driveway.

He hummed his own remix of Tom Cochrane, making life a driveway instead of a highway.

He lined up another ball on the right-hand corner of the goal box and thought of his other childhood mates in town, like Jase and Brayden, now reduced to faraway Facebook images of sunburnt stubble, Arnette sunnies, tribal tatts on biceps and AR-15s, all set against monochrome backdrops of clay huts and sand horizons.

This time the three steps to the ball lined up perfectly and he felt his left foot take his full weight before his right – one second coiled behind him – came swinging down. The satisfying sound of the strike gave him a full-body sensation. He watched the ball's tiny blur of a logo spin back at him then it disappeared into a strained section of the net at the goal's left edge before suddenly dropping like a shot bird.

'Wonder how many army careers could have been stopped just by longer driveways,' Phinn murmured to himself.

Chapter 7

Claudia: I can't wait for you to get here.

Dylan: Uh oh. I hope your family is being nice to you.

Claudia: Not really. I just wish you were here.

Dylan: Not long now my love.

Claudia: Aren't you even going to ask me what's wrong?!

Dylan: Um, I thought you would call.

Claudia: I hate my family.

Dylan: Your mind is like the Earth when men thought it was flat and they could sail off it and didn't go certain places because of dragons. Terrifying.

Claudia: You're meant to be on my side.

Dylan: I am. I will call you in a few hours.

Claudia: Great.

Dylan: Amazing.

Claudia: Fantastic.

Dylan: Super.

Claudia: SPLENDID.

Chapter 8

'A broken heart at a wedding is like an ugly baby: everyone will put up with it but keep it out of their face.'

'A broken heart at a wedding is like ice cream for dinner, incredibly indulgent.'

'A broken heart at a wedding is like your nine-to-five job, a fact of life not worth whining about.'

Nora leaned back in her train seat. The scenery had not changed much since she had left the city. She was four hours in with five hours to go.

She looked down at her diary, seeing that the fifteen lines or so beginning, 'A broken heart at a wedding is like ...' seemed rather pathetic once she put the pen down.

She glanced at her watch: like her handwritten diary, it seemed a relic. She assumed her friends kept their diaries in their Google drives, accessible from any device. That is if they kept diaries; she didn't even know if they did. Nora thought it was important to be aware of how much she had forgotten, which she was reminded whenever she read a diary from her teen years and marvelled at the names. She would revisit what at the time of writing had seemed like a life-changing event, but when she tried to conjure an image of it would come up with zilch.

The intricate brass minute-hand on Nora's watch ticked over to midday, a vertical exclamation point on top of its shorter, fatter counterpart. She almost leaped up from her chair in glee. It was a respectable time.

She walked to the dining cart where two young men, probably backpackers, were leaning against the counter watching some kind of sports game on a small screen held closely between them.

Nora smoothed her already crisp jeans. She was wearing a navy soft cotton down T-shirt, but her linen blazer remained draped over her seat in case it got cold later. Her chestnut-coloured hair had been blow-dried two days before so it was that sort of no-effort-ruffled-chic that she so enjoyed.

She watched the two men – adult-sized boys actually, she thought to herself – for another thirty seconds and cleared her throat. They looked up simultaneously, and seeing who was in front of them each tried to serve her at the same time.

'What would you like?'

'How are you today?'

'What can I get you?'

Nora caught the eye of the shorter one, just to save her the hassle of craning her neck slightly more, and smiled without showing any teeth.

'I'll just have a chardonnay, thanks.'

The shorter one beamed. 'Certainly, ma'am.' He turned around and, as he retrieved a miniature bottle from the fridge,

Nora felt a wave of relief to see it was 500 millilitres and not one of the tinier ones. He gave her the bottle with a defeated-looking plastic cup on top as she handed over her credit card.

He winked at her. 'See you again soon, no doubt.'

Nora took the bottle and cup and let the comment bother her all the way back to her seat. What did he mean by that? That because she was buying wine at midday she would certainly be back again before the train reached its destination? She could have a glass of wine on the train. It was one of the reasons she had decided on the train: it seemed old-fashioned, kind of exciting. Time for a sit and a long think. A sit, a long think and a drink. They wouldn't offer it on the train if it was a problem, would they?

Nora was having this conversation with herself more and more lately. Did she need to drink wine at every dinner she went to? Could she have a lunch with someone without a bottle of something? Was two nights in a row booze-free enough? Did she need to drink at the cinema? At the China Town food court? At baby showers?

But everywhere she looked at these places, at these events, people were drinking as well. When she googled it a multitude of blogs came up, people who drank socially, were never told they had a problem and they gave up alcohol and then wrote about how it was a problem, an easily disguised problem if you're not drinking at six a.m. and still holding down your full-time job. The bar for being labelled not-a-problem-drinker is in fact very low.

All the blogs said that people who drank 'normally' never thought about drinking. They didn't count their alcohol-free nights and they didn't ask anyone else if they thought they drank normally. But Nora wasn't so sure. She also monitored how much meat she ate, how much sugar she consumed.

As long as she could remember, as a child at the lonely dinner table with just her mother, she ate her dinner faster than anyone she knew and then stared longingly at their full plate, just like she did in adulthood with her glass of wine.

She twisted the cap on her Jacob's Creek chardonnay and poured it into her little glass. She took the first wonderful sip and exhaled. Now was not the time to be thinking about her drinking. Now was the time to enjoy the surge of energy and hopefulness of the first sip, the low and euphoric hum that surged through her veins as she began to shake off all that kept her up at three a.m. She would focus only on the next blissful few hours. Now that she had a little armour, it was time to get out her laptop. Balancing the cup on her knee she slid it out of its simple black case and opened it up on the tray table in front of her. Taking a moment to whir to life, she dutifully typed in her password. MrsTran. It had long been a private joke with herself, a play on other girls' obsessions with what they thought marriage meant and other things she felt intellectually above, as well as a joke about her obsession with her boyfriend. Hamming it up, even when there was no one there to 'get' it.

She hesitated, took a swig of her wine, and opened her email. She clicked on the last email from Tom Tran. It had already been opened but remained without a response. She drained the rest of her glass, glanced sideways at the woman in her fifties beside her who had boarded at one of the larger and affluent coastal towns and was now eyeing her, poured the rest of the bottle into the glass and began to read:

The fact is, in my heart, I know that I have generally taken you for a figurative ride for four years with little to no intention of marriage or children with you, which has forced me to take a hard look at myself. And I don't like what I see. Especially for you. I think the fact of the matter is you wanted this so badly you looked past the fact I am a pretty small person at the heart of it. And I know it's a cliché, but I am so sorry and I know that there is someone out there who does deserve you a lot more than I do, especially when I look at what I have done and the fact I pushed these things to the side to be "a good guy". I appreciate now, ironically, that blinding yourself to the fact you love someone, but not enough to give as much of yourself to them that they are giving to you, means that you are NOT A NICE GUY, but an emotionally retarded fuckwit (to paraphrase from Helen Fielding, I guess).

Another thing I don't like about the email exchange is how absolutely cold and impassive this all sounds, when this whole mess has been dragging me into a deep, dark funk for the last ten days. I don't want you to think this isn't devastating for me (leaving aside the whole "poor-me I can't emote, boo-fucking-hoo" confessional at the top there). In the time we've been together, we've done so much, and you have been at my side for so many important things in my life (career change, the six-month healing process of a broken leg, family estrangements, etc.). I can't repay you for that. I wish I could.

And I guess that's the point. I believe this whole situation has seen us become different people. You are growing into your role as one of the country's leading young lawyers. You are also growing into yourself as a young woman, and not the, ah, brash but brilliant teen I first met. And sometimes, like it or not, I feel I am in the way of this because I cannot give you what you want as you grow (and I try desperately to stay in place). Once again, it is not fair to you. And I feel like a terrible person because I have been with you for four years, giving hope to you that something would happen along these avenues when it wasn't in me to start with, and is definitely drifting further away now.'

Nora shuddered and let out a low groan. She put down the glass and gently pressed the edge of her palms against her forehead. Reading it physically hurt. She could genuinely feel her heart contract tightly in her chest. She still couldn't quite believe it each time she read it. And she read it much more than she should. She hadn't even told Claudia she had broken it off with Tom. She had done it half as a lark. To try on singledom like slightly different underwear before returning to faithful briefs. Tom was still the man she was supposed to have her babies with, an actual life with. It would have been one last hurrah before settling down. If she was being brutally honest with herself it was also to sleep with one of her colleagues without feeling any guilt. And somehow it had spiralled out into this. An email telling her he had never really loved her. He did say he was devastated and blah blah blah. But that was the essentials of the message. He'd never loved her.

And now she was on her way to her best friend's wedding, unable to talk to the person she was closest to in the world about the break-up because it was happening in the most turbulent week of Claudia's life. Nora assumed it was the most chaotic; she hadn't spoken to Claudia since she had arrived in her home town. But Nora had been friends with her long enough to know what to expect. She was half prepared for an emotional wretch to meet her at the train station. It couldn't be a meeting of two emotional wretches, so Nora really needed to pull herself together.

Just one more read of the email, she told herself.

But first, she thought, standing up, another drink.

Chapter 9

Claudia stood on the platform with a bunch of cheap clearance-style roses in her hands. Flowers at airports, at bus and train stations, were a long time in-joke between the two friends. Neither of them could remember what the punchline was anymore ... was it to do with romantic comedies and men never buying flowers in real life? But they carried on. She shifted from one foot to the other and ran her hands through her hair, flicking the band on her wrist and untucking and tucking her pale pink shirt into her high-waisted black cigarette pants. Despite Nora's obvious distaste for them, Claudia was standing in the same black and white trainers she almost always wore, which she thought went with everything and added a bit of funk. Claudia was not nervous about seeing Nora. It did not matter if Nora thought her shoes were dreadful, or if Claudia had not showered this morning, or if she used phrases such as 'more better', which she was prone to do when very relaxed.

A best friend cannot make you nervous: there is too much of yourself poured into them staring back out at you and it is difficult to find yourself particularly dazzling or intimidating.

What Claudia was worried about was the delicate familial ecosystem that Nora's arrival was about to interrupt. A once-closed natural balance comprising her and her sisters: of ego, of competition over each other's feelings, of insecurities, and some painful memories. The thought that the hurt of some recollections and the dull collective ache they provoked are not just shared with each other exclusively anymore. The realisation that as you get older there are other people you love enough that you can suffer with them too.

It works in reverse too. Secret languages, whatever truly brings you joy, jokes coded for a select few, your most hilarious shames – all once the province of sisters alone – can be shared with an expanded circle as you get older.

Between sisters, their emotions, their feelings for each other, a tricky tenderness, they're all spinning plates – but ornately inscribed, like ancient Chinese artefacts bearing narratives.

Here is the plate that represents you as the person I love most in the world.

Here is the plate showing how suffocated you can make me feel.

Here is the plate holding the memory of us as teenagers, when you told me you pity me and it was the most savage thing anyone has ever said to me and I will never forget it.

Here is the plate that holds a childhood full of fun and mutual adoration.

Here is the plate that only the two of us know about.

Here is the plate holding the constant feeling you are the only adult in the world I have ever wanted to smack in the head.

Simultaneously, your sister is the one with whom you are your most authentic self, who you don't have to watch what you say to, who knows everything you think, but is also the one who can be thrown into a rage at the most oblique reference, the most subtle dig. She knows everything you mean. She knows what everything you say means.

Now Claudia was about to add to this already precarious array of spinning plates, with relationships with people she had grown to love outside the family circle. A husband or wife can mostly provoke ambivalence. They're almost ornaments or accessories in family get-togethers, of complete uninterest to even the most passionate of siblings, who have no quibbles with ignoring the status of their in-laws. Nobody wants to have sex with their sibling, so why would you worry about the person who does?

But a friend. A friend is much more complicated territory.

Claudia could hear the rumble of the train before at last it came into view and she beamed to herself, thrilled at the thought of an arrival whose job essentially was to be in her corner.

The train stopped, shuddering to a final mechanical sigh. Shading her eyes against the sun, she looked down the silver and orange carriages as people began to get off. It was the usual older crowd: chubby older women in tracksuits, with hair that had been set at the hairdresser's just for the trip; young, harried parents with sunken eyes reflecting a ten-hour stint keeping toddlers captive in a ten-metre by four-metre box. Ecstatic children covered in chocolate and sausage-roll crumbs finally tasting freedom. Gloomy middle-aged women and men, who had escaped their home town decades ago and were unsurprised to be back. And Nora.

Nora stepped off a carriage halfway down the platform. She looked her usual cool, calm and collected self, dressed in the uniform of the eternally unruffled and calmer friend. Jeans, unwrinkled shirt, blazer. She wheeled a sleek monogrammed hard black suitcase next to her. Claudia shouted her name, waving enthusiastically, and started bounding towards her friend.

Nora turned towards her, grinning. But as she stepped forward her boot seemed to get mixed up with her suitcase, her foot turned at an odd angle and as she tried to lean on the suitcase for balance it slid out from beneath her, taking her leg with it. Suddenly she was sprawled on the ground.

Claudia hooted as she got to her friend's feet and put out her arm.

'Get it together!' she yelled – an old refrain between the two, but usually reserved for other people's pitfalls.

Nora quickly looked up and down the platform for people who were staring at her. Only a man in his seventies, wearing shorts with knee-high socks, was chuckling and not bothering to pretend it was about anything else but Nora's tumble. Nora took Claudia's hand and jumped to her feet.

'Jesus Christ, spare me,' she mumbled as Claudia pulled her in for a hug.

'You're here!' Claudia, a few inches taller than Nora, nuzzled Nora's neck, inhaling her scent. She stopped and held Nora out at arm's length, studying her face. 'Have you been drinking?'

'Why yes I have, thank you for asking,' Nora responded, laughing. 'What else am I going to do on a godforsaken thousand-year train trip I've taken purely for you?'

Claudia smiled and nodded, picking up Nora's suitcase.

'Let's get you checked into your crappy motel and you can scrub the smell of cheap chardonnay from your skin.'

∽

'This is glamorous in a B-grade movie kind of way. I could see interesting things happening to you while you stay here.' Claudia surveyed the Motor Inn room the pair were forced to push their way into after the water-damaged door jammed.

'Interesting things like sexual assault?' Nora said, looking into the bathroom. The beige tiles were clean-ish. The brown carpet had been vacuumed strenuously, but she could already see that under the beds and down the side of the television cabinet had not had the same treatment. 'Make me a coffee would you?' Nora said, gesturing to the corner where a bar fridge squatted. On top sat a kettle and black sachets of Nescafé Blend 43 and white sugar.

Claudia flicked the white plastic kettle's switch. 'Need to sober up for the dress fitting?'

'Oh, rack off.' Nora was busy in the bathroom, taking out her various potions and gels. Claudia listened to the jet-like sound of the tap running, Nora squirting something onto her hands, the slap of skin on skin and the splashing of the water again.

She reappeared looking five years younger.

'You need to put mascara on and fill in your eyebrows; you look like a teenager,' Claudia said, stretching out on one of the single beds in the room. 'Why did you book a room with single beds?'

'In case you need rescuing,' Nora said deadpan, lying down on the other.

She rolled onto her back and stared at the fake wood panelling across the ceiling.

'How you doin', kid?' she asked the fan. She listened as Claudia let out a low sigh.

'I don't know.'

Nora rolled to her side, facing Claudia.

'You don't know?'

'Yeah, I don't know. I don't feel like I think I should. I should feel excited. I feel dread. Should I be feeling this is the surest thing I've ever done? Because I don't know if I've just allowed myself to be corralled into this and just gone along with it. I don't feel like I've made any actual decisions in this.'

'You feel dread? Is that because of Dylan? Or is it because you have to be here for a week? Is it because you're getting married or because you're at the centre of some weird emotional tug of war between your parents?'

'Well, a five year old could tell I'm not enjoying the guilt trips being laid on me by each of my parents in both their blatant and subtle ways. But maybe I am feeling a bit, I don't know, inconclusive about Dylan? Is this really the man I want to be married to? Do I really even want to be married? It's not very cool.'

Nora snorted.

'I'm not sure what your doubts are. Maybe you are just a walking and talking cliché at the moment and it's cold feet.'

'Hmmm, well maybe the week before their wedding would be exactly the time someone *would* reflect on their life.' Claudia sat up and poured two sachets of sugar into a mug with the instant coffee and picked up the kettle.

'You don't have time to reflect on your life this week.' Nora manoeuvred herself into a sitting position and put out her hand for the mug.

'There's no milk, be careful,' Claudia said, handing it to her. 'You know, I thought you would be more sympathetic, for some reason.'

'I'm here to give you what you need.'

Chapter 10

There is plenty to witness when you spend eighteen years living with the same people. Such as, watching them evolve from loving The Wiggles to loving Wilco and thinking that is an extremely individual act, along with approximately three million other teenagers at the time. If you are lucky, your siblings are the only people you ever really belt, that you fight with so ferociously there is hair and bits and skin scattered down hallways for months. Offspring watch their parents eternally commit the sin of being imperfect. Even though their humanness is demonstrated almost daily, the older you get, it still comes as a shock.

When you grow up with people, as opposed to just live with them, when you love them enough to show how enraged you are at their bathroom transgressions, then an unavoidable consequence is knowing them. Really knowing them. A movement of the mouth, the way a hand brushes away a bit of hair, the way their shoulders are set. Undetectable to most, but to those who truly know them, who have grown up with them, the way someone moves their eyebrow can say a hundred different things. I'm mad. I'm sad. I'm bored. I don't like this person. I am attracted to that person. Entire moods can shift within families on the way one of them has moved their hand. There is nowhere to hide from your siblings, from your parents, from your children.

This is how Claudia knew Poppy was going to be a complete cunt at her dress fitting.

Claudia was already standing with Nora in the light-filled upstairs room of the dress shop when her younger sister arrived. The pair were idly flicking through wedding magazines, trying to deduce the differences between the forty-five or so strapless white gowns filling the pages, when the door swung open. Claudia looked up and locked eyes with Poppy and knew. Poppy had her mouth closed, one of the sure signs of her infamous foul moods. It wasn't just closed, it was shut with purpose. She bowed her head slightly as she entered and leaned against a wall after giving her sister and friend a slight wave. She was wearing a short black skirt and a shirt with the logo of a band that had been in their prime when she had been in nappies, but it was her thongs that provided the most extreme visible provocation. She knew Claudia hated thongs. She also knew the final wedding-dress fitting was an event that merited actual shoes. But there she was. She raised her phone and started scrolling through it. Claudia glanced at Nora: beautiful, oblivious Nora. 'Hey Poppy,' she said cheerily. Her enthusiasm was rewarded with silence. Poppy looked Nora up and down, drinking in her ironed white-collared shirt, her espadrilles, her tapered dark jeans, cutting off neatly just above the ankle. She raised an eyebrow but – luckily – she didn't have the kind of cruelty in her to make a seemingly offhand remark that would have the victim thinking about it for three days, that would make someone weep into their pillow at three a.m. while the tormentor forgot what she had said almost immediately. That was Zoe's specialty.

As a silence was settling between them – one Claudia would call uncomfortable, Nora would call innocuous and Poppy wouldn't even notice – a cascade of red tulle entered the room.

It stopped in front of Claudia and the head of a doll emerged from the top of it. It took the trio a moment to realise it was just the woman at the centre of the red tulle dropping her enormous skirt now that she had stopped.

'Clauddddiaaaaaaa,' she squealed.

'Amelia,' Claudia responded meekly, while grasping for something else to say. 'Mum isn't here yet.' Claudia stepped back involuntarily. There was just so much of Amelia; she filled the room.

She wore a ball gown. A red ball gown with a full tulle skirt she had to lift so high when she was walking that it obscured her head, bringing to mind visions of a classic seventies crocheted toilet doily, with its dress billowing out just below its plastic bosoms. The bodice was fitted to her waist and there seemed to be at least three petticoats underneath. An intricate, gold-thread diamond pattern was punctured by different jewels. Her dark hair was pulled back in a severe bun and she wore full make-up of red lipstick, foundation that was half a shade too dark, cat-eye eyeliner, bronzer and blush, both in shades slightly too dark and slightly too bright for her skin. The overall effect left one wondering if she was quite mad or if she was so lacking in personality that this was her way of making up for it.

'It's so refreshing to have a bride who doesn't feel the need to diet before her wedding,' Amelia said with a bright smile while looking Claudia up and down.

Amelia was a bitch.

Nora opened her mouth and then quickly closed it again, the manners so ingrained into her as a child once again short-circuiting her stinging response. Poppy snorted while Claudia, in the absence of any appropriate comeback, just thanked the boutique owner.

'I don't think we should start until Mum gets here,' Claudia added.

Amelia's eyes narrowed slightly. 'This is a very busy shop.'

'We can see that,' Nora said, looking around the space that was entirely empty except for the four women.

'It's okay, Mum would've been out the door but just wanted to put on a load of washing,' Poppy said, speaking for the first time. Claudia looked to her hopefully but Poppy was scrolling on her phone again. Like a menacing stray cat, her crankiness had looked around the room and settled in, making itself comfortable on the green velvet chaise longue. It was here for the morning.

'Are you going to offer us some tea? Maybe some champagne?' Nora asked, inherently scary by the sheer neatness of her clothes and hair. She was trying to fill the room with her 48-kilogram frame, to show Amelia she was committing the most heinous of sins – being a bad host. She wanted Amelia to feel small.

'Oh of course,' Amelia said breezily. 'I just thought since the appointment was for nine thirty a.m. we would have everyone here at nine thirty a.m. and I could offer refreshments at nine thirty-five a.m. Now I think of it, it's been so long that the tea I prepared for you might be cold. Eeeesssssiiieeee,' she called.

A plain woman in her fifties appeared, hair cropped, rimless glasses on, holding a tray with five crystal glasses of champagne, a teapot and five mugs.

'Help yourself while we wait,' Amelia said, cocking her head to emphasise the wait. Nora defiantly picked up a champagne glass and found a spot on the chaise longue. Poppy jumped away from the wall, an animation brought to life.

'Hold on! Let's get a photo before we drink them,' she said, reaching her phone out awkwardly in front of her and sitting down so close to Nora she was almost in her lap. She grabbed a champagne glass and beckoned to Claudia.

'I'm not drinking this morning,' her sister said.

'That's okay, just hold the glass for the photo.'

'What is this photo for?'

'Just Snapchat; we don't have a money shot for Insta yet.'

It was on the tip of Claudia's tongue, so close that the way she clamped on it was almost violent. But she didn't say it. She picked up a glass and sat on the other side of Nora, tilting her head just so for the photo.

Poppy returned to her sulk corner as soon as she'd uploaded it. Nora took a swig of her champagne. Claudia's chest tightened as she tried to think of something to say to pull Poppy from her mood. Amelia continued to glare.

Finally, finally, finally, after a century had passed, after the tides had adjusted to a new distance from the moon, after dynasties had risen to power and died out due to infertility, after another planet had been discovered and dismissed from the solar system like an unwanted child, the door opened.

Rachel never apologised for being late. Not because she thought it was not her fault, or because she thought of it as a power play, or because it was so rare. She never apologised because it never occurred to her it was rude to be late – or even that she was tardy at all. She was such a chronically late person it was as if the concept of seconds, minutes and hours did not apply to her: like someone in a pulp sci-fi novel she was exempt from time's terrible, inexorable powers. And if it did somehow apply to her, then nobody else's time would be more valuable than hers anyway.

Trailed by Zoe, she walked in, as excited as Carole Middleton on learning who else would be going to St Andrews.

'She had to hang some washing out before we left,' Zoe said dryly, looking Poppy up and down. Zoe nodded towards Claudia, holding eye contact for a moment and a half. That was the length of time it took to convey, 'Don't blow up at Mum; at least we aren't here an hour late. I see Poppy is in a foul mood so this is going to be a fun morning, but at least I am here for you, don't worry.' If she'd had the time she would have also set her face into delivering an addendum: 'I don't know why you have to bring Nora everywhere when you have me,' but, mercifully, she broke eye contact.

'Hello sweeeeetie,' Rachel said, giving Poppy a hug before the bride, which they all knew meant she had registered Poppy's cloud of scorn as well.

'Aw shit, man, I wish I was dead,' Zoe said, staring Poppy straight in the eyes.

Amelia finally interrupted.

'Let's get in this dress, shall we?' she said sharply.

Nora looked from Amelia to Claudia to Rachel and, after being certain nobody was looking, picked up a second glass of champagne.

∽

Claudia had disappeared, whisked away to a changing room, pulled away by a tide of red tulle. Rachel faced the other women and weighed up her options: she was now bored with Zoe and, after quickly noting Poppy's combative stance, turned to Nora.

'It's so nice you could come, to be here in the days before it really gets manic,' she trilled, unable to help herself. 'Claudia needs all the support she can get.'

Nora, having known Rachel for years, knew that all that was required of her was a nod and smile. Conversation with the matriarch did not need a verbal participant, just some faint sounds of agreement and an adequately interested-looking face.

Zoe cut her eyes at her mother in warning. But Rachel forged on obliviously in her bid to pull her youngest daughter out of her scary funk, while bypassing the well-worn path of confrontation, screams, tears and apologies.

'Have you seen the veil we think will go perfectly with the dress? Poppy made it! She's so clever. Claudia wants flowers in her hair, for some reason. I think it looks so common; you can wear flowers in your hair to your birthday party, why wouldn't you wear a veil on your wedding day? You only get married once – well, that's the ambition. She wasn't letting go of this flower idea and I said why don't you try a veil with a little bit of flower embroidered on it? Well, Amelia said that was impossible to get, that she would order it in for about $220 but Poppy said to leave it with her. Why should tulle be so difficult to sew into? And she did it! She's so clever. Aren't you, Poppy? Just watched a video on the internet, it looks so beautiful, but I haven't seen Claudia try it on yet. It was only $11 to make!'

Rachel used the time she needed to draw breath and look at her two daughters. It was pathetic and desperate the lengths one would go to in an attempt to pull Poppy out of a mood while steadfastly maintaining the pretence that she wasn't in one to start with. It was a complicated process. Often those involved would end up walking around her as if on an unpredictable platform of rotten wooden floorboards, gently testing where they could place their feet with each treacherous step.

Putting aside prior inclinations and private promises, Zoe joined in the pantomime. 'I didn't know Poppy made the veil!'

Which basically translated to: 'Please crack a smile. Don't you want to feel good? Please don't ruin the afternoon. Please don't ruin the week.' It was half-begging, half-praying.

'I just looked it up on YouTube,' Poppy said, glancing up from her phone. 'Hey, that's a cool photo. You're all at equal distance apart. Stay there.'

Rachel and Zoe didn't move, but there was a certain eagerness to how still they stood. Nora turned towards the camera and Poppy took the requisite eight frames.

Oblivious to the desperate motivations behind the impassioned interplay, Nora actually asked how long it had taken to craft the veil out of genuine curiosity rather than any desire to placate her. Nora didn't even know Poppy had to be placated.

She did not get any response, though. Poppy was already hunched over her phone in a blur of thumbs, ticking sounds and raw intent.

Zoe felt her back pocket buzz with an Instagram notification.

@PoppyBangBang had tagged her in a photo. Zoe read the caption: 'Dress fittings with my Ma and @noranotephron @ZoeYouShould for the most beautiful bride ever #forwhom thebelltulles'. The tips of Zoe's ears went red.

'Wow, that's some real bullshit right there,' she said, looking directly at Poppy while gesturing to the screen. 'Why you gotta do that? Post a photo on social media like you're having an amazing time when you've barely spoken to us the entire time. That's some boring and clichéd bullshit there.'

Poppy raised her eyebrows. 'Well, unlike you I've been to plenty of fittings, so excuse me if I'm not as thrilled by the novelty as you seem to be.'

'You're a real brat, you know that,' Zoe shot back, pointedly ignoring her mother's pleading glances. 'A freakin' class A, Mariah Carey ticket-holding, Prince George mimicking, Bieber entourage member brat.' Zoe's tipping point had been reached somewhere between Rachel's obvious hand-wringing desperation and the delicate sugar-coating that everyone – except Nora – had been trying to apply to a benign discussion on bridal accessories.

'Well, I've actually been here. Some of us don't get to swan in with overpriced handbags, creating an illusion of a personality and then expect everyone to get along with us,' Poppy replied, provoking a sharp intake of breath from Nora, the only reminder she was still in the room.

Zoe responded with the most infuriating thing a sibling can do during a violent crossfire of harsh home truths. She laughed. She didn't think it was funny. It was merely a basic battle strategy, launched for maximum impact on Poppy's fury.

'Girls, girls, stop it, I swear to God, I will tell your father,' Rachel whispered, invoking a long impotent threat that had survived the divorce and remained out of habit.

She was interrupted by the salon door swinging open. In the doorway stood the cheesecloth-clad figure easily capable of restoring Zoe and Poppy's sisterly affection via a well of mutual spite. 'Helllooo sweeeeties!'

'Helllooo!' Mary bellowed. 'Rachel, I know this was a girls' afternoon, but you told me about the fitting and I thought – well, I'm in the neighbourhood – I might as well pop my head in … And I'm a girl!'

Poppy's eyes narrowed as Zoe muttered, 'So your purpose for being in the neighbourhood is to crash things you were specifically not invited to?'

Rachel, who came from a long tradition of bestowing her best graces on those least deserving of them, hugged her sister, the previous shouting match now a distant memory. 'Of course you're welcome! Here comes Amelia; I think Claudie has just put on the dress.'

Zoe looked from Mary to the emerging Amelia in horror: she knew Claudia would be just behind her. Amelia did a dramatic bow, took a dainty sidestep and held out her arms for the bride to emerge. Nora idly wondered if the circus-master style that Amelia employed for such grand entrances was not the teeniest bit ironic in the current circumstances.

Claudia stepped out from behind the curtain, a vision resplendent in ivory. She glanced around the room and quickly clocked the distance between Zoe and Poppy, but it was only after she had registered Mary's presence that her face really began to fall.

Poppy turned on her heel and left.

But Claudia was already in tears.

'Why is Mary seeing my dress before Dad does?'

Chapter 11

Poppy stormed down the street, fists clenched, chest stretched tight. She could hear her heart. It was compressed and beating madly. Her ears filled with roiling blood. She was muttering under her breath. Nobody walking past could quite catch what she was saying but it was to a steady, basic beat: 'And up two, three, four, five, six, seven, eight, and down two, three, four, five, six, seven, eight, and up two, three, four, five, six, seven, eight.' It was a mantra she had learned when she was teaching barre classes – just one of her fly-by-night jobs that never seemed to involve discussions of contracts, sick pay and holiday leave. It was incredibly easy to convince people you knew about the combination of yoga, Pilates and ballet, and people in the city were willing to pay $25 for the pleasure of being fooled. She would count three sets of eight leg raises to the beat she was reciting, three sets of eight turned-out pulses, three sets of eight making little circles with your arms. She swore she did the counts in her sleep. She also used it to try to calm her anxiety.

She didn't know why she always had to be so awful when there were too many members of her family in one space. She felt there was no room to breathe; she felt herself regressing the minute she was with both of her sisters and mother. The more she told herself before the event that she would behave, that she would be happy, the more the anxiety would move from her stomach to her chest to her limbs – so they wouldn't move – and finally to her mouth, which would inevitably fix in a pout. Something would infuriate her, a flippant remark about her bedroom, a comment on her clothes, a question about her job(s), and all the anxiety, at this point a rapidly whizzing internal combustion of bristling nerve endings, would once again strike the flint of her open heart and become that familiar iron spark before the explosion about to force its way out. Blind rage. Even while she was spitting insults at her sisters, refusing to speak at a lunch table, there would be a small part of her asking, 'Why, why are you doing this?' but a bigger part of her, the part in charge, would be too furious to respond.

She had ruined the dress fitting. She knew that. But her perfect sisters with their perfect lives would get over it. Arseholes.

Poppy continued walking and counting down the beats until the white-hot flare of anger bubbled down and became manageable, a small dark stress ball she could toss from hand to hand until it turned to guilt. Poppy got out her phone and sent a text. Within a minute a message had flashed on her screen. She read it and let out a small sigh, before turning on her heel in the direction of the pub.

∽

Poppy pressed her palm flat to her fringe. She had read somewhere that it was preferable to running your fingers through it because that just made it greasy. She wondered if that was bullshit, like primer before foundation. Probably.

She looked down. She was wearing a long loose black dress with pink patterns of lipstick all over it. After years of dressing in jeans and shirts in an attempt to prove her sexuality – an unconscious plea to those she had come out to: 'See, I am serious about being a lesbian; this shirt is from the men's section!' – she had become more comfortable embracing her *femme* side. She did not know if the dress looked like a shapeless sack or very chic, though. It was slightly irrational given the medium, but if she had known she was going to text Leah today she would've worn something entirely different. Something that accurately conveyed that she was unaffected, and sartorially savvy, but without trying too hard. But anyway. Here she was. She had told Leah she was busy with wedding preparations when she left her house the other morning, so she knew it was her responsibility to make next contact. She just hadn't thought she actually would.

Leah was perched in the corner when Poppy walked in. She sat on a high stool at a small round table – her feet not quite reaching the bar below her – with her spine stiff, sitting ruler straight. Her black shirt read 'Pissed Jeans doesn't care about YOU people' in plain white type. Only because of Dylan did Poppy know this was a reference to yet another band of skinny white men-children with loud guitars. She smiled. Leah hadn't even been halfway through primary school by the time the nineties finished.

Leah looked up, saw Poppy, and they greeted each other with the acute awkwardness of two almost-strangers who have exchanged bodily fluids.

There's the awkwardness of a confessed crush, a drunken kiss with a colleague, or telling an acquaintance they have something in their teeth: awkwardness is a spectrum. On the spectrum, Leah and Poppy were at the fairly niche end where you have sucked their titties and lost your virginity to their brother.

'Tough day?' Leah asked after Poppy's mumbled greeting. They both directed their glances towards vague points of the pub and paused, each waiting for the other to keep talking.

After a beat too long Poppy turned back and pointed to Leah's empty schooner glass. Leah nodded.

∽

Three empty glasses later, a slightly more relaxed Leah was finishing her medium-sized story about how she had decided to run a small-sized business from her parents' house, selling earrings in the shapes of icy poles and book covers.

'Because of copyright, maybe the second worst law after defamation, I can't do iconic book covers, so they are puns on famous book titles. You know, *Grater Expectations* with Pip and a little cheese grater? *Couching Towards Bethlehem*? *One Hundred Beers of Solitude* with an old Spanish guy sitting at a bar?'

Poppy laughed. 'That's clever. You should branch into CD covers next. You can do *Don't Look Back in Hunger* with the Gallagher brothers tucking into a cake or *Nevermime* with the French clown guy in the pool instead of the floating baby.'

Leah laughed and grabbed the table to steady herself on the stool. 'Holy shit, that's good! Maybe you can be my chief strategist. I need to market as well, which basically means I don't know how to use Instagram.'

'Just post a sunset at least once a week and only put up pictures before nine a.m. and after six thirty p.m. Your followers will quadruple.'

'See, you're a natural.' Leah smiled coyly.

'Well, I do have a degree in journalism, which is essentially marketing. And I follow Selena Gomez on Instagram. Really, Selena taught me everything I know.'

'Amen.'

Poppy looked at a corner of the roof of the pub as she addressed Leah.

'It's brave what you've done.'

'What? Starting my own business? The overheads are incredibly low when it is run out of your parents' garage.'

'Hmmm, that and coming back. Knowing when the time was to come back.'

Leah stopped smiling and sagged her shoulders. 'Knowing when to give up, you mean.'

Poppy moved her gaze from the corner to a rag lying on a chair three tables away from them.

'Yes. That's brave too. Knowing when to give up.' She looked at Leah. 'The ground has become sand beneath us. It's falling away. The city isn't made for us anymore, it's a fortress for the wealthy. You want to live in the city now, you have to be born in the city, or come from the kind of wealth that could fill Olympic swimming pools with cash. I haven't quite accepted that yet.'

'How long ago did you graduate?'

'Two years. Two years and seven months. And three weeks. Two years seven months and three weeks and I still don't have a proper job. Just a bunch of gigs. A bunch of gigs in the gig economy.'

Leah nodded empathetically. Truly. She had been there.

'What kind of gigs?'

'Copywriting. A bit of reception work. Delivering pizzas on my bike. I used to Uber but had to sell my car. I'm so tired. I thought I would have a job by now. I am supposed to have a job by now. But I don't even know what the industry is going to look like in five years' time. Where are journalists meant to fit in all of this? You can flog your product direct to the customer online now. I know journalists should exist, sometimes I think they have to exist, but I just have no idea how they are meant to fit into the new model. What is supposed to fund us? Do we just rely on benevolent millionaires? Subscriptions? I honestly can't even see at the moment how something like the press gallery is supposed to exist. I can't see the market demand for it.'

'I just couldn't get a real job. I know people want illustrators; a few years ago you could eke out a living doing it. But now you eke out the same living and rent is five times as much as it was just five years ago.'

'And the planet is being destroyed; the Great Barrier Reef is being bleached. RIP the Great Barrier Reef. We can't have housing and we can't snorkel.'

The conversation had taken the inevitable turn. Their own destruction.

Poppy took a swig of her beer. 'I don't know how we are going to survive. I don't know what the jobs of the future will look like. I don't know how we can save ourselves from being poor.'

'I can't penetrate the future either. I have no idea what we'll look like in five years, what the country will look like.'

'Do you want to know how I comfort myself? Surely America collapses first? We'll get the warning, won't we? We'll have a warning and it will be America. That country will fail first and then we will know what to look out for. Then we will know what's coming.'

Leah sat up straighter. 'I've been doing boxing four times a week – I'm ready for the war.' She grinned and raised her beer to clink Poppy's.

'To being ready for the war,' they chanted.

They were so miserable there was no option but to go home together.

Chapter 12

Reasons People Are Wrong, by Claudia Carter, an exercise in being committed to passive aggression and not yelling at my family:

Mum bought blue cheese.

Poppy does not believe in compromise.

Phinn won't stop playing the guitar.

Zoe said I was not interesting when I was talking about the superiority of plunger coffee over Nespresso.

I feel like a moody bitch.

Nobody appreciates it when I'm a decent human being.

The house is already trashed.

It's really windy.

We have a fridge full of beer and the only cold ones are fucking Stella.

Poppy is just a bitch.

I can't think of any more failings for myself. I am just moody.

I thought I saw a dolphin once but it was just wind.

I can't find a candle to light so I can pray Poppy dies next time she goes on an overseas holiday she can supposedly not afford.

Poppy taking my beer despite there being cold Stella in the fridge. She doesn't want anything unless it's mine, then she needs it badly and is obviously entitled to it. Apparently she is not capable of deciding she wants a Bighead and putting one in the freezer herself and waiting for it to be cold. Apparently I should be taking care of her needs at all times. Allowing her to be in my bridal party and choose her own dress is obviously not doing enough for her; I should be making her beer (which she also didn't pay for) cold too.

I pulled Poppy's hair for a not-very-good reason. It's just a beer. Should save the violence for when she commits credit-card fraud in my name for an ugly It Bag or something of the sort.

Phinn took photos of a serious fight.

Dylan is the only decent human being in the family, and that includes me.

I told Poppy I didn't want her here. Which in the moment was true, but in the balance of things isn't.

Poppy will not say sorry for taking my beer.

I am being uncharacteristically passive aggressive but it might be allowed because I am at least funny.

There was no last-minute accommodation in town midweek. That would have showed them.

Chapter 13

To say that Dylan was a simple man was to say that the sun is bright. It is true on a very basic level but it's ignoring a hell of a lot of complexity. Dylan possessed those characteristics that are most underrated in human beings. He was funny and intelligent – attributes recited monotonously around the world when people talk about what's important to them. Because it's true but, on the other hand, it's unacceptable to also say, 'I want someone who will ignore my polite requests during sex and just throw me down' or, 'I want someone who will always take my side against my reasonable mother' or, 'I want someone who will accept me as a little bit sexist and racist but fundamentally a decent human being'.

Dylan fulfilled the criteria one usually simply forgot to acknowledge out loud. It was an overlooked quality due to it being slightly out of fashion, a little bit boring and just plain taken-for-granted – he was kind.

When he was seven years old, much to his father's horror, he donned a pair of rabbit ears and hopped up and down his street leaving chocolate eggs on the neighbours' doorsteps.

When he was thirteen he asked the tallest girl in the class to dance after watching her stare at the floor for an hour at the disco.

When he was sixteen he spent six weeks mowing the lawn of a teacher with a broken leg because he knew he had not made any friends in his town yet.

When he was nineteen he would rub his girlfriend's back when she suffered period pain and fetch her a hot-water bottle instead of dismissing it as yucky, whiny women's business like most of his peers.

His kindness wasn't ostentatious, or extravagant, or even worthy of any notable praise, as most of it fell in the category of Decent Thing To Do. But being kind is much more difficult than most of us who have never practised kindness assume it to be.

It was this sweet, kind, slightly awkward man who now walked into the jaws of the Carter family.

∽

Dylan had obligingly made the nine-hour trip by car to Claudia's home town. It was easier if they had their own getaway wheels. In a stupendous mood after uninterrupted hours of listening to Mclusky and Future of the Left, he hummed along to the opening strains of 'She Will Only Bring You Happiness' as he pulled into George's street. The week was going to be fine; difficult at times, but fine, he thought to himself, an unsurprising stance given his perennially sunny disposition.

He turned down the music as he pulled into George's driveway. He was never quite sure if it was the right low brick bungalow he was entering, and liked to turn down any noise for concentration, just like when he turned off the radio to focus on his parallel parking. But this time he knew he was right. The garage door was slightly raised and through the bottom he could see three pairs of bright pink Adidas shoes. Matching anything was a classic Carter giveaway, despite everyone demonstrably being older than five, and was something even the parents joined in on. Dylan allowed himself a sigh. Even from here he could tell they were up to something; they had the whiff of mischief as unity. He wouldn't be walking into a brawl, sulky silences and bruised egos; instead, today, it would be scheming. As he edged the car up the driveway he could see the owners of the pink sneakers had registered his approach. The stances changed and a head appeared at the bottom of the garage door, bending over to get a good look. He saw the ruffled head of his fiancée. Claudia's blonde hair, almost bleached into oblivion, fell over her dark eyebrows and ill-advised grey-rimmed glasses. She saw Dylan and a huge smile broke out as she lay down on the ground and wriggled beneath the garage door.

'Dylan! Love of my life, eternal joy of my soul! You came running back to me!'

She leaped into his arms and wrapped her legs around him.

For a moment there were no doubts. Dylan kissed her nose and placed her on the ground, glancing towards the other two pairs of feet visible in the garage.

'What's going on in there?' he asked.

Claudia cocked her head. 'Family bonding time.'

'Hoo boy.'

Dylan walked over to the roller door and bent to lift it.

'NO!' Claudia stopped him. 'We can't open the door; we can't let anyone see what's going on in there. Wriggle under.'

So it begins, Dylan thought to himself. He briefly considered a protest but he was not wired that way. He lay down on the ground and rolled under the door, coming to rest on his back inside the garage.

'Dylan!'

Poppy and George spoke in unison as their heads appeared in his vision. Despite the weather, Poppy seemed to be wearing a dark polo neck, beanie and sunglasses. George was in a pale blue shirt that read 'This is what a feminist looks like', something he probably found hilarious.

'I don't want to give you the satisfaction of asking,' Dylan said, looking at Poppy as he scrambled to his feet. He shook George's hand as Claudia finished rolling beneath the garage door.

'What are the three of you up to?' Dylan looked around and saw a bright blue Mercedes. 'Whose car is that?'

He walked closer and saw that it seemed lopsided.

'It's kind of a long story,' George said thoughtfully as Dylan walked to the side and noted the two flat tyres.

'Do you think we should deflate all of them, or is two enough?'

'All of them will be a much bigger pain in the arse,' Poppy said, heading to the other side of the car and crouching down. Dylan heard the not-quite whistle of air escaping a tyre.

'This is a nice car,' he said, pressing the edge of his shoe against the rubber, as if he was double-checking it was real.

'It's Lisa's,' Claudia said cheerfully. 'She left Dad.'

'Again,' Poppy interjected.

'She wanted to keep some plates in a different cupboard, and it was just the last straw,' George said, rubbing his jaw.

'So you're letting down the tyres of her car?'

'Well, we paid for it together but it's in her name. I don't want her coming during the night and taking it.'

'What is the likelihood of that?'

'You never know with women; they can turn into real bitches at times like this.'

Dylan looked at Poppy, but she continued to concentrate on the air escaping every tyre. As usual, her staunch feminist credentials evaporated in the presence of the men in her family. Poppy felt Dylan's stare and looked up at him.

'What? She is a bitch.'

George stood up abruptly, brushing down his garish shirt with the palms of his hands. 'You know that you are quite "misfeatured" to Dylan?' he said, looking down at his youngest daughter.

'What?'

'I read it in a book the other day. Zadie Smith, I think. She basically said that the siblings of the people we desire are uglier versions. I thought that was very good. What do you think, Dylan? Do you think Poppy is an uglier, misfeatured version of Claudie?'

Dylan paused. 'I've never looked at Poppy.'

George roared with laughter. 'Pitiful dodge. Come inside and I'll feed you.'

∽

Claudia trailed behind Dylan and George as they made their way to the kitchen, leaving a satisfied Poppy with one last tyre to deflate. Through the side door they went down a hallway lined with eccentric decorative drawings and paintings – not many would stoop to call it art. Mostly they were gifts from his children. Shaky paintings of mountains bought from gypsies in some overly frequented European city that made them feel worldly; sketches from the country, and pictures and pictures and pictures of pelicans, a joke that had long ago run its course, but still they persisted in buying a postcard or painting or drawing of one whenever it was spotted.

The hall opened to the kitchen where a giant bowl of tomatoes sat on an otherwise bare table.

'It's a real treat to have you with me today; I get to cook with one of the most tasty and diverse vegetables there is, but which I was forbidden from even mentioning for twenty-one long years,' George said, picking up three tomatoes and lightly squeezing the skin. 'I'm going to make you strapatsada – a little treat, just for you and me.'

Claudia walked over to her father and peered into the bowl. 'I like tomatoes,' she said.

George looked at her, horrified. 'No you don't.'

'Yes I do.'

'No you don't.'

'Yes I do.'

'Since when?'

'For a few years now.'

'You've never liked them.'

'Well, I didn't when I was a kid, but I have been an adult outside of your house for many years now and I like tomatoes. I feel like I'm hitting you over the head with a metaphor now.'

George stared at his second child for a moment too long.

'I feel bad for you and pity me,' he said finally. 'You can have some strapatsada.'

Strapatsada, for when your child is still breaking your heart twenty-eight years on and you are reasonably sure she is going to break the heart of the lovely young man at your table:

Chop up eight tomatoes and put them in a heavy-based pan that is already hot with a little olive oil. Stir for five minutes and watch as they reduce. Put the toast on and pour into the mixture a tablespoon of tomato puree with some sugar and some salt. Stir. Crack two eggs into the tomato mixture and stir as if scrambling for another five minutes as the skins of the tomatoes come off. Take off heat. Spread generously across toast and crumble sharp cheddar and basil leaves on top.

Serve.

Try not to look too devastated at the realisation that – for the 482nd time – you are not the expert on your daughter.

George sat down with Claudia and Dylan as they hoed in. Dinner-table manners are one of the first things eschewed as surplus to requirements once the third child comes along, before you start letting go of frivolities such as daily hygiene with the fourth.

'Mary has a new boyfriend,' Claudia said over their chomping.

Dylan raised an eyebrow. 'Hmmmmmm.'

'It could be a big drama for the wedding.'

Dylan finally looked attentive.

'It's Dad's brother.'

Dylan snorted and George stood up. 'It's not a drama. She can see whoever she wants to see.'

'But she wants to bring him to the wedding.'

George waved a hand as if dismissing his court. 'But she's not.'

Claudia looked at Dylan and nodded towards him. 'See, drama.'

George had already sulkily started to scrape his uneaten strapatsada into a bin and was out the door before anyone had the time to start on a second piece of toast.

'As you are well aware, my family is notorious for how reasonably and well they handle the slightest hint of emotional upheaval,' Claudia said, pretending very badly she was not shaken by her father's hasty exit. Dylan reached over and grabbed her hand, tenderly rubbing his thumb over the top of her knuckles.

'What's the deal with Mick?' Dylan asked, hating himself a little bit.

'It's a long and involved and boring story, but basically Mick cheated on his wife in a very visible and humiliating fashion and Dad has never forgiven him. He took her side. She is invited to our wedding; he is not. Dad hasn't spoken to his brother in about five years, I think; won't even be in the same room.'

'What about birthdays? Surely your family has had some birthdays?'

'Oh, you think the fact it is someone else's birthday would get in the way of his grudge?' Claudia laughed her meanest laugh. 'No, it is for the rest of us to work around.'

Dylan picked at the last of his eggs and tomatoes, as he liked to call George's Greek creation. 'Three sleeps until the wedding. Is there anything you would like?'

Claudia brightened. 'A contract!'

'Well, technically I think we are entering a contract.'

'No, like Kurt Vonnegut, he wrote his wife a contract. Basically saying she could only yell at him after he had failed to do something for three days and that he would scrub the bath after every use so it didn't leave a mucky ring.'

'Hmmm, okay, you want a contract?'

'Yes please. Also can you check in with Nora and make sure she is going okay? She is having some Nora time at the moment but she seems a little ... odd.'

'Anything else?'

'Yes, come here,' Claudia said, patting the space beside her.

Dylan slid closer. 'I am here.'

Chapter 14

Dylan's contract for Claudia, part 1.

So, new contracts. Just the thing. I already promised you one contract and now I am already agreeing to another. I don't know how I feel about that.

Caveat emptor! That's how I feel. Wait, once more with caps: *CAVEAT EMPTOR!!!*

Sounds so authoritative, Latin. I mean, you could probably have built the empire, ornate columns and all, with just the lingo. In much the same way that French gives off that imperceptible balance of sexiness and disdain, I get the feeling that even mentioning cleaning the toilet in Latin loudly enough would somehow conjure up images of Anthony Hopkins sharpening a vintage paring knife in a distant mansion's private library.

PLACERE MUNDATIS LATRINA!!!

Ah, maybe I'm wrong. That should be part of the contractual obligation as well, I guess. Admitting my fault.

I am severely wrong.

(sad face)

EGO SUM SEVERE (pauses, clasps toga over chest, glares at Senate) ... *INIURIAM!!*

All RIIIGGHT!! Even the stupid Caesarean salad days of this lingo are helping me with what is going to be tough. Law. Contract.

So, in the interest of things being fair at the outset before you move into my leaky, creaky 140-year-old home, I will try and put forward the terms of a contract. Seems like a good excuse to look at the tenets of contract law.

Contract law. Ahem. (Googles quickly.)

Anyhoo. A quick revision of my anti-net stance and some judicious use of ctrl + V shows us that contract law is about regulations directed towards enforcing certain promises.

So, certain promises.

1. I promise (sighs deeeeeply, stares at ceiling) as long as you are in my house I will clean the toilet. *Placere mundatis latrina.* There you go.

   And I will scrub without complaint! Not even in Latin, or its latter-day sleazy unemployed uncle, Italian.

   And I will scrub without looking back on what I have done in that same ivory-coloured locale, not stopping until it is clean and clear and something which a clichéd *Full Metal Jacket* (I know you don't watch war movies, growing up in a household so heavy on the X chromosome) -style drill sergeant would feel good about shouting at some hapless private.

2. I promise I will not say anything about how chores are divided in our household (70 per cent to 30 per cent me to

you, just so we have it recorded in writing somewhere other than the census) when you are talking about how women are socialised to be the carer and placate in all their adult relationships. Because you are right! They are! It's just you were too clever to fall for that.

3. I promise I will always give you a kiss at night when I get home, even if you are asleep, because I know it means something to you that I kiss you at night.

Hmmmmm, this is a lot of promising what I will do, while ignoring what can be equally important – maybe even more important, but possibly less important: what I will NOT do!

1. I will not try to fathom you. Because, as you so often like to declare when you have had five proseccos: *You are not here to be fathomed!!*

2. I will not remind you of melodramatic declarations made when you are drunk. Except for just then.

3. I truly, truly will not use a new towel every single time I have a shower.

4. I will not say 'she seems nice' every time you introduce me to a female friend who I think is batshit insane therefore making you feel like you are also going batshit insane interpreting a banal general comment as a vaguely misogynistic sledge.

5. I will not, ever, stop loving you.

Chapter 15

Poppy: I love Dylan.

Claudia: You can marry him then.

Poppy: Aren't you going to ask me why?

Claudia: I know why.

Poppy: Why?

Claudia: You read that crazy fucking contract. A small window into a fantastic and incredibly weird mind.

Poppy: I know he was weird, but my god, what a gift.

Phinn: I have always loved Dylan.

Claudia: All I asked for was a contract!

Chapter 16

Zoe leaned over her mother's sink and tilted her head back. She mussed her hair, ran her finger along her chin and, finding exactly what she was looking for, raised the tweezers. Three swift movements later she bent down to survey the bounty · against the off-white porcelain of the sink.

She shook her head ruefully. A year ago she had two chin hairs. Now she had four. Dark, curly follicles which resolutely returned to her chin almost the night after being plucked out, emulating the kind of endless punishment doled out to one of the errant gods in her ancient Greek mythology.

Was this the beginning of the long and slow decline? Would she wake up tomorrow and see her mother's startled face staring back at her from the gold-plated mirror frame? Ha! She wished. She would more likely see her father's face staring back at her.

It had almost lulled her into a false sense of security, thinking that the worst thing that could happen to her would be turning into her mother. She idly wondered if there was a psychology field in this called Gilmorephobia or the Lorelai Syndrome.

She sighed and turned from the sink, bending at the waist so her knotty hair would gather over her head to be coaxed more easily into a ponytail. She was sceptical about the value of the beach outing, but Claudia had effusively declared a sibling morning ocean swim would be good for the group, and for the week she was trying to give Claudia whatever she wanted. For the week at least. Zoe had held the refrain 'you get one day' on the tip of her tongue like a clenched fist held tightly within a pocket. She had tried to tell Claudia she was taking unnecessary risks organising any group activity in the week leading up to the wedding, that it was taunting fate to have the siblings spending long chunks of allocated time together, but she had the feeling that the success of the pub outing the other night had made her sister cocky, instilled in her a belief she could pull off a situation where everyone would briefly put down their figurative weapons, like Christmas Day on the Western Front.

She had not asked why Nora was not coming. She assumed it was because she was not invited – one of the many tokens of peace extended towards Poppy for the week.

She jumped at the dull thud against the door before the knot in the pit of her stomach unravelled at Phinn's rising baritone.

'Women and the bathroom. I am so sick of women and the bathroom.'

Zoe yanked the door open and laughed as her brother almost fell onto the chessboard tiles while following through on a third knock.

'There's your precious bathroom,' she said, dropping her shoulder into her off-kilter brother's ribcage. Phinn clutched his side, begrudgingly marvelled at his sibling's footy-style hit-and-spin, and held in his painful groan until Zoe was out of earshot.

He quickly put the body-check behind him and strode to the mirror. He surveyed himself admiringly, in the unselfconscious manner that most women could only dream of in some far-off future where their chin is smaller and their blemishes gone and their eyelashes a bit curlier and their nose not so 'strong' and, and, and ...

He had not even finished lathering his jaw in shaving cream when the door opened – this time without knock or warning – and his mother was standing beside him in what he instantly knew was nothing but her dressing-gown. Rachel always had been, and remained, the most mortifying on the scale of what people's mothers were like at home – a naked mum. Other people had cake mums, business mums, shy mums, conservative mums, hippy mums, health-nut mums, and a relatively new breed that was also swelling its ranks: Facebook mums.

The Carters had grown up with Naked Mum. The kind who does not close the door when using the toilet and thinks nothing of her children's deep shame when dashing from the shower to the bedroom to get changed after failing to register the empty towel rack beforehand. The ease she had with her body was brought into sharpest contrast when the girls hit the minefield of adolescence and wouldn't even get out of the shower by themselves without first wrapping themselves in a Sheridan-tagged cocoon so as not to do anything as deeply embarrassing as glance at their awkward, rebellious bodies in a mirror.

Regardless, Rachel was Naked Mum when they were children, when they were teenagers, and she definitely saw no reason for that to change now they were adults. They were lucky she threw them the occasional concession of a flimsy nightgown when Dylan was visiting. Small mercies, thought Phinn.

She nudged her son sideways so she took up half of the mirror and reached for her toothbrush and toothpaste.

'Ma!'

'What?'

'Privacy!'

Rachel rolled her eyes and raised the toothbrush to her mouth. 'I wiped your arse for five years; you can shave the pathetic seven hairs on your face with me in the same room.'

Phinn gave a slight shake of his head and, after letting the creeping blush across his cheeks settle, returned the razor to his face.

❧

Zoe checked her phone and allowed herself what she would now consider an uncharacteristic moment of exasperation. It took so many years to lose it, to soothe it, to pretend her incendiary temper was not lurking just below the surface, an impatient shark patrolling a small tank. Years of hard work quickly unravelling as she waited for her brother and her sisters to get in the goddamn fucking car. She leaned over, and in a movement that brought back an entire youth spent sitting behind cracked faux-leather dashboards waiting for her siblings, leaned heavily on the horn.

Somehow, over the blare, she could still hear her mother's voice cut through the front door to her '... and tell that impatient sister of yours not to touch the goddamn horn, there's no goddamn clock at the beach.'

Zoe paused and leaned on the horn again, ignoring the sudden twitch of the white lace curtains of the neighbours' house. She had never learned their names.

She glanced back at the green front door with a small degree of satisfaction as Phinn sprinted out and leaped over the hedge, quickly making up the metres between the yard's edge and the car. He wore bright green shorts patterned with peacock feathers, a blue shirt that looked two sizes too small and, Zoe realised with a mix of horror and bemusement, a red cap that said 'Make Winston Great Again'.

'You know people think they are so clever wearing the Trump parody hats, but all that anyone thinks when they look at you is, "Look, a dickhead Trump supporter",' Zoe said, adjusting her blue singlet to cover more of her chest from the sun.

'Who said I was being ironic?' Her panting brother grinned as he gave himself another once-over in the rear-view mirror. Then it was his turn to study the door. 'Where are your dumb effing sisters?'

'Mate, I'm the one sitting in the car on time,' Zoe responded. 'They were swapping shorts last time I saw them.'

Phinn kept staring at the door, willing his sisters to materialise, while Zoe fiddled with the wires in the car, trying to tune it to her phone so she could play her own music free of inevitable sibling interjection. While her focus was on choosing between the Yeah Yeah Yeahs and the Liars, Phinn

143

looked back and asked as casually as he could, 'Are you, uh, seeing anyone?'

Zoe slid her sunglasses from her head to her face and surveyed her brother. 'Why would you ask that?'

'I'm trying to be a good brother! Interested. In your life.' He nonchalantly pointed towards her. 'All of that.'

Zoe tapped her phone and Nick Zinner's needling guitar line signalled the familiar opening bars of 'Maps'. She cocked her head lightly and squinted as her sisters came barrelling down the front steps, Claudia shoving Poppy a little too hard out of the way.

'Nothing I would tell you about,' Zoe murmured, as the girls reached the car's blazing hot door handles.

Claudia looked hopefully at the front seat where Zoe was perched and shook her head, as if to clear herself of the notion before clambering into the seat behind Phinn.

Poppy instead dawdled to a light jog, before taking exaggeratedly slow-motion steps around the boot to the other side of the vehicle and then finally wrenching open the door and settling down behind her older sister. It had the desired effect. Zoe turned in her seat and looked at Poppy sharply. 'Are we running on Rachel time, or what?'

Phinn sighed and revved the car, reversing slowly onto the road. 'Lovely day at the beach in T -minus forty-seven minutes,' he mumbled.

Poppy, still weighing Zoe's comment, instead looked out of the window.

Rachel loomed so large in their lives that everything was compared to her – a bad mood, an offhand remark, the way they wore their hair; when they were infuriating each other, when they were emotional, even what they chose to eat and how they drank water (three quarters filled, ice-cold). It was 'just like Rachel', they would tell each other in a tone of rote reprimand. They invoked her name on a daily basis, whether it was internally comparing each other to the omnipotent matriarch, or imagining her disapproval in the morning in their respective homes as they guiltily poured their third coffee.

Unable to stomach butter on your toast? Just like Rachel.

Find yourself so moved by the shuffle function on your iTunes that you start crying in the street for a song from thirteen years ago? Just like Rachel.

Late getting to the car to go to the beach? Rachel.

While the invocations of their largely un-silent but definitely long-suffering Madonna figure bore mocking tones, there was no denying she still made up the scaffolding they hung their days and their selves off.

The siblings rode for the first twenty minutes in silence, Claudia preoccupied with marriage, Phinn enjoying the serenity, Zoe trying to think of safe topics of conversation and Poppy thinking about what she looked like staring stonily out the window. Moody? Beyond reach? Melancholy? (She just looked like someone staring stonily out of the window.)

They could smell the salt in the air when the conversational ceasefire was enthusiastically broken by Poppy. 'Hey Zoe,' she thumped the back of the seat in front of her, 'Mary said something funny this morning when we were leaving.'

'Was it that she needed some wart of toad and hair of virgin for the next time she had her cauldron out? Was she thinking of buying a Dyson V6 because her arse is getting too big for her broomstick?'

The four of them allowed themselves a snigger before Poppy continued, 'No, it was something about a postcard.'

Zoe raised her eyebrows as the corners of her mouth pulled up. 'What did she say about postcards?'

Poppy looked searchingly at Claudia for backup. 'She was talking to Mum and she said something about Zoe being good at writing nasty postcards.'

Zoe's smile was wide and genuine. 'Did she now?'

Poppy leaned in. 'Yeah, she did, what was she talking about?'

'Do you remember a few years ago when Mum was having a hard time at work? They kept cutting her hours?'

Her sisters nodded. Everyone remembered. Rachel had tried to start a union at the credit union where she worked as a cleaner, and her boss, a 52-year-old man in a white short-sleeved shirt and pocket pen protector in another town, responded by cutting her hours to the sixteen-hour weekly minimum. A useful lesson in socialism for some of them and the vital importance of personal finance for others. They all remembered a lot of soup and toast for dinner.

Well, Zoe told them, during that time, Rachel actually needed her sister a bit. Mary was living a couple of hours away, rent-free with some poor sucker in one of those hill village-towns full of exhausted middle-aged tree-changers, and Rachel kept calling her. But after the first conversation Mary just ignored the calls. A Rachel in need was a burden indeed, in her sister's mind.

'I was in the area, I forget why, it might have been for work, or I could have just been road-tripping. I don't know why I was in that town; I don't think I've been back since. Anyway, I knew where she was living; I think I had saved the address from when Mum had posted her some things she'd needed a few months before. I was walking past the poky little village news agency and saw postcards for the area. I don't know why but I lost it, I was just so furious, so I bought a postcard and wrote one to Mary. It said something like, "You are a terrible human being, a bottomless emotional abyss with no empathy for the suffering of those closest to you and you need to apologise to my mother.'"

The car was silent, apart from Karen O's constant yelp about good things happening in bad towns.

Poppy cackled. 'You *what*?'

'I wrote her a postcard telling her she was a terrible human being. I still don't know why. She has never said anything to me about it. Does Mum know about it?'

It was Claudia's turn to start snorting. 'Oh, she knows about it. She didn't tell me what happened but I remember her telling me you had done something she thought you shouldn't have. Then ... Then she told me a story.'

Claudia paused, long enough to make sure she had everyone's attention, but short enough that their notoriously unreliable attention spans did not wander to a road sign bearing a decades-old double entendre or, even worse, their phones.

'Do you remember that beautiful postcard Mum used to have on the fridge? That she bought in Beirut in the seventies?'

The siblings all remembered the gold-fringed relic from their childhoods. Something they had all gazed at either privately or in concert at least daily, enchanted by the gilded edges, the crystal blue Mediterranean taken from above, a beach club dotted with glamorous young Arabs and sweaty Eastern Euros lazing around in bikinis and dick stickers, glittering chains around their necks and Jackie Onassis-inspired sunglasses on the faces of the women, gold-rimmed Wayfarers on the men. Everyone looked so young and beautiful and impossibly far away.

They had not seen the postcard in years, but none of them could actually recall when it had gone missing. Like so much of their youths – primary school best friends, final-year exams, teenage despair – it had loomed monolithic in their lives until suddenly, inexplicably, it didn't.

Now Claudia had the answer to a question they had never thought to ask.

Roadwork sites and their high-vis sunburnt caretakers whizzed past as she grinned and relayed the tale of her first heartbreak.

She had been nineteen. They all remembered him: a bit lovely, a bit dumb, a bit fundamental. His interests spanned cars, MDMA, never ever letting his feelings show, the gym, and occasionally Claudia. His sister had died in her early teens, which Claudia shamelessly found morbidly attractive. She married this fact with an emotional hinterland for the boy almost entirely confected by herself. In hindsight a lot of imagination hung on his square jaw, tight delts and sad eyes. But he had been her first boyfriend and she had quite an attachment to him. Zoe, Phinn and Poppy all remembered, though even now Claudia would not portray the relationship in such unflinching terms.

He seemed sweet, albeit temporary, until one day he did something both completely unexpected and terribly predictable, and slept with a woman who was not Claudia. She found out within three days on the trusted Winston bush telegraph, and retired to her bedroom for a week to cry, more out of sheer humiliation and bruised ego than actual heartbreak. One night, drunk on self-pity and one and a half bottles of wine, she confessed to Rachel the reasons for the relationship's demise.

Rachel, who even at the best of times could be magnanimously described as 'smother superior', was blind with fury. In Claudia's retelling she looked wildly through the kitchen drawers, scrabbling through scissors, bobby pins and old vinyl-embossed refidexes. Finally, she turned to the fridge in exasperation and ripped down the azure and white postcard before fiercely hunkering down at the kitchen table to write. Claudia did not see exactly what was written but she had been able to deduce from text messages from the victim days later that it called him a piece of shit, said he was lucky Rachel did not tell the boy's mother – 'a beautiful member of her parish who was unworthy of such heartless offspring' – and said she hoped his beloved bonsai plants died in a huge effing fire involving his car.

Zoe interrupted in disbelief: 'So she actually sent it?'

Claudia giggled even more. 'Of course she sent it! Can you believe it? That beautiful, intricate homage to 1970s Beirut – in its Paris of the Middle East phase – which she had saved for thirty years. And then just to finally send it, turning it into a psycho postcard.'

'I can absolutely believe it,' Phinn said dryly, shifting the gears down as they snaked through the impossibly wide back streets of the beach town to the ocean.

'I wonder what it was like for him. This stunning relic arrives in the post – such a dreamy scene, exotic even – and then he turns it over to read it and it's just pure savagery. A Trojan horse of an absolute bollocking.'

Zoe smiled at the idea of Claudia's vain Adonis going down to another Grecian analogy. 'I think the most savage part of it is that anyone in the house could have read it before he got to it; it was a postcard.'

The siblings burst into new peals of laughter, awed by the most diabolical aspect of their mother's revenge. Phinn tried not to dwell on the fact that Poppy's laugh was the first to cut out seconds later.

'So psycho postcards is a family trait,' he mused as he pulled into a takeaway-wrapper-strewn car park facing an unpatrolled section of mildly undulating surf. The three rusty four-wheel drives with shining roof racks suggested the placid water wasn't providing much incentive for the locals, while a look towards the east revealed just four board riders perched on the water, pointedly looking away from the forty-something paddleboard rider flailing away nearby. Claudia and Zoe opened their doors in time with each other and breathed the air deeply. Poppy was slower, infuriatingly so. Somewhere well after Winston, and almost immediately following the communal joy of psychotic postcards, a heavy mood passed over her – almost as if the quickly changing atmospheric pressure of the sky over the suddenly open water had drawn a coastal cumulonimbus directly down to her.

Straight away her sisters knew they were not going to get more than two syllables from her at a time. As always, Phinn was happy to cheerfully ignore it, but the pall had fallen. The tension was obvious to all four, the chatter died down and the jokes became more forced.

On the beach, Poppy sat on a towel with her silver one-piece swimsuit pointedly beside her. She was not going to put it on.

Phinn sprinted towards the waves and dived under in a graceful arc. Suddenly he was behind the sets and swimming lazy lengths parallel to the beach.

Zoe pulled out her sunscreen and took off her shirt, offering her back to Claudia without bothering to look at her youngest sister. The two fell into an old game, tracing symbols on creamy backs in the hopes they might tan along the same lines. Zoe drew four roses on Claudia's back, while in return she gave Zoe a planet, some stars, and even part of a moon.

'Are you coming in?' Zoe said to the space beside Poppy's shoulder.

'No,' Poppy responded, lifting her sunglasses, Ray-Ban rip-offs, so she could squint at her phone properly.

'The water looks like it's the perfect temperature,' Claudia ventured pathetically.

Poppy held her phone a bit closer to her face so her head shaded the screen from the sun's glare. Zoe shrugged and took off her denim skirt, folding it neatly on top of her sandals to reveal a violently red bikini in a design that tied in a series of knots at her hips and neck. Claudia pulled off her old blue cotton dress and pushed her growing fringe out of her face, giving the effect of a tween boy's body in a black one-piece. She linked one of her arms through Zoe's and walked carefully towards the water's edge, so they could complete the female Carter ritual of entering the water, inch by painful inch, step by tiny step, stopping and grimacing for each freezing wave, no matter how small, to break around their shins, then their thighs, then their stomachs. Finally, when it had reached their armpits, they would duck their heads under, muffling squeals with the foamy tide.

They trod water between sets looking at each other. Claudia glanced anxiously back at the shore.

'Do you think she's all right?' she asked, searching for her sister's horizontal figure on the sand, which she supposed was baking evenly in the sun.

'Oh, she just wants to sit moodily on the beach where we can all see her so we know she's staring moodily at the ocean,' Zoe said, leaning back so she was half floating in the water.

'Do you think I should marry Dylan?'

Zoe swung her legs through the water so she was upright, bobbing like a cork in an Esky of melted ice, and looked at her sister. Claudia was staring straight back at her, eyes glazed.

'I don't have any opinion on who you should marry, Clauds, unless he is hitting you or is a Tory,' Zoe said gently. 'What's going on?'

'Thinking about that break-up when I was younger and Mum's postcard. That was a relationship that looking back was so obviously a disaster, so completely wrong, and I didn't really see it at the time. What if that's happening again?'

Zoe looked out at their brother, the clean strokes of his arm as he calmly freestyled past the impassive surfers towards a rocky outcrop, his head turning every two strokes for one breath.

'I don't think this relationship is the same as that, but I don't know how normal it is to think you don't want to get married a few days before your wedding. What do you think you would miss about him if you did break up?'

'I loved your crooked sleep beside me and never dreamed afraid.' Claudia ducked her head under a wave.

'Huh?' Zoe stared at Claudia as she surfaced, showing her teeth in a forced smile.

'It's a line from a poem about a break-up, called "One Last Poem for Richard", I think. I often think about it when I think about Dylan. The poem talks about how they should have champagne for surviving their break-up, basically.'

'It's only me out here, kid, you don't have to impress anyone with poetry, you can just tell me how you feel.'

'I don't know how I feel.'

Zoe paused to consider Claudia, her relationship, her options. She honestly had no opinion. Claudia attempted to interpret her older sister's silence.

'This is a first-world problem, isn't it?'

Zoe shook her head. 'That's not useful. First-world problems are not enough money for all of the luxuries you covet, slow service at a restaurant, UberEATS not reaching your suburb. Relationships still matter; the people we love matter; our feelings matter. It's true we have more time to think about these things, but do you think the most oppressed people sit around just focused on their oppression? Of course it dictates their lives, but they still have room to fret about the people they love: who's not loving them back, who's loving them the wrong way. This is not a time to check your privilege; you can always go and find someone who needs to check it more and less than you.'

Claudia took in Zoe's words gratefully. 'So what should I do?'

'I don't know, that's up to—'

Zoe's response was cut short as she was suddenly dragged under the water, disappearing with a series of bubbles marking where she had just been.

Claudia tried to scream but rasped instead as she looked around wildly for anyone else in the water. She was just two metres from where Zoe had last been, and instinctively she swam towards the spot before stopping and frantically looking back to the shore, then to her right to the surfers and up at an endless sky.

It seemed there was a wide silence, only punctuated by the slow and regular roll of the waves and the tight uneven spacing of her short, hurried breaths.

Her eyes were suddenly stinging as the sound of a huge break in the water shattered the terrible quiet. When she opened them up again, Zoe was spluttering beside her, joined half a second later by a burly figure laughing hysterically.

'PHINNNNN,' Zoe screamed in fury. She grabbed her brother ineffectively by the shoulders. His body kept rocking in the surf with laughter.

'Got ya,' he said, before turning and cutting through the water towards the shore.

Claudia looked at her sodden sister, still trying to push her wet mop of hair out of her eyes. 'Sweet Jesus that scared the hell out of me.'

Zoe just turned wordlessly and calmly swam in the direction of her brother who was already on dry land, walking towards towels.

∽

By the time Zoe and Claudia reached the towels, Poppy was already yelling.

'Fuck you! What is your problem? Can't you just leave me the fuck alone?'

Phinn bashfully tried to rub his hair dry. Zoe looked at her sister, now shirtless, the straps of her bra pulled down to avoid tan lines on her shoulders. Poppy had both of her fists clenched and was huffing in Phinn's general direction. Still, it took a few seconds for Zoe to notice the spattering of salt water on Poppy's face and hair.

She turned to her brother. 'Did you shake your wet hair over Poppy while she was sunbaking?'

Phinn didn't respond but his enraged sibling snapped back, 'He's such a fucking arsehole.'

'Aw come on, Poppy, what's really the matter? I know he's annoying but you seem to be having a bad time anyway.' Claudia attempted to sound reassuring. Poppy blinked as her face flushed an endearing pink.

'I'm fine! I just don't think we have to do everything together all of the time. I need some quiet from you guys sometimes; I don't have to come into the water if I don't want to.'

'I know, I know, you just seem really cranky this morning.' Claudia kept her tone neutral, like a zookeeper to a tiger who has had a fright.

Poppy seemed on the verge of tears. 'I'm just not like you guys, I can't be as happy.'

'Oh Jesus, calm down.' Zoe picked up her towel and wrapped it around her. 'It's just a bit of water.'

Poppy let out a scream and, grabbing her bag, stalked off towards a bush track. Claudia looked at Phinn and Zoe, but none of them tried to stop Poppy straight away as her figure shrunk towards the headland.

'What is her problem?' Claudia said, directing her question to nobody in particular.

'She's just a messy bitch who loves drama,' Zoe said. She was already walking towards the car.

What it came down to was this: Poppy was offended by the overwhelming physicality of her siblings. In the real world you were not rough with other adults: you did not grab them, you did not drop your shoulder or elbow into them as you passed by, tickle them or, indeed, pinch them. All of this was supposed to be left in the primary school playground, but it took longer, so much longer, when it came to brothers and sisters. They were still considered young enough to be fair game for a sneakily outstretched ankle while walking around a coffee table, to be shouldered aside while trying to grab a sausage off a barbecue, to be suddenly hoisted, kicking and screaming, in a bruising bear hug from behind.

Don't touch me. Get out of my space. It was hard to assert boundaries, to hold on to yourself when there was so much familiarity. And everyone else seemed to know what familiarity breeds.

The three watched Poppy's retreating figure, her melodramatic stomping, the tension in her balled shoulders as she half ran away.

'Pops! Wait,' Claudia wailed.

She tried to catch up but Poppy raised one hand without turning around to reveal only her middle finger. Claudia reluctantly gave up, knowing better than to try to talk Poppy down from her almighty wrath at these moments. She turned back to the other two who were both casually rubbing themselves raw with their ratty towels.

Zoe leaned forward at the hips to towel her salt-frizzed hair and returned Claudia's pleading gestures with rolled eyes.

'Let Christian Bale over there walk it off. The performance must be *tiring* when so much has to be put into it.'

Phinn shook his head and set his mouth. Not just an ominous sign; the subdued jaw-grind was an unconscious familial callback to a long-dead grandfather they had never known – a Carter tic that would need a member of the clan's previous generation to verify it. Phinn would not be swayed to sympathy today: that was it, his sisters knew it. They slowly gathered their things and headed to the car, the playful air of the morning fully punctured and now deflating at the regular rate.

In the front seat Zoe checked her phone. 'Well, we have to meet Mum for lunch in forty-five minutes so leave here in twenty. Surely the sulk and dash will be done by then?'

Phinn just sighed deeply, shut his eyes and leaned back in the driver's seat, tapping the steering wheel. Claudia attempted to furtively type out a text in a painfully obvious way, an SOS screed to Dylan, no doubt. Zoe tried to tilt her head to see what was on Claudia's screen, but she was thwarted by the glare so instead she opened her car door again.

'I'm going to try to find her; she can't be far.'

Zoe pulled her top over her head and slid her Birkenstocks back on. On her, the iconic sandals looked the way their namesake designer probably intended when he had created them in 1963 – like giant paddles signalling to onlookers that the wearer had given up on many things in life, but mainly style for comfort. They had seemed more attractive when she bought them, ironic in their ugliness.

She faced the road and looked right, searching down the visible kilometre-straight before the corner rose into coastal scrubland. Several neat brick bungalows lay towards the end of the bitumen, betraying how their owners had little of the laidback beach village attitude associated with such coastal communities in previous decades. To her left was more beach scrub canopy and, she knew, a beaten track that people used for walks to a couple of saltwater lakes, which teenagers used as cover for their pot smoking. Zoe headed to the small thirty-centimetre outline of sand and waffle-tread shoeprints set against the patchy green border.

Phinn opened his door, and for a moment Zoe thought he was going to join her for the grand retrieval mission. But instead he hung one leg over the door and manoeuvred his bulky frame into a more comfortable position to laze in the two p.m. glare.

Claudia stayed on her phone.

Zoe was now slipping on rocks not made for the thick soles of the German sandals, while tentatively calling Poppy's name, in between cursing to herself in exasperation. Dried leaves and sticks crackled beneath her feet, and above her the gum leaves continued to wither and yellow in the dry heat. She watched as the light became more dappled and after 700 metres finally let out a scream.

'*Poppy!*'

The only response was the high-pitched pipe of a stray plover.

Zoe looked at the sky, becoming more sparse through the dense canopy, and down at the moist dirt track. She bent down to examine the ground more closely, looking for recent signs of movement. Apart from her own sandal treads, which were already fading, there were no footprints she could decipher, nor freshly disturbed rocks. She found her focus fading into that all-too-familiar creeping sense of futility. On the other hand, she guessed that she had been gone for ten minutes, so it would mean she had also used up all the time they had left before having to leave to meet their mother.

She picked up her pace, fretting as she finally approached the car.

She thought about how supremely annoying her youngest sister was, while also reluctantly acknowledging how that surface emotion of irritation was grimly anchored by a pit of dread, quietly shared, that was dragging down all the siblings. Deep down she also worried about why Poppy was behaving like this; just how unhappy she could be; how Poppy felt about the form her life was failing to take, like shaping water with her hands; and finally how gruelling this was for Claudia.

When she got back to the car, Phinn was still there, mouth still set in a thin line, listening to New Order. The overall effect was a vaguely menacing counterpoint to Phinn's usual breezy demeanour. Zoe peered into the back seat.

'Where's Claudia?'

'She went looking the other way.' As Phinn finished, Claudia came into view on the other side of the car, her face slightly sheened.

'You didn't find her?' Claudia was slightly puffed.

'No, have you tried calling her?'

Claudia shook her head and Zoe made an exasperated murmur as she pulled the phone from her pocket and scrolled through her Favourites. Despite keeping contact to the bare minimum, she kept her siblings at the top of the starred list in some gesture of loyalty she still did not quite understand.

The phone rang out as she climbed back in the front seat and Claudia took her position behind. Zoe looked over her shoulder. 'I guess we should do a quick drive around to see if we can see her.'

Phinn grunted and slammed his door shut, taking his sweet time to put his seatbelt on before they were trundling down the road. Five minutes later they had completed two laps of the dormant township – both with no sign of their sister.

Zoe could see Claudia's breathing become shallower as her chest tightened. Meanwhile she was trying to suppress the frantic edge to her voice as she raised her phone to her ear every forty seconds to listen to the ringing die out again.

'What should we do?'

Phinn shrugged. 'Fuck her. She's probably got Mum to pick her up and is already at the café. Who cares?'

Claudia and Zoe cared, but they were trying hard not to. This, as always, was the problem.

∽

The trio rode the twenty minutes in silence along the same ochre-bordered bitumen that had delivered them to the coast, but the hysterics they had shared on the eastern run now simply hung in the air as a stark juxtaposition. In unison, both sisters sighed as Phinn rolled to a stop across the road from the café and Zoe finally put her phone in her bag after her last attempted call.

Claudia paused at the bottom of the stairs and shielded her eyes from the sun as she gestured to the other two. 'How much do you think it would piss Poppy off if we took a selfie here and put it on Phinn's Snapchat story?'

Zoe snorted, while Phinn, refusing to surface from his mood, shook his head and kept walking up the stairs. 'Sounds incredibly productive.'

Inside, their mother was already at a table next to a window, her head held close to Mary's as the two whispered to each other. Phinn quickly clocked the midway-level of the yellowing pinot gris in both women's wine glasses, and was forced to pull his slumped shoulders up and make his choice: half full or half empty?

'Yeah Mum, get on it!' he boomed at Rachel, as his slightly stunned sisters took their seats opposite her.

They made no attempt to hide the absence of Rachel's youngest daughter. That didn't quell their vain hopes it would escape her notice, though.

'Where's Poppy?'

Rachel hadn't even said hello. She addressed Phinn, suddenly deflated. He had never been able to lie and looked imploringly at Zoe.

'She's meeting us here; you haven't seen her?' Zoe replied.

Rachel's eyes narrowed. 'Why is she meeting us here?'

'She wanted to go look for something.' Zoe knew the best strategy for a moderately successful lie was vagueness: scant detail meant what had to be remembered and offered up to Rachel's deductive powers was also minimal. The biggest trick was avoiding any specific destination, object or other person, which their mother could quickly check off through an algorithm of elimination honed from the four children's marathon upbringing. 'I thought maybe she would beat us here.'

'Where did you drop her off?'

'Well, it's not so much that we dropped her off ...' Claudia tried to back her sister up. 'It's more that she dropped us.'

Mary drained her wine glass and waved her hand at a staff member for a refill. The young waiter looked up from the counter briefly and returned to wiping forks, beside the red-lettered sign urging patrons to ORDER AT THE COUNTER. Mary was too delighted to take much notice.

'You don't know where your sister is, do you?'

The three paused for a moment.

'We know the vicinity ...'

'We know where we last saw her ...'

Phinn stared at the glass stem reaching up at the transparent bowl above, distorting his view of Rachel's index finger, impatiently tapping away. Glass fully empty. Fuck it.

'She's a bitch, anyway; we don't need her for lunch.'

'PHINN!' Rachel and her daughters reprimanded him as a choir – the matriarch's high-pitched outrage cutting above the emotional exhaustion of his sisters' duller voices. Mary buzzed with satisfaction.

Eyebrows raised, Rachel reached for her bag and got out her phone. She half-stood up but then sat back down.

'Just before we start lunch, Claudie, where are you staying tonight?'

'I, um, I think we were going to go to Dad's after the beach.'

Rachel sighed. 'Typical. Rushing off to your father's again.'

Zoe cut in. 'We've been at your house the past few nights, Mum! We are having lunch with you right now.'

Rachel raised her hand as she stood up and put her phone to an ear. 'I just feel like an afterthought. You're fitting me in around your father.'

All three siblings lowered their heads. Despite the glaring evidence they had been spending time with their mother, she could still invoke guilt in them. They could clearly hear the dial tone on Rachel's phone and the familiar voice after just two rings.

'Poppy, sweetie.' Their mother walked away.

Chapter 17

Dylan: YOU'VE MISSED THIS.

Claudia: NOT AS MUCH AS YOU THINK.

Chapter 18

Claudia leaned out of the taxi and furtively looked each way before pushing a $20 note into the driver's hand and darting under the streetlight and into the motel car park. Each hand bore two bottles cocooned in a brown paper bag. Basking in the paranoia, she looked over her shoulder and took the stairs to her right, two at a time.

After ending the ascent with a little jump, she looked down the row of myrtle green doors and found what she was looking for. Holding the four bottles, she kicked the door three times.

A moment later it swung back to reveal a sliver of Nora, in her version of house clothes, before jamming awkwardly with a clunk. The length of chain pulled taut between door and frame at eye level. Nora's face quickly split with a grin as she ducked back behind the green frame. Claudia could hear the chain rattling from its hook before the door opened again properly, giving a full view of Nora barefoot in tan capris and a bamboo cotton T-shirt.

How very like Nora, she thought, glancing at the now limp security chain.

Claudia took one last look behind to make sure nobody knew she was there and stepped over the threshold, raising the brown packages triumphantly. 'I couldn't find anything in this town but prosecco, but look what Mary had squirrelled away for a special occasion.' She pulled open the bags to reveal Veuve Clicquot labels on warm dark green bottles.

Nora squealed. 'It's our secret hen's! Secret hen's, secret hen's,' she hummed the mantra to an obscure tune. Claudia giggled and opened the tiny freezer compartment of the bar fridge, inelegantly jamming one bottle in and leaving two others on the grimy white shelf inside the door and another still warm on top of the fridge.

Claudia gingerly took off her shoes and flopped down on the bed, ignoring the slightest of frowns that crossed Nora's face as she realised her friend was wearing her beloved leggings as pants. Claudia stared at the ceiling and began her run-down of the day, which Nora had already known would somehow centre around Poppy. They fell into the easy repartee built over years of female friendship, gossip, Icelandic politics (always weird how the Euros love to have heads of state who can completely over-rule a separate head of government – what is the point?), their pick for the colour of the summer, loneliness, long-ago bosses.

Claudia told her friend how Poppy had slunk into the café after calling a taxi to the small beach town for something in the ballpark of $130.

'Worst of all, I end up being the one who feels guilty,' she said, staring into the moderately expensive champagne in the cheap hotel room tumbler. 'I know she loves me, I can feel how much she wants to be close to me again, and it's almost as if I have run out of patience with her. I can't allow her to be close to me. Every time she has a small fuck-up I shut down from her; there is something about her at the moment I just find so profoundly irritating.'

Nora raised an eyebrow. 'Her personality?'

Claudia ignored the jibe. 'She just wants to love me so much and I can't forgive her for an offence that I can't seem to articulate. I'm sure she wonders what she has done wrong.'

'I can provide her with a list if she needs,' replied Nora, refusing to let it go. 'Maybe she can choose at least one to say sorry for.'

Claudia felt the friction in the air, the tension between friend and family, trying to explain your sister to an only child. She sighed inwardly: you might as well be trying to explain the concept of the ocean to a landlocked desert tribe.

There were plenty of apologies between the sisters; they were just not the kind where you say sorry. In fact they were relationships built on the refusal to say sorry; instead contrition was signalled with a casual text hours later. Had they seen the latest episode of *Broad City*? Or a simple screenshot of a quote; the last between Claudia and Poppy had been: 'It's not enough for me to succeed, my friends have to fail.' A simple 'haha' in response and all was forgiven; it was time to move on without the need to dissect hurt feelings.

The olive branch takes many forms: for the Carter sisters it was communication about entirely mundane subjects that transcended issues invisible to the impartial observer. But none of them ever mentioned the truth that olive trees take a decade to actually bear fruit.

An upbeat declaration that 'I just saw a koala in a tree next to the highway!' invited a response that could mean 'It's all good', 'I'm not going to fight with you anymore', 'I don't feel like holding on to the anger that had me hang up on you last night', 'I'm still talking to you but you're still a dickhead' or even, 'I forgive you'.

Claudia wondered if it was possible for a group of people to put together a complete picture of a person. What would be known about her if Poppy and Zoe and Dylan and Nora walked into a room and laid out everything they each knew about her? All the things they would discover they did not know about someone they considered themselves to be closest to in the world. An imperfect collage.

She was interrupted by Nora clinking her glass. 'You're thinking about your sister again. Can you stop for just one night? I know you say she loves you, but it's really not that difficult to avoid upsetting you so much.'

Claudia smiled and thought about the desert dwellers surrounded by dunes, blissfully ignorant that the wide expanse of sky over their heads could ever run into a shimmering liquid horizon. But she obediently changed the subject. 'What do you think the worst thing about being single was?'

She dipped her head to the champagne, inadvertently missing the brief stoniness around Nora's mouth at the question.

'What is there to miss? It depends on your partner what you miss, I guess. I miss what everyone misses: making my own decisions.'

Claudia nodded. 'Not knowing where the night would take you.'

Nora was careful choosing her words. 'I think that is something where the concept or the memory is looked upon a little too fondly compared to the reality, not knowing where the night would take you. Most of the time it takes you home to bed alone.'

Claudia sat up suddenly. 'Let's download Tinder!'

'What? Why?'

Claudia ran her hand through her hair nervously. Her blonde crop had begun to get greasy at the roots but she was too distracted to care. Her cheeks flushed, filling in the remnants of blush applied a morning ago with brushstrokes gleaned from long-ago YouTube tutorials. She picked up her phone. 'I want to see what's out there.'

The mechanics of creating a Tinder profile were quickly figured out: after a brief hesitation about it possibly being linked to Claudia's Facebook profile they switched her photo to a generic shot and set their net for a 100-kilometre radius – they figured it had to be cast wide in a town like Winston.

It was dumb, but the girls (ahem, the women) had suddenly repossessed the bulletproof recklessness only available for a brief period to those in their twenties fortunate enough to have avoided real tragedy.

They were also a bit drunk.

Claudia flicked through profile after profile of what seemed the same four men smiling from the black rectangle again and again and again and again, variations on a limited number of themes.

A man with his shirt off in one photo, on a boat in another, with a large group of men and beers in hand, sunglasses on for most of them, describing himself as an 'adventure junkie' (read: he has a lot of disposable income and a lack of imagination).

A man with a mystery child in his photo who was obviously not his but a prop being used in what he thought was some kind of ingenious honey-trap.

A man here 'for a good time, not a long time'.

A man who didn't like women with 'to [sic] much make-up' (read: I think the only reason women wear make-up is for men).

There were so many, like children pulling themselves up as high as possible, chest out, for their first school photo. This one grinning in what was obviously his first selfie, or another using a mediocre photo because he thought it was a nice picture. It could be sweet and it could be a bit sad or it could be soul-destroying. Claudia and Nora spent two hours emptying the Veuve bottles and going through the ceaseless options.

'This is a wicked hen's night,' Nora said.

'Wow.' Claudia didn't look up. 'That is some old-school slang I haven't heard in a while – wicked, man.'

'No, I mean this is a wicked thing you are doing, as in Witch-of-the-West-dear-Dorothy thing we are doing. It's kind of evil.'

Claudia looked up, more hurt than she had a right to be. 'Are you trying to be my moral compass?'

Nora sighed and slid off the bed, walking to the fridge for the final champagne bottle. 'I'm not trying to be a moral anything, but what are you playing at? Why are you downloading Tinder and getting married on Saturday?'

Claudia sighed. 'I don't think I'm going to marry Dylan. I'm almost positive I'm not going to.'

It was the closest to a decision she had got. Nora silently popped the cork on the bottle and measured out their glasses, a purposefulness to her quiet as she waited for Claudia to fill it.

'Why shouldn't I have a look at what's out there before I make the jump?'

'Because you're getting married in a few nights. It's kind of tacky. Very tacky.' Nora sat down on the edge of the bed again and shrugged. 'But I can stand tacky more than people realise.'

'You're not going to ask me why I don't want to marry him?'

Nora felt suffocated by the question. She shifted on the bed, steeling herself for a list of reasons why having a man who loved you was somehow not enough. Claudia asked her if she remembered Simon and Gabe. Nora not only remembered them but also the fallout that left her and Claudia in a three-month perpetual hangover.

Two boyfriends, one after the other, who Claudia had let completely envelop her. Simon had been tall and, with the benefit of hindsight, really hated women. He loved to make promises, from plans to spend the morning at the beach to elaborate weekends away, and then not turn up. Whenever Claudia had dared complain he would say her clinginess was unbecoming. But, she was wildly attracted to him, and any time he texted she would drop whatever she was doing (usually Nora) and go to see him.

She met Gabe when Simon was giving her the silent treatment, and at the time he seemed the polar opposite, but it turned out he was just at the other end of the toxic spectrum. He bought her gifts every time he saw her and bombarded her with messages about how beautiful she was. After a month or so, the messages would become vaguely threatening if she didn't respond within minutes, and then outright threatening. 'But my body wants his body,' Claudia would explain it, as if that was an explanation.

Yes, Nora remembered Gabe and Simon.

'Remember how lovely Dylan seemed in comparison? How sweet? How normal?'

Nora snorted. 'Because he *is* lovely and normal in comparison.'

'Well, what if that's all he is? Just lovely and normal in comparison to these men I had these insane attractions to? I've sort of fallen into this relationship that I think is great because he doesn't harass me or ignore me. He's just nice. Is that all I'm supposed to be grateful for?'

'Yes,' Nora snapped. 'If you feel lucky, it's because you are lucky. It's only going to get more desolate out there. You have someone to hold your hand through it; that's all a lot of people want.'

There was a viciousness in Nora's voice that Claudia was not used to. But Nora was also a bit drunk. Maybe she didn't get it, and that was fine.

Claudia signalled the end of the conversation by returning to her hands, swiping ordinary-looking men on her phone.

'Someone's written to me!'

Nora rolled her eyes. 'They've *messaged* you, they haven't *written* to you.' She took the phone and studied Claudia's inbox.

Hi ☺

If you could choose only three types of cuisine to eat for the rest of your life, what would you choose?

Nora furrowed her brow. 'Well at least he's trying. Kind of.'

Claudia looked up quizzically. 'You don't think he's one of those white slavers, some freak with women in his basement?' She returned to the screen and took a careful sip. 'And a very active Menulog account?'

⁕

A few kilometres away from the pair – say, a third of the daily distance of his long-lapsed running regime – Phinn's feet lay over the edge of a single bed at the back of their father's house. It was in a room supposed to be a laundry but, given the option between enough bedrooms for all adult children to visit at once and a garden, George chose the intermittent rewards of loamy flowerbeds and a frustratingly fickle herb garden. The house was empty except for Phinn: George was at the local watching reruns of the previous week's rugby league games, despite having seen them broadcast live, or he was visiting his sister, or he was tom-catting – Phinn did not really care. His phone vibrated to signal a new WhatsApp from a name he associated with high school, hazy pot smoke in bike sheds and other ancient history.

> Yr sista single now?

Phinn frowned and scrolled down to the attached photo. It was a screenshot with Claudia's name, her age, and a blurry photo of her taken from a few metres away. Underneath it was a single quote: 'The only thing that might be wrong with you: the human condition.' He rolled his eyes.

It was a screenshot from Tinder.

Phinn moved onto his stomach and studied it again. Then he deleted it and went back to the Sportsbet app, momentarily wondering about joining the old man at the pub for the second half. Amazing how his sisters would all make a huge show out of leaving for big cities, but always seemed to end up in tiny, tiny global villages where everyone knew you all along.

∞

At the motel Nora was invigorated, she was inspired, she was galvanised. What this really meant was, she was lecturing. She had not quite told Claudia what she was doing – how she was behaving – was wrong, but she was getting close. She hadn't told Claudia about Tom either; that was not so close. Claudia was propped up against the dreary headboard of one of the beds, her leggings long ago discarded on the floor along with her bra; her cotton dress now worn like a nightgown. She fanned herself with an issue of *WHO* magazine from twenty-three months before – the same coterie of curvy family members staring reassuringly out from the cover – and sipped her champagne every time she remembered it was in her hand.

Nora was telling her about Kanye and Taylor Swift, making her decide who she wanted to be.

'Look at what drives Taylor: fame. Fame and self-interest, that's it. The friends she has, the lyrics she writes, the clothes she wears, it's all with one goal in mind, to promote herself. To be richer. Taylor and capitalism go together like *Sex and the City* and white feminism. She makes everyone think that's what they want a piece of. I doubt she's made a decision in years that was actually driven by her own taste or preference or even her own

176

happiness. What she has is a fundamentally outwardly directed life; it's self-indulgence at the expense of fulfilment. It's all to feed her self-interest first and foremost.'

Nora rocked back proudly on her heels. She was not usually someone with a spiel, but she had been thinking a lot lately. And listening to *1989*, *Reputation* and *Yeezus* exclusively.

'Kanye, on the other hand – anyone who calls him arrogant is an idiot. You have to think about what drives him, why he acts the way he does, and he's a very funny man, by the way, incredibly self-deprecating. He talks about bringing rap back wearing a backpack with a pink polo shirt! He is making fun of himself!

'But what is he driven by? Love. Love and anger. And his anger isn't just on his own behalf; he's not just angry about what happens to him. He's angry about how other people are treated, he's angry about the poor black victims of Hurricane Katrina and he's angry Beyoncé didn't get the recognition she deserved at the 2009 MTV awards – which she didn't, by the way. Everyone knows that now. He's angry about a lot of injustice for a lot of people and he loves Kim so much. You want your life to have meaning? You need to commit to something. It can be a man, or a woman, or a cause, or a creative output bigger than yourself.'

Nora's speech was starting to drag around the edges. Some of her words were running into each other, her eyeliner was smudged, but Claudia had to concede she had a point. She didn't have much choice.

'Do you want to be driven by love and anger? Or self-interest? Do you want to spend the next few days being a huge brat and agonising over a man who loves you?'

Claudia considered the question like she would consider the question of whether a horse could fly or whether trickle-down economics actually worked. She was completely baffled it was even being asked in the first place. Baffled that she was confiding her deepest fear to her best friend and was being berated in return.

A woman can be forgiven myriad sins and stupid decisions by her friends: hubris, condom-less sex, nights given away to MDMA, extravagant grieving over unreturned calls, devotion to BritPop; but breaking up with a nice guy? That was an incomprehensible act of stupidity. There had to be concrete transgressions, proof the relationship was doomed, knowledge that they had tried. Claudia thought of all the middle-aged couples she knew who were pleasant enough to each other but seemed to have nothing in common. It was courtesy that kept them in loveless relationships for decades. She was beginning to realise how difficult it was to explain the demise of a commitment to a 'good guy'.

'It would be a lot easier for you if Dylan hit me, wouldn't it?'

Nora spat the champagne she had just sipped back into her glass. 'What?'

'You need a reason so badly; I don't know why you are so desperate for me to justify maybe not loving him. You need a list of faults that I can't provide.'

'I'm just trying to understand why you are deciding to dump Dylan the week before your wedding.'

'Well.' Claudia looked down at her empty glass. 'You are acting really strangely; I thought you would be on my team. You're presenting me with a false dilemma: I can be Taylor Swift or Kanye. Maybe the ordinariness of the life I am going to have is not bad, but it's not what you're painting. I'm not Kanye West and Dylan is not Kim Kardashian.'

Nora sighed and attempted a reset. 'I just don't know what you think you are missing out on, what you think your life will be like single.'

Claudia accepted the shaky attempt at a truce.

'I feel tethered, is all. What if I want to go live in Lisbon?'

'You have never mentioned wanting to even holiday in Lisbon.'

'What if I want to have sex with a woman? I've never done that.'

'I didn't know you wanted to have sex with a woman.'

'I don't! But I could! Isn't that the point? I don't think it would be anything in particular; I think it could be a lot of things. Maybe I would travel to Malta by myself; maybe I would go and do some work in the Philippines. I might go hang out at Quintana Roo. I might sleep with a few more men. I would just be free. More free.'

'You would do precisely none of those things. Oh, maybe you would sleep with some randoms. I thought you were better than romanticising your life. You sound ridiculous; you sound worse than ridiculous, you sound bourgeoise. In the absence of any real problems you have created a pathetic one: your fiancé is too nice.'

Nora's tone was sharp and furious. Claudia was stunned.

'Where is this coming from? Why are you so angry at me?'

'Mate, take your Tinder and your self-pity and take a think for yourself. Even Taylor Swift would be embarrassed by this.'

Nora stood up a little too quickly and for a moment almost finished her rebuke with a wobble. She caught herself and, after making sure both feet were on the ground, she walked towards the door, picking up her wallet from the side table.

'I'm going out for cigarettes.'

Claudia was left with just the champagne bottles for company. Then she noticed her phone flashing.

Chapter 19

Sometimes Rachel hated her kids. She thought about this as she picked up a soft pink onesie in size 0000. Just looking at it made her ache. Just below her bully button. The ache she got when she saw one of her children driving by themselves, or paying for underwear, or telling her three weeks after the fact that they were sick and had to stay in bed a few days. It was the ache of not being needed. Of a womb with a permanent vacancy sign.

She would never tell her kids that she hated them, but sometimes it was true. She sometimes thought about the kind of person she would be if she had not been a mother, the way that people married for twenty-three years romanticise the kind of person they would be unattached. Novels written, spontaneous trips to New Zealand, perhaps half a language learned. Of course in reality it would never measure up like this. You would probably still be disappointed in yourself. Maybe a bit unhappier. Rachel did not put much stock in this rationale, though. She liked to think if she had not been a mother she would have a flat stomach. She'd be almost inconceivably rich. All that money spent on sustaining life!

When she was pregnant with Zoe, her sisters, Mary and Wanda, both convinced themselves that Rachel was carrying a child before she even knew. Rachel had yelled at the pair over some long forgotten slight – a completely standard occurrence at the time. But they liked to pretend it was rare to lose control of their tempers. This time they pinned it on hormones. Not just any old hormones; they knew they were so close to Rachel that they could feel her baby. They harassed her for three weeks about whether she had her period before they finally revealed the motive, overshadowing her pregnancy announcement at lunch with explanations of how they just *knew*.

When she was pregnant with Phinn she got fat. Sometimes pregnant women just get pregnant, a volleyball atop firm thighs. Sometimes they gain thirty kilograms with no explanation. Rachel still crossed herself whenever she saw a fat woman. There but for the grace of God.

Carrying Claudia she ate olives every day. That was it.

And Poppy, Poppy she breastfed for almost two years and we all know how that turned out. Also, she slept with another man when she was about six weeks pregnant but nobody ever found out. Sometimes you can be bored, lonely, and make catastrophic decisions. Sometimes your actions have no consequences.

Rachel stood up straight at the thought, as if being called to attention, to account. She looked around and discovered she was still in the shopping centre. Still standing in the children's section, running her hands down size 0000 onesies, which was how she soothed herself when her hatred of her children was particularly intense. She turned to her sister. 'Isn't this darling?'

'As long as you can accept it's darling empty and not full of baby, then yes, it's darling.'

Mary was bored. She had accompanied her sister to the shops with ulterior motives but was finding her routine almost too much to bear.

'Do you really think one of your children is going to give you the satisfaction of a grandchild?' Mary asked, holding up a pack of three bibs for effect.

'Well, I'm sure if they do, it won't be to make me happy. You know how often they think of my happiness.'

Mary nodded thoughtfully, pulling her black handbag over her black shirt, which was tucked into her flowing black skirt. The children liked to compare the colour of her uniform to her soul, it was too easy, but really Mary had just been taken by surprise by what a fifty-year-old body looks like. It wasn't pretty.

'You're always the one making compromises for them,' she continued slowly. Claudia was the one having a wedding 650 kilometres from her preferred venue for Rachel but Mary put the facts to the side.

'They never call you ...' The longest Rachel had gone without speaking to one of her children on the phone since they left home was five days.

'I just don't know how you do it. They treat you like shit.'

They were in the thrall of their mother in the way most people are. They were connected through the belly buttons. There is a shelf in your soul reserved for your mother, whether she is quite mad, sub-par or cruel. Especially if she is cruel. Rachel was not cruel but she could be quite maddening at times.

She turned to her sister and started weeping. 'I just feel so powerless, so alone. I don't know what more I could do for them.' She discarded the onesie.

'Mick just marvels at you, says you are one of the strongest women he has ever met,' Mary continued, steering her sister by the elbow towards a more interesting section of the shop.

'That's so lovely of Mick. You're lucky to find such a good man, I have always had time for him, even after he ...' Rachel wiped her eyes and looked sideways at her sister. '... had all that business with his wife.'

'How are you feeling about Saturday? Your dress is gorgeous; you are going to look gorgeous, even if we haven't seen hide nor tail of any of your daughters since they have been here.' (Claudia had spent four of the past six nights at her mother's house.)

'I'm excited for Claudia, she is a beautiful girl, Dylan is a beautiful man. I won't lie, I could never lie, I do wish there was someone special for me to take along. George will have Lisa; I do miss having someone to celebrate with.'

'Well, you will have me, and wouldn't it be nice to have Mick as well? He speaks so fondly of you; you two have always had a special bond.'

Rachel gave a small nod. 'That would be nice.'

'Everyone else has someone,' Mary reminded her. 'You should have two people.'

Mary had struck the indignant spot. The soft flesh only your sister knows the location of. Where it not only hurts to be struck, but a bruise is left, and nobody else even sees a mark.

'Mary, you're right. I do so much, and ask for so little in return. I think I would like to sit with you and Mick. I'm sure Mick is invited; I'll make sure his seat is next to mine. In fact, Dylan's dad and stepmum arrive tomorrow. Why don't you bring Mick to dinner? I'll let George know.'

Mary nodded and picked up a black dress she had been eyeing off all week. 'You are too kind.'

Chapter 20

Petunia's was a restaurant nestled in the middle of the main street of Winston, which – despite the slightly cloying name – was regarded as palatial by the town's standards. But that was simply because it boasted an upstairs *and* a downstairs seating area. It retained a reliable if stodgy menu, one of the last balconies in the town not directly attached to a bowling green that welcomed smokers, and still included an unpredictable microphone in the space's rental cost. It was the natural venue for the wedding reception.

Dylan and Claudia had been paying for it in small instalments for eleven months, with the understanding Petunia's had absolutely no responsibility for how it would look on the night. Claudia could find no wedding decorators, only wedding 'stylists', within a 180-kilometre radius – a distinction that seemed to mean they charged three times as much as decorators would for filling the space with empty jam jars and molasses-scented candles. In yet another boundlessly optimistic act of delegation loosely agreed upon since the initial booking, the seemingly simple job of deciding the final destination of flowers and tablecloth patterns had fallen to Claudia's brother and sisters.

George had arrived that morning at ten in an effort to at least ensure some decorating got done. The move was largely sparked by a chance encounter with one of his old schoolmates, who had stopped his Hilux, laden with his battered tinny, at a service station several days beforehand. After some small talk about Cedric's fishing trip, George glanced into the bow at the plastic bucket holding the mud crabs frantically scuttling over each other in a futile bid for freedom beyond the white curved walls. The sight instantly led George to an ungenerous but probably accurate comparison with his children's organisational capabilities and his realisation that he'd have to step into the interior-decorating role.

He nodded to the owner as he walked past the front counter without saying a word and began his ascent up the curved stairs. He could hear his children before he saw them.

'I'm her sister; I know she will love it.'

'I'm her brother and that means jackshit. When was the last time you saw which flowers were in her house?'

'She said we could do whatever we wanted with the flowers.'

'Yes, but I don't think she envisioned we would try to dye them blue.'

At the top of the stairs, George was confronted with twenty bare tables and what he assumed were twenty pale pink table-cloths thrown carelessly in the corner. He knew they had been dry-cleaned and folded before pick-up. However, one of his offspring who had escaped any kind of relationship with an iron had failed to consider what happened when they were simply emptied out of the plastic bags onto the ground instead of put on the tables. He allowed himself a deep sigh. It was exactly as he expected.

In the middle of the room, Poppy was holding a bunch of daisies as a prop in one hand while gesticulating wildly to Phinn, who was standing forlornly beside a table bearing hundreds of brown paper packages of the same blooms.

'Dad!'

Poppy was excited to see George emerge, assuming he was a natural ally. George gingerly made his way through the tables and hugged his daughter, patting Phinn on the head.

'Hey Dad, welcome to the floral derangements,' Phinn quipped to his darkening old man.

Before George could respond, Poppy had already started on him. 'I've had this amazing idea. Remember when we were kids and we used to dye the flowers blue each week? Wouldn't it be incredible to dye the daisies for Claudia, as a surprise?'

George paused as Phinn shot back at his youngest sister, 'Wouldn't it be incredible if we just did what we were supposed to do?'

Eyebrow arched, George surveyed the room and realised the tables were not in any kind of formation and the sound system remained in the box. Before he could referee the brewing argument, the door from the kitchen swung open and Nora walked in with her head still facing the kitchen entrance.

'Thank you! You're very kind!' she called back to a staff member hurrying out of sight.

In an effort to be as unthreatening as possible, she had made the concession of wearing denim shorts cut off just above her knees. With her leather loafers and ironed cotton T-shirt the overall effect was still more Nice, France, than nice-and-placating, but she was trying. In her hands was a cardboard tray of styrofoam cups, some bearing the small browning stains from the trip up the stairs. She turned her head to the small crew and called out sunnily, 'Good morning! I thought you might like some help. I've brought coffees.'

Phinn rushed over to take the tray from her hands while George broke out into a smile and finally broke his silence. 'Nora, that's very kind!'

'I didn't know what you all drank but I figured a tray of lattes would be safe, and there's sugar in here too.'

It might have been her optimistic survey of the room that led Nora to miss Poppy's deepening scowl. The youngest Carter threw down her handful of daisies and edged around one of the tables.

'I thought Claudia just asked *us* to decorate,' she said in place of a greeting.

'Yes, well, she mentioned to me that you would all be here this morning and I thought maybe I could make it easier.' Nora now weighed up Poppy coldly, with the latter quickly realising that she had heard about the beach the day before. Claudia must have been upset.

Poppy silently picked up a coffee while Phinn sucked his gut in and threw his arm around his sister's friend.

'There's plenty of work for you to do. You can actually settle a, uh, contest of ideas we are having.'

Nora shrugged Phinn's arm off and stepped towards the corner with the tablecloths.

'Are these clean?'

'Do you think we should dye the daisies blue?'

Nora turned back to Phinn, startled. 'The daisies blue? Those daisies? The daisies for the wedding?'

'Yes.'

Poppy had flinched each time Nora uttered the flower's name, her harsh inflection on the first syllable gradually rising.

'How would you dye them blue?'

Poppy rolled her eyes and interrupted. 'It's very simple, you put blue dye in the water of the vases.'

'Why would you dye them blue?'

'Well,' Phinn said, raising his coffee to his lips, 'why indeed.'

Poppy struggled to maintain an even tone. 'Claudia would love it; we used to do it when we were kids – it was so much fun.'

Nora seemed to weigh the response and everything she knew about manners and diplomacy in the seconds that followed, before her eyes brightened at a welcome new distraction heading across the floor.

'Zoe! Rachel! Hello!'

'I'm going to find an iron,' George said, heading towards the kitchen as he scooped up a pile of the tablecloths in his arms. He didn't turn at any point.

Rachel and Zoe picked their way through the chairs from the stairway with the matriarch leading the way in tight white trousers and a hibiscus pink top that made no pretence at her being coy about her figure. By contrast it appeared that Zoe, in a light-blue T-shirt dress, hair tied back from her face and stepping out in Nike joggers, had taken cues from Nora's breezy style, while also trying to dress for the menial tasks of the day. She looked at Nora uneasily and then to Poppy.

'Hiiiiiiiii, I didn't know you were decorating too, I thought it was a ...' She bit her lip. 'A family thing.'

'Well, Claudia told me about the decorating and I thought I could come and just see if you needed help.'

Rachel grabbed a bunch of daisies.

'I see my ex-husband is here as well.'

Poppy finally spoke. 'Our dad is here, yes,'

'These daisies are pretty. They're not the only flowers though, are they?'

The flowers had officially been marked for battle. In one corner were Nora and Claudia's current tastes; in another corner were Poppy and Claudia's tastes from long before there was ever her friendship, adulthood, distance, independence. And creating another battlefront was Rachel, who simply couldn't see past her own taste to bother considering what Claudia might prefer.

Rachel picked up a few of the daisies and sniffed them. 'Do they seem a bit old to you?'

Phinn volunteered. 'We watched them being picked this morning; they couldn't be fresher.'

'Did anyone think to get some baby's breath? That would be lovely with the daisies. And we need some colour. Do you know what's in season? Gerberas – Claudia loves them.'

Claudia had bought gerberas weekly for her room for an entire spring when she was fifteen. The phase seemed to end with the close of that one solitary season and she had never mentioned or paid for them again, but it didn't matter. She had been doomed to receive bunches of the gaudy flowers every birthday since.

Nora physically stopped herself from gasping. 'I don't think we can have gerberas at a wedding.'

'Actually Mum, I agree on the colour thing. I was just saying we could dye the daisies blue, remember like when we were kids?'

'Yes, I showed you how to do that!'

It was really George who had dyed the flowers with them, but everyone knew better than to correct the record, given the current Cold War dynamic between the parents. Poppy was talking to her mother, who could be relied on for reinforcement when they were not personally warring, but all the time kept her emboldened gaze fixed on Nora, daring this relative outsider to disagree. Daring her to try to prove she knew what was best or who loved Claudia more. No matter how much she was told it wasn't a competition, Poppy was determined to win against her sister's chic shielding interloper.

'I think the baby's breath is a really good idea,' Nora finally responded, sparking a staccato burst from Rachel.

'I'm going to get some blue dye and order some gerberas. Where is the seating plan? I haven't signed off on it. I kept asking Claudia for it but she must have forgotten to show it to me.' Rachel was a bright pink blur speeding towards the kitchen when the doors swung open to reveal Phinn with tablecloths draped carefully over his arms. He leaned towards his mother to kiss her, then started on the first useful task of the morning.

The girls watched in silence as he laid a cloth across a table and moved around it to even out the sides. Nora put her coffee down next to the dreaded daisies and, hoping it was a neutral task, walked over to take one of the cloths for the next table.

'Are you a tablecloth expert now as well?' Poppy almost spat.

Zoe, who had been waiting for the inevitable boil-over as soon as she had seen Nora, quickly moved towards appeasement.

'She's just trying to help; she's here for our sister.'

'She's here because she thinks she's an expert in Claudia and everything else. We're her sisters; this is our job.'

Phinn rolled his eyes. 'You're obsessed with this sisters thing, like it gives you some special magic. *It's just fucking DNA and chromosomes.*'

Zoe and Nora both caught their breaths. Nora, without the aforementioned biological bonds to Poppy, was already fed up. Poppy seemed to share her mother's propensity for intense moods and the dog-like faith that she knew what was best, without it being tempered by Rachel's consideration for others (George notwithstanding). Nora's new strategy was simply to ignore the youngest Carter. She couldn't give a solitary flying ibis if her presence riled her anymore.

'Look, Claudia asked for daisies, shouldn't we just get daisies?' she said mildly.

'We need more tablecloths,' Phinn said emphatically, heading towards the kitchen doors they had all last seen Rachel enter. Momentarily distracted by his self-loathing at getting involved in the women's squabbling, he had actually forgotten he had passed his mother on the way out. So it took him by surprise when he opened the door and heard her voice. Contrary to his usual instinct, instead of noisily making himself known this time, he paused.

Rachel was trying to speak in a low voice but it was beyond her capabilities. Her son's ears pricked up at the sound of his uncle's name.

'He has a right to be there, you know. It's supposed to be a family dinner and he is family, and I haven't seen Mary so happy in so long. And you know what, I couldn't care less what you think; you just have to deal with it. She deserves to bring a partner and he is your brother.'

Phinn could see his father through the stainless-steel shelves on the kitchen island, looking down as he concentrated fiercely on the edges of a tablecloth with his iron.

'He's going to be there, anyway.'

Rachel reached over and patted George on the shoulder, purposefully making him flinch as Phinn stepped forward, letting the door slam noisily behind him.

'I've got to go sort out these flowers now,' Rachel said as way of farewell. 'Hello son.' She breezed past Phinn, who watched his father shake his head slowly, dourly. Without a word, Phinn ducked down to pick up the newly ironed tablecloths but, to his surprise, it was his father who broke the silence.

'What's going on with the flowers?'

'Uh, Claudia wants daisies, Rachel wants gerberas, Poppy wants to dye the daisies blue.'

George had watched his children acquiesce to Rachel's interminable whims and demands for years; he knew come Saturday night which flowers would be on the tables.

'Well, that would be something blue, and it sounds like your aunt Mary is bringing something borrowed,' he said as Phinn hurried out.

In the dining room, the table of daisies sat untouched as Nora and Zoe stood on the other side holding one of the round tables between them. Zoe was gingerly stepping backwards while Nora guided her with what seemed to the Carter girl a very boring version of the 'Time Warp': 'step back and to the left, there's nothing behind you yet, now just wriggle it a little to the right, hmmm maybe to the left again'.

Zoe followed obediently but her uncertain steps still gave the impression of a five year old attempting to waltz with her grandfather. That would be the closest thing to a traditional wedding trope we'll be seeing around here, Phinn thought, as he hauled the tablecloths over.

'Are you sure that table is okay there?' Poppy, arms crossed, leaned against another table so heavily she was almost in a combat crouch.

'Take one more big step back,' Nora said to Zoe as a way of response.

She was happy with her defence mechanism. Nora the Ignorer. Just like cartoon Dora the Explorer's sullen little sister, who cared for neither exploring nor remonstrating with a kleptomaniac fox.

The two women put the table down and Nora turned and surveyed the room. 'We don't want the tables lined up perfectly; it works much better if they are kind of scattered so it doesn't look so regimented.'

Phinn dropped the two ironed cloths on the table. 'Do you want to lay these out now or wait until the tables are arranged?'

Behind him thunder crossed Poppy's face as he waited for Nora's verdict.

'Lay them out now so they stay nice and smooth.' Nora carefully pulled on the cloth to start spreading it across the table and before Phinn could start helping her Poppy had the other side.

'These are rectangular tablecloths; we should make them square so they look even,' she said, lifting the edge.

Nora narrowed her eyes and gave a little tug on the other side.

'The rectangle is fine; as long as it covers the entire table, nobody will notice. If we make them square it will be easier for them to ride up.'

'It's okay,' yelled Phinn. 'This marriage is literally all about round pegs in square holes! All marriages are! It's what makes the speeches interesting.'

Poppy ignored both Nora and her brother and began folding the other side.

'Don't fold that! You will just cause another crease.' Nora pulled back the cloth to try to get the other side out of Poppy's reach, but she had a surprisingly tight hold of it. Poppy gave a violent pull back.

'The square will look better,' she said defiantly.

Suddenly Nora went from Ignorer to Warrior. 'Can you just let us put the fucking tablecloths on the tables without making it a statement about your fucking influence?'

As soon as she had said it she looked taken aback at her own swearing.

If Poppy was shocked she didn't show it. Instead she planted her feet squarely for maximum effectiveness and she yanked back on the cloth fiercely. Nora, ready for it, dipped her shoulders and pulled back at the exact same time, leaving the two held upright only by the tension of the (now-not-just-creased-but-twisted) tablecloth as they both jerked on it.

Phinn's jaw dropped to create an exaggerated 'O' as he stopped and gaped, while Zoe put her hand over her chin, first to stifle her gasps and then her giggles. The wide-eyed brother instantly thought of the shared silence of wildlife documentary makers trying to record a big cat bringing down a buffalo as he stood still next to his sister in a bid to take in the spectacle while desperately hoping not to be the next target.

It wasn't an inaccurate analogy: by now a visibly agitated Poppy had scrunched up the corners at her end into balls so she could get a better grip, while Nora's mouth was set in a determined line as she refused to cede an inch of her side.

'Did ... did she just growl?' Phinn whispered to Zoe.

Zoe grabbed her mouth in a bid to stop her silent giggling fit.

Poppy and Nora refused to break eye contact as they each violently pulled on their side of the tablecloth.

'Just let it go!'

'What is your fuckin' problem?'

'Ooh good swearing,' murmured Phinn.

'Old school, dropping the "g" there,' Zoe replied under her hand. 'Loike it, mate, loike it.'

'I swear to God!' Nora bellowed.

'Why are you even here?' her opponent shrieked back.

A deeper voice joined the fray, booming behind them. 'What are you doing to that tablecloth?'

Nora jumped, momentarily missing a step as her foot landed behind her, but still did not drop the cloth. Poppy didn't even turn to face her dad. Her hands ached.

George stood with four other tablecloths carefully draped across his arms, which were raised to stop the sheets trailing on the ground. He shook his head and asked again.

'*I said*,' he yelled before softening slightly, 'what are you doing to the tablecloth? I just ironed that.'

The girls both let go; Nora, turning the colour of beetroot, tried to delicately smooth the edges on her side.

Phinn finally answered for them. 'It's like a brawl in King Arthur's Camelot, Dad,' he said before comically drawing himself up to full height. 'Welcome to the fights of the round table. For some reason these two think Claudia will care if the tablecloths are folded into squares or a hexagon or something like that.'

His father opened his mouth and then thought better of it and turned back towards the kitchen in preparation for more ironing.

'I guess,' Zoe smirked soberly, 'this is what Ma meant at the engagement party when she got drunk and told us Carter marriages are really a vicious circle.'

Chapter 21

Zoe stood outside of the door and raised her fist. Then she put it back down again. A casual observer would see an expensive-looking woman trying to convince herself to knock on a lover's door. Zoe had the right clothes to be sophisticated but something wasn't quite right. She wore Italian brogues, handmade, leather, beautiful. But she wore them because she had seen Amal Clooney wearing a pair in a paparazzi shot and had immediately bought them online despite the fact they were $400.

It was that type of sophistication. Affected. Unnatural. Like criticising hip-hop as shallow without ever having listened to *The College Dropout*. The fundamentals were not there. The taste.

Zoe was not convincing herself to confront a lover; it was worse. A woman she admired was on the other side of the door. A woman she was a little bit in love with in a very specific way heterosexual women can become obsessed with other women. It has to be a woman you do not know well (how can you truly be devoted to someone you *know*?), but have some personal connection to so you have access to their Instagram, Facebook page and enough personal contact to keep you interested.

You don't want to have sex with them. It's far more intense than that. You want to wear their skin.

Zoe pulled her hair out from its messy bun and scraped through her fingers to create a messy ponytail instead. Then she knocked.

'Who is it?' a voice on the other side immediately called out.

'Zoe,' came the squeak back.

Zoe could tell by the way the door handle was turned that Nora was exasperated. Nonetheless it opened to reveal white linen pants patterned with navy flowers, a crop top that sensibly met the top of the high-waisted pants, only hinting at the toned stomach (Reformer Pilates, Zoe already knew) and Nora's head of damp hair.

'Claudia sent me,' Zoe said briskly.

'Where is she?' Nora remained in the doorway.

'At Dad's. I think she is dodging everyone. She's already heard about the venue.' Zoe stuck a foot in the door. 'Poppy is there too; all is forgiven.'

'What do you mean "all is forgiven"? How can it all be forgiven?'

Zoe started laughing. 'Five minutes passed, that's what happened. You know how willing Claudia is to overlook the fact Poppy is a complete and utter arsehole. Being held to account for one's behaviour is very boring for some people.'

As she spoke, Zoe stepped forward so her foot in the door became two feet in the room and Nora stepped back to avoid coming nose to nose with her friend's sister. Not that Zoe would've minded. She surveyed the room. As suspected it was meticulous. For these straight-girl obsessions to work, the object has to have something out of reach to you, but only slightly. She has to have enough money to fly business class if that's the pinnacle of glamour for you. She has to work as a yoga instructor if you were so bad at sport your grandfather refused to come to your netball games it was 'such a waste of time'. She has to have bouncing curls and an oval face to your lanky thin mane. For Zoe she had to be so particular and organised and clean that she ironed her sheets.

Nora had hung a silk dressing-gown on the hook on the wall for that specific purpose and her silk dresses hung in the wardrobe with three pairs of shoes lined underneath. Next to her pink leather hand luggage was a pink leather structured make-up bag with various lotions and bottles, and next to that was a pink leather pouch with various eyeliners and lipsticks. Heaven for the chronically messy.

Zoe looked up from the two copies of the *New Yorker* sitting perfectly square to the *Gourmet Traveller* and noticed behind Nora in the bathroom was a hairdryer and a bottle of white wine.

'Have you been drinking?'

'Why yes I have, thank you for asking.'

Zoe smirked. 'Righto, what's the occasion?'

'The occasion is being stuck in this town for my best friend's wedding watching her sisters skilfully guide her to the brink of a breakdown. Would you like one?'

Zoe shrugged and sat down on the bed Nora had been sleeping in (she could tell because it had been made with far more care than the other bed, which had obviously just been made up by the professional cleaners).

'Sure, why not?'

Drinking in the daytime. Always a thrill, until the third glass. Zoe had (gladly, gleefully) been dispatched by Claudia to check on Nora. Apparently she had not been quite right since arriving in town, and while Claudia had intuited this she was also very busy with the small question of whether she would in fact marry Dylan or not. Zoe relayed all of this – apart from the gladly gleefully bit – while Nora bent over with a hairdryer that had all the force of a two year old blowing out birthday candles, occasionally staying upright to sip on her chardonnay.

She finally conceded defeat, switching it off with her hair still damp.

'Hmmmmmmmm,' was her considered response.

'We don't have to talk about your feelings, although I have noticed you are not your usual ...' Zoe paused. 'Your usual *sparkling* self.'

There was no way to say that without sounding sarcastic.

'We can talk about things far more interesting than your feelings,' Zoe continued, swigging her drink to arrive at the stage of thought where daytime drinking is an excellent idea leading to resolutions to do it every day. 'We can talk about what's more important in the struggle – race or class. I am white, so I will of course conclude class, but you can argue your side. We can talk about the most overrated mascara we have tried. We can talk about things we have eaten in Paris. We can talk about football. There is literally an infinite list of things we can talk about that are not your feelings so don't feel pressured.'

'Tom and I broke up.'

'Ah.'

Zoe shifted on the bed. She knew what she shouldn't say. She knew the rules of that. Never tell your friend to break up with their partner. Never slag off your friend's ex-partner. Never reveal how much you disliked your friend's ex-partner. Tell your friend how amazing and beautiful and intelligent they are.

But the problem: these were all rules for your friend. There were no such basic guidelines for your sister's friend with whom you are slightly obsessed.

'He wrote me an email.' Nora leaned on the chest of drawers opposite Zoe.

'Ah.'

'Do you want to see?'

'Sure.'

Nora opened the drawer under the television (of course her laptop was in a safe place where she wouldn't sit on it and thieves would not check first!) and passed the computer to Zoe. A small piece of her heart, in her friend's sister's hands, because she was the imperfect understudy at the moment.

∞

Zoe may have been lacking a rule book but she had some experience here. She knew the only way to tell someone that they were the most annoying person in the world. She had been in Sicily when she'd discovered this.

A longed-for holiday. The Mediterranean, her French-speaking boyfriend, balmy nights eating fresh bread and the most perfect steak she had ever tasted. And she couldn't stop being a bitch. There was no real reason; she was just hot and permanently bloated and too comfortable in the relationship. Everything he did annoyed her. She remembered one particular day when he had breathed wrong. The worst! Half a holiday spent with every figurative peace offering slapped from his hands. And for what? No solid reason. He just annoyed her. He annoyed her before she realised part of a relationship is being the most annoyed person in the world. Part of a relationship is looking at someone and accepting, as Ask Polly once put it in a long-forgotten column, 'You are fucking wretched and a huge disappointment in almost every way, and I love you like crazy anyway.'

It was too late when Zoe realised all that. It was too late and she was not sure if she should relay the information to Nora anyway. She did not know if this was the time for relationship revelations or the time for embracing being single. These are the types of things you know if the person spilling their guts to you is actually your friend.

∽

Zoe thought about this while she read the email. She thought about this while being careful to hide the sound of her heart breaking repeatedly for Nora while she read the email. She wanted to tell her everything she knew but she did not know if Nora could be trusted.

Nora, in showing a minute of vulnerability had also inevitably become less attractive to Zoe as some weird and complicated crush.

Zoe was careful. 'It's quite cruel.'

Nora nodded.

'It is quite cruel,' she repeated, almost as an affirmation from a Chinese fortune cookie. 'I obviously haven't told Claudia this. I think this whole crisis,' Nora waved vaguely at her laptop, 'can wait until she is back from the wedding. Then she can devote herself more readily to being my emotional crutch.'

Zoe kindly laughed. 'What are your general thoughts on this? Is this it?'

'You mean are we broken up forever? I can't see us coming back, no.' Nora pointedly didn't elaborate.

'How do you feel about being single?'

'Excited. Lonely. The usual. Being single is more of an identity for me than a reality. I like the idea of it. In practice, I'm not so good at it.'

'Well, almost all of us want to be in a relationship. Whether people admit it or not, it's pretty self-evident. It's nice to have someone who always has to be on your side. It's nice to be known, in your bones known. It's nice to touch another human being. It's not really something to be embarrassed about.'

Zoe talked the talk but at the walk she was pretty pathetic. There was her single status and complete aversion to dating as testament to that. Nora pointed this out, albeit a touch more delicately.

'Oh yeah, but I have the cliché of my parents' marriage breakdown to justify that. I didn't even know the extent of it until my first boyfriend snapped at me over accidentally leaving his oven on and I had a complete emotional shutdown and was inconsolable for hours because I was convinced one disagreement meant we would be screaming the most intimate abuse at each other within twenty minutes.'

That was not something Zoe revealed often and, feeling the warmth of traded intimacies, and half a bottle of wine, she decided to tell Nora about the staircase.

'If happiness is a staircase – if happiness is coupledom, to be specific – then at the top you obviously have happy couples. Those arseholes who have it good, pretty much through no fault of their own. They might be good people, sure, but they basically got lucky. Nonetheless, they're at the top. So where do you think you as a single person – a freshly dumped single person, to be precise – where do you think you are?'

'Ummmmmm, in the depressing nightclub, a thirty-dollar Uber ride away from the airport, which is a four-hour flight away from the palace with the staircase?'

'I'll laugh, but only because I'm feeling charitable. Ha ha! No, my friend, my sister's friend. You're not at the bottom of the staircase, you're three quarters down. At the bottom are unhappy couples. Because they are so far away from a happy partnership. They first have to split up and then work through their issues and figure out what they want and the kind of person they are and then meet someone and then they will get to the top. It's a hell of a journey. You, you have some work to do on yourself, but you're already single. Single people who have sorted their shit out, they're halfway to the top, not at the bottom. So comfort yourself with that. You think a happy relationship is light years away, so far out of reach, but really you're in a better place than people stuck in unhappy relationships that will eventually end. You can at least start looking for a decent relationship soon.'

Nora considered the staircase. 'That's the most pretentious thing I've ever heard.'

Zoe was fine but she was no Claudia. Nora thought she would feel a pressure valve released, or even a vague weight lifted after talking about Tom, but there was still only emptiness. Emptiness and day wine. Zoe was a poor stand-in for her sister; she was a sub-par stand-in for being Nora's actual friend. She needed real consoling, genuine advice, some intimacy in the wake of her devastation. Instead she was stuck listening to self-help pep talks about imaginary staircases.

Chapter 22

Claudia lay on her side looking at Dylan's profile. His phone was propped on his chest and his headphones were in, his viewing platform shuddering every few seconds as he laughed at skateboarders falling over in a stunning variety of ways. She put her arm around him and squeezed. Dylan, taking the cue, pulled his earphones out and turned to face her.

She moved closer still. 'Come here,' she muttered.

He wriggled in. 'I am here.'

It was years-old call-and-response between the two, Claudia demanding physical and emotional proximity and Dylan assuring her he couldn't be any closer. He laid his hand flat on her face. 'How are you holding up?'

It sounded simple enough but Claudia knew what he meant.

'I am fine; it's fine.'

She rested her forehead on his and the two lay still against each other. Claudia thought about his question. He always looked out for her. It had been Dylan years before who had first tried to warn her when her moods turned dark and she couldn't get out of bed. Who begged her to see a doctor. Who cooked her endless pots of bastardised pad thai, heavy with soy sauce and lime, the only thing she would pick at. Despite the clichés, it didn't feel like falling into a dark hole, or being followed around by a dog. It felt like nothing. She didn't want to die, but she didn't quite care if she stuck around either; she just wanted to feel something. When she couldn't remember the last time she showered and Dylan found the razor, it was him who made her call her mother, who brought her home to recover.

Every time he asked her how she was 'holding up', she knew what he was really asking. Are you normal upset or going crazy upset? Are we going to go through this again? How could Claudia ever repay him for looking after her, for sticking around? In the furthest corner of herself she questioned her lovability; surely she'd lost a few points of desirability in all of that; who else would want her?

She opened her eyes, her forehead still pressed to Dylan's forehead and his dark eyes doubled to four as she tried to focus while still lying so close. He laughed and kissed her on the forehead, pulling away but grabbing her hand as compensation.

'What are you thinking about?'

It was another one of their private games: the responder got to list three things.

'Ummmm.' Claudia thought better of saying 'the time I went insane and you stayed with me, for some reason'. 'My sisters, how many sleeps it is until we can leave, aannnnddd Maltesers ice cream. What are you thinking about?'

'Corpus Christi, a skater in the 1980s.'

'That's it?'

'That's it. Do you want me to go get you a Maltesers ice cream?'

Claudia sighed and rolled away from him. She shook her head and instead picked up her phone. He had his, by her standards, ancient skateboarding videos; she had her own personal quest to find Beyoncé's Snapchat.

∽

For three weeks when Claudia was fifteen years old she had decided to go on a diet. Every day she ran 11.5 kilometres and ate only oranges. She dropped a staggering 9 kilograms in that time but then perceived the path she had set out on and changed course, instead becoming obsessive about making sure the sugar content was under 12 per cent in everything she ate.

Such was the power of her addictive personality.

She was careful what she tried, what she decided to do more than once, for fear of fixation. She studiously avoided even a toke of a joint throughout her teenage years and never ate chocolate more than two days in a row because of the destruction she knew would eventually be wrought.

But she had been cavalier, careless; she had stopped paying attention for a minute.

Which is how she found herself barricaded in the bathroom, sitting on the edge of the closed lid of the toilet while Dylan snored softly in the bedroom. Claudia was hunched over her lap so the light of the iPhone illuminated her features, the remnants of mascara lying stubbornly beneath her eyes and her furrowed brow. She was swiping.

Shirtless man, after shirtless man, after man in a suit with sunglasses on his head at the races.

She had been caught off guard by how attractive she found the men on Tinder, an attraction that lay easily beside her guilt. It had been so long since she'd flirted, so long since she had been so viscerally attracted to a body. According to the app in the palm of her hand there were more than plenty of fish in the sea; there were so many opportunities for an easy ego boost, or even an easy lay, they could populate another planet. No matter how many she swiped, there were always more: men visiting from overseas, weirdly defensive men 'not looking for a wife on here', sweet men who put photos of their mum in their profiles, so many men mooning the camera from on top of a mountain, and a lot of men listing their height, for some reason. Claudia found it intoxicating, and she was only swiping, she told herself. There was no harm done in swiping. The men were swiping right back: it had been the rush of notifications in the hour after she'd left Nora's during which she had experienced the first dangerous pulls to open the app again and again. Men swiping right on her, matching with her, signalling they found her attractive. She had not initiated any conversation with them, she told herself. At the moment it was just two adults confirming to each other they would absolutely go there.

But she was feeling something she had not realised was missing until the old familiar tingle had returned. Anticipation.

Her inbox was filling up with hellos and winky faces, but they were easy to ignore; they weren't real messages, just one of the many lines these men were casting out into the night in the hope of a nibble.

Footsteps in the hallway broke the hypnotic hold her phone had on her and she looked up. Someone had just walked past the bathroom and down the stairs. She sighed and glanced at her phone again: 2.45 a.m.

She flushed the toilet and ran the taps for anyone outside who might need convincing her bathroom visit was entirely functional. Someone could be listening in this house at any time. She stepped quietly into the hallway and ducked across to the bedroom where Dylan lay on his stomach, a pillow beneath his head and a pillow beneath his cocked knee. She crawled in next to him and put the phone on the floor, lying on her back and then on her side again. Instinctively, he rolled over and rested his arm across her. She was used to falling asleep in his embrace.

Chapter 23

Claudia: Dylan says can you please bring him a tie clip (????) when you come to dinner tonight. Please.

George: I have a tie clip for him. I will bring it for him in the morning. I can't make tonight.

Claudia: Why?

George: Too much to do.

Chapter 24

Rachel walked into the living room where her sister was sprawled across a ridiculous green velvet couch. Ridiculous and fantastic. She lowered her book and swung one stockinged leg over the side so she could half sit up.

'I have something to read you,' Mary said as she propped herself up on her elbow and thumbed through the book; Rachel could make out Helen Garner's name on the front. 'Here it is.'

'A crime novelist spoke at a conference about the unsuitability of his usual sardonic tone for the war story he was trying to write, "about young men with their stomachs torn open who cry all night for their mothers and then die". An old man told me, after he had had open-heart surgery, that he and a ward full of other men his age woke in the dark from hideous nightmares, screaming for their mothers. I have never read or heard of a woman in extremis who called for her mother.'

Rachel walked out of the room.

Chapter 25

Claudia crouched down in the corner where the kitchen benches met across from the island. She would've preferred to be under the dining table surrounded by tucked-in chairs, but in one of a series of betrayals by her body over the past twenty-eight years she had grown too tall to sit comfortably under there. Instead she crouched in her black boots, staring down at her pale blue socks, a fried egg drawn on each side. She had on a loose white cotton T-shirt with giant roses in yellow, pink and blue drawn all over it, and tucked into her dark denim cut-offs. 'I look good,' she thought to herself as she quietly wept. She heard the footsteps of Phinn coming down the hallway followed by Rachel (you live in a house for eighteen years with the same people and you too would be able to distinguish between the footsteps of the 28-year-old kind male and the 65-year-old frustrated mother). She pulled the top of her shirt over her face so she could not see them for a few more seconds and squeezed her last tears out of her eyes.

'I am going to write a letter to the shopping centre. You can't just put a pole there; they really should pay for it to be fixed.'

'You can't back into a pole and seriously blame the shopping centre for putting it there!'

'There's so much concrete, it's very bright, you can't see properly and there's no reason to put the pole—' Rachel's sentence fell off a cliff. 'Claudia?'

Her second daughter wiped her face while still focusing on her ankles and then looked up.

'What are you doing down there, you dumb doob?' Phinn asked.

Despite her best intentions and efforts up until that point, Claudia sniffed and a fresh burst of tears came on.

'Dad's not coming to the dinner tonight,' she said, putting her face back in her arms.

'Oh sweetie.' Rachel crouched down next to Claudia and rubbed her back, only triggering another cascade of tears. 'Sweetie, why isn't he coming? How do you know?'

'He texted me. He didn't tell me why; he said he had too much to do. I was really looking forward to this. I'm not going to get to hang out with any of you much on Saturday. Tonight was supposed to be the night for a proper family dinner; now he's not even coming.'

Rachel cocked her head. 'Well, you know what he's like. He doesn't mean anything, this is just the way he is.' She traced her fingers up Claudia's spine, a spine she had been tracing since it was an hour old, a spine she had been tracing since before Claudia could even remember.

'You know, sometimes I get the feeling Dad doesn't even like me.'

'Sweetie, of course he loves you, you're his daughter.'

'Of course he loves me, that's not what I said. Sometimes I think he doesn't like me. I know he loves me, but I get the feeling he doesn't like me as a person. I think he finds me high maintenance. Or too foreign to him. Or something. He never seems to feel obligated to make the effort for me. It's like, just because I'm not as oversensitive as my siblings, he can be mean to me.'

'Your siblings are not oversensitive.' As ever Rachel was unbothered by the actual point of the conversation; she only heard descriptors she objected to. You could tell her that your best friend was dead, but if you used a nickname all you would get is scolded for not using the name your best friend's mother had given them.

Rachel stood up, dragging Claudia by the elbow with her. 'Your dad does like you; he's just a grumpy old man sometimes. It's been a big week. You'll still have a great night. We will all be there – don't let it ruin your special night.'

Claudia nodded into her mother's shoulder.

'Now, sweetie, if your father isn't coming, why don't you let Mick come along? It will be nice. You like Mick, he's a lovely man, and it would be nice to have him at one of the celebrations.'

Claudia nodded again. 'Sure, if Dad's not coming, then Mick could at least have dinner with us.'

She did not notice Phinn had not said a word the entire time.

Phinn waited until Claudia had left the kitchen and glared at his mother. 'Why didn't you tell her?'

Rachel pulled eggs and tinned food out of the same shopping bag, shaking her head at the ineptitude of the packing skills of the woman at the checkout. 'She doesn't need to know the car is scratched. She's already stressed.'

Phinn shook his head and followed his sister. His steps slowed as he reached the bedroom door. He was a lifelong student of conflict avoidance. While his sisters had raged around him as children, he had counted how many times he could hit a tennis ball against the water tank with a cricket wicket.

If Phinn had been Queen Victoria, Ireland would have been under Home Rule in 1849, just so she would not have had to undertake an awkward propaganda visit to the country. If he had been in the Iraqi prison Camp Bucca with Abu Bakr al-Baghdadi, the caliphate would never have been declared because he would've distracted the future Islamic State leader with a game of cards rather than get involved in a political discussion.

⚭

When Phinn was fifteen and his long-awaited growth spurt was still very much delayed, he had been in the main street with his mother when his mate Tony had yelled at him from across the street. Tony was a year older and three times bigger. He was a surf lifesaver who fancied himself as a bit of a hometown hero but, as he did with most people, Phinn had always got along with him. They were mates. He yelled some insult that was muffled by two cars but Phinn got the general gist. This is how boys communicated; this is how mates spoke to each other.

'You dumb piece of shit!' Tony hollered. Phinn, forgetting he was standing with Rachel for a second, exuberantly yelled back, 'You're ugly!' Tony crossed the street.

Phinn bounced towards him, holding his skateboard under his arm. He held out his hand for their traditional bump of acknowledgement. That's when Tony punched him in the face. Dazed, Phinn staggered forward and dropped his skateboard.

'Mate?'

Tony hit him again, this time in the chest, winding Phinn for a few seconds. The next punch landed under his right eye. The next one was the one that got him on the ground. Rachel stood on the footpath screaming

'Tony, you son of a bitch, I know your mother, get off him! What are you doing?'

Phinn felt Tony's shoe in his ribs and, from his horizontal vantage point, watched him walk away. He let his eyes sting with tears for a moment but blinked them away before Rachel dragged him up by his elbow and spent the car trip home yelling at him for fighting.

Rachel didn't seem to understand that Phinn had just been beaten up in front of his mother. He hadn't landed a single punch. He didn't care about the physical pain. Nobody gives a shit about that. It was another reminder he was small.

Phinn never found out why Tony suddenly turned on him, and for some reason it was Tony who he thought of as he walked towards his sister's room to detonate a bomb because it was the right thing to do.

He leaned on the doorframe as his sister lay across her bed scrolling through Twitter. Sensing his presence, Claudia rolled over and, without looking up, said, 'Phinn! Listen to this tweet from @dril: "This whole thing smacks of gender," I holler as I overturn my uncle's barbeque grill and turn the 4th of July into the 4th of Shit.' Claudia cackled to herself and finally looked up. 'What's wrong?'

He sighed and sat down on the bed. 'Mum told Dad that Mick was coming to the dinner tonight.'

Claudia shrugged. 'She can tell him whatever she wants; he's the one who isn't coming.'

'No, she told him that before he said he wasn't coming.'

Claudia sat up straight. 'What?'

'When we were at the restaurant decorating it for the reception tomorrow, Mum came up and was talking to Dad. She said she was going to bring Mick since he probably won't be allowed to come to the wedding and it was the right thing to do.'

'What did Dad say?'

'Nothing.'

'Did they see you?'

'I don't know; I had walked into the kitchen but Mum knew I was there when she walked out.'

'So she just watched me cry about how Dad doesn't like me, and she just stood there and pretended she didn't know a thing about it?'

Phinn sighed and moved closer to his sister so he could put an arm around her. 'Yep.'

'Unfuckingbelievable; that woman is unbelievable.' Claudia put her head in her hands. 'So, I am getting married, his daughter is getting married, and there is meant to be a dinner so the parents can all meet each other and we can have a nice time, and really it should just be us and our parents but fucking Mary is coming along because she sees no issue in crashing her niece's special night and she wants to bring Mick, and Dad is so fucking immature that he can't just suck it up for his daughter and be in the same room as someone he doesn't like? Instead he just doesn't show up because he doesn't like somebody; it doesn't matter that it might mean something to me.'

Phinn looked out of the window and on the street envisioned George and Rachel as human beings. As their own individuals, who were not – as the siblings mostly believed – an extension of themselves, whose lives did not surge and recede on the whims of their children. It is not unique to discover your parents are fallible, but it can be savage.

Phinn took a breath.

'Both of our parents are arseholes, yes.'

Chapter 26

Nora: Zoe and I can't decide on a wedding topper. How do you feel about one with blue hair?

Claudia: I don't care.

Nora: *Star Wars* themed?

Claudia: I don't care.

Nora: The greater Left project fails unless you choose a wedding cake topper.

Claudia: I don't care.

Nora: Trump just got a second term.

Chapter 27

Claudia was forever threatening to do something melodramatic and memorable. And here she finally was, and there was nobody around to witness it.

Claudia walked into a supermarket and started sobbing over the broccoli. She went into a clothes boutique and wept quietly as she looked at shoes. In the Reject Shop she picked up plastic flowers and started laughing because she knew crying while holding on to a $2 fake petunia was too much, even for her.

She sat in the food court and ate a burger and still the tears came.

A part of her was secretly enjoying the image of herself walking around town with tears streaming down her face the day before her wedding. But she did it so discreetly there was nobody to enjoy the performance. It was only a tiny part a performance anyway. Mostly, she was just truly sobbing before her wedding day.

Claudia did not know how she felt about marriage. She felt like a passenger in her own life. She had just let things happen to her so much that now she was getting married. She had always had a vague sense of wanting to wear the dress and have the ring and the day where all the attention was on her. She'd also had the vague sense that marriage was a flawed institution, certainly, and possibly an empty one.

But she loved Dylan. She nodded vigorously as she cried outside a shopfront where people could get their keys cut. She definitely loved him. She also had the creeping suspicion that her happy relationship was weakening her staunch (on paper) feminist beliefs and stunting her moral imagination.

It was hard to be angry at men when you got to kiss Dylan every day.

They had built their relationship, like everyone else, on a thousand small intimacies. They knew each other in their bones.

A year into their relationship his mother had got sick. As vibrant 24-year-olds they had the ringside seats as her cancer caused rapid deterioration. Together they couldn't decide what was worse: the sheer indignity of it all (nobody really talks about that; people are always 'battling' and 'brave', but in reality an adult child ends up spoon-feeding their parent and putting on their clean underwear after a shower), or being robbed of appetite. When someone knows the end is near, when their health has already gone to shit, by rights they should be able to eat and drink whatever they want. Cholesterol and calorie content is irrelevant when death is already assured within months. But instead, cruelly, Dylan's mother was too nauseated even for iced water.

Claudia had watched over Dylan as he fed his mother. She had been beside him when he found out she was dead. They all thought they were prepared for it. They had been in the hospital with her for months. But Dylan told her it was still like a cricket bat over the back of the head.

'Nobody cares if I am cold now,' he had sobbed to Claudia. 'Mum was the only person in the world who gave a shit if I was wearing a jumper or not. There is nobody who cares about me like that.'

It was true, Claudia conceded. She never noticed if he was wearing a jumper or not. She was not going to see a photo of him as a grown man in winter and ask where his coat was. That's not what lovers are for.

She was there when, a week after the funeral, Dylan's sister, Elaine, asked when they would be coming back to visit.

'Why have you got to be such a *cunt!?*' Dylan screamed, kicking Elaine's toddler's toys across the kitchen.

Later Dylan would say Claudia was horrified he called his sister a cunt in front of her two year old. Claudia was actually more concerned about the six year old.

She had once asked him, 'When does it start to feel okay? How long is it unbearable for?'

He hadn't even paused. 'Four years.'

The fourth anniversary of his mother's death had been the month before.

'It's okay, we are in year five now,' he told her cheerfully, turning away.

But it isn't these big moments that make a relationship. They help, kind of, but really it's about all the mundane stuff. Can you go to the shops together for the 480th time? Can you sit on the couch eating stir-fry for the 693rd time? Can you spend 4000 days washing their toothpaste out of the sink?

Can you still make each other laugh after 2894 days?

A few weeks before, a Lexus had pulled out in front of Dylan when he was driving and Claudia began berating him for braking hard. Shifting into second gear, Dylan had snapped at her, 'Maybe when we are married you should take my side against strangers in Lexuses. It isn't in the vows but it's implied.'

Claudia collapsed in laughter every time she thought about it. Including now as she walked past a shoe shop weeping. She thought about Aesop's dog and telling Poppy about it. She thought of bones rotting on the ground around her as she stood paralysed. Maybe eating an apple.

She thought about this as she walked in circles around underwear racks in a shop, eventually picking up green silk briefs. They were nice.

She recited her favourite Philip Larkin poem to herself like a mantra:

In times when nothing stood
But worsened, or grew strange,
There was one constant good:
she did not change.

She made a decision and walked towards the counter. The girl had dark curly hair piled on top of her head, seemingly thousands of bobby pins holding it all together. She wore a denim jacket with a koala brooch on it.

'Hello! How! Are! You! Today!'

She was the last of a rare breed, the enthusiastic shop girl. Claudia smiled despite herself, suddenly self-conscious of her puffy eyes.

'I'm well.'

The girl smiled and folded the underwear. 'These are nice; what are you up to today?'

Claudia shifted from one foot to the other.

'Actually, I'm getting married tomorrow. So just doing some shopping.'

The girl squealed.

'That's SO! Exciting! How are you feeling? The weather looks really good!'

Claudia allowed a smile.

'Good, I feel good. It is exciting.'

Chapter 28

Zoe typed her sister's name into her phone and watched as the map slowly updated.

'She's still moping around the main street, more than likely thinking about how romantic and crestfallen she looks.'

Phinn had Zoe's dark satin and polka-dotted skirt spread out in front of him while he frowned and studied the iron. He looked up at his older sister.

'You can tell that from your phone?'

'I've told you we should share locations. Claudia is the only one who will do it with me. I have Dad and Mum's too and about eight of my friends.'

'I'm not sharing my location with you. It's incredibly psycho. Why do you need your sister's location?'

'So when she storms off in a huff on the day before her wedding you and I don't have to waste time looking for her.' Zoe pinched her two fingers together and zoomed in. 'I can tell you the exact shop she is in. It's Shabby Chic. I bet you that she is buying underwear. Crying and buying underwear. I would put a cheeky tenner on it.'

Phinn picked the skirt up by the waist and extended his arms in front of him while shaking it out. He examined it again and inspected the temperature gauge on the iron before pressing it cautiously on the material of the skirt.

'This is an absolute bastard to iron.'

Zoe leaned back on the wall, using it to prop herself up as she stretched her legs out in front of her.

'Thank you, Phinny, I appreciate it. I just can't do it myself – you know ironing is not in my nature.'

The pair fell back into the silence they had learned more than twenty-seven years ago when Phinn first began to talk. It was a silence like an embrace, familiar and comforting and brimming with habit. They knew they were both thinking about their younger sister. Ensconced in their old battle lines, they had stuck with each other when Claudia had slammed the front door, ensuring everyone inside knew she was ignoring them. They were concerned for her from a distance, the way any family member should be. Claudia didn't need their comforting words; she needed to sulk it out. While years ago they might have stealthily taken turns keeping an eye on her from behind street signs and trees, now they had a smartphone and moment of weakness when Claudia shared her location and then promptly forgot about it.

When the kids were nervous they returned to the same conversation topics: recounting blow-by-blow physical brawls from their proper childhood years (the teen brawls were still too emotionally fraught for exploration); how to divide $1 million between them (inevitably someone was cut out of a will); and death. Death was their absolute favourite: who had died, how they had died and the scenarios in which they themselves would die.

The kids loved any hypothetical life-altering situation – pregnancy, long-lost half-siblings, loss of limb, financial windfall; but the best one, the biggest treat, the one they returned to most often, and had done since they were all in primary school at the same time so could meet at lunchtime for earnest discussions, was death.

'What would you do if Claudia was diagnosed with cancer next year?' Zoe asked, glancing up from watching her sister move, as a blue dot, north from Shabby Chic.

Phinn warmed to the topic immediately. 'Well, you earn the most money in whatever it is you do, so you would have to keep working to send us money. You'd be a useless-as-tits nurse as well. So I would take personal leave, unlimited, maybe even sublet the apartment.'

'I could maybe negotiate nine-day fortnights, or working from home every second week, and then every second weekend I could come down on the Friday until the Sunday while she was resting from the chemo.'

'Yeah, yeah, and it would obviously be best for Claudia to come home. She could come back here and sit up in Mum's house. She would be too weak to shuttle between both so Dad would have to come here to see her. And she would get her treatment – you could pay for any extra drugs she needed – and I would stay with her so Mary didn't drive her insane—'

Zoe interrupted, 'Mary wouldn't matter. Claudia would be dying, civility would be dead. No need to be civil, civility is absolutely the worst hangover from the twentieth century. Civility would be dead; we could just sit around and watch Claudia be rude to Mary all day every day.'

'Right! Mary would be irrelevant. She fades away, not even a footnote in this story. I bet she would try to throw herself over Claudia, really work up some emotional capital. There'd always be one of us with Claudia, though. We'd do shifts, make sure she wasn't by herself.'

Zoe skipped ahead to the most wrenching part, the best part. 'And *the funeral.* It would be unbearable, little Claudie's funeral. I almost would not want to go.'

Phinn picked the skirt up and ruffled it around the ironing board to expose the unironed back, looking at it mournfully.

'It would be so hard. Almost unbearable, but we would have to go.'

'For Mum and Dad,' Zoe agreed.

'We might even have to do a reading,' Phinn continued. 'I would want to wear black. A black shirt, a black tie – silk – with my black suit, maybe about five days' worth of facial growth.'

'I would wear pink, something really joyful, to celebrate our Clauds. I would read something eloquent about how nothing would be the same again. Something like W. H. Auden but not as well known.'

Phinn nodded. 'It is a great poem, but every man and his dog has it read at their funeral. We'd be shattered. What music would she want?'

Zoe cocked her head. 'Well, she liked tools of manipulation, so at the beginning something really over the top, something that just has the entire congregation sobbing. "Into My Arms" is a good one. "Into My Arms", or maybe, maybe "Little Dreamer".'

'"Little Dreamer"?'

'I've been listening to it every night, by Future Islands; it's very haunting; it goes "I found you dreaming, I'm dreaming of you always".' Zoe began humming. '"And as we say goodnight, I hold you close and tight, No more raging suns, only waning ones, Like the waxing scar where my lonely heart, Once bloomed before I met you".'

Phinn winced. 'Ooft, that's good. Please stop destroying it by trying to sing.'

Their intimate silence returned as they both thought about their lives minus Claudia. Poor, weak Claudia. A wisp in the wind after her brave endurance of cancer – not a battle, never a battle. One just endures. And then she would be gone and they would be three. Inconceivable.

One of the most addictive bits of hypothetical deaths was how much you could emotionally wring yourself out, get to places barely conceived of in your soul, be enveloped in sadness. Almost convince yourself the death had happened and get to stand thrillingly on the edge of the abyss of grief before returning safely to the land of the living and healthy.

What they both refused to factor into this comforting and twisted game of yore was that it would not be them at the centre of the funeral. It would not matter if they wore black or pink, really. They wouldn't be at the forefront as they once would've been. They wouldn't get to pick the music. They wouldn't even get a couple of thousand dollars from Claudia's superannuation.

Phinn and Zoe both looked at each other sadly.

It would be Dylan making the decisions.

Phinn pulled out the skirt and clipped it to a hanger before handing it to Zoe.

'If you die I am leaving the family. Sorry Mum, you're on your own; you have to deal with the girls and Dad for the rest of your life.'

Chapter 29

Rachel and Mary were giggling. Whole body-sobbing, can't-breathe, borderline-hysterical giggling. Perched on the end of Rachel's bed, they were holding each other as they gasped for air, laughing.

It was not clear what was so funny, but a bottle of Moët sat between them, the beacon of the lower middle-class looking for posh signifiers.

'I was on my knees!' Rachel screamed. 'I thought: Jesus, Mary and Joseph, Our Lady is appearing before me, I'm having a vision, she's here.'

Mary held on to her arm as she half slid off the bed, laughing. 'You thought Our Lady was appearing!'

'I swear to God, I was even scared, I couldn't believe it.'

Mary pointed across the room to a small globe emblazoned with the word 'Medjugorje', a holy site in Bosnia-Herzegovina. Inside the globe was a plastic white figurine in the shape of the Virgin Mary. A gift from Zoe, beneath it was a switch, which triggered a flashing light that changed from pink to blue to purple to green as it lit up the figurine.

The night before, Rachel had got out of bed at two a.m. to find it flashing in the hallway and dropped to her knees in prayer while thinking about the pilgrims who would arrive at her house over the next 1000 years seeking the healing powers of the Mother of God who had appeared to Rachel, the patron saint of lost causes, taking the mantle from Jude. It was a holy moment, and her first prayer was for her children, but she was also forecasting her future glory.

Forty seconds on the ground and she realised it was just a flashing light. Her sainthood was revoked; she returned to life as an ordinary mother of ungrateful adults. Now she sat on her bed, slightly drunk, clutching her sister while she relayed the tale. Her halo well and truly diminished.

Rachel laughed harder.

'You, you are a wild bit of gear,' Mary said through giggles. She opened her mouth to say something but thought better of it and closed it again. Her laughing had ceased. She stood up, wobbled a moment, and looked down at her feet to get her grip, realising the bottle of champagne on the floor was empty.

The movement evoked Rachel's children to her. Her children when they were learning to walk. Her children when she thought of them as tiny morons, marvelled at how useless a human child was for so long. Her children when they used to chase her around the house squealing, 'Mummy, are you walking away from me?' but in a language only she could interpret. Their toddler English.

'You know the minute your children finally are interesting is the same minute they don't want to hang out with you anymore,'

Rachel said in the general direction of her sister who was now rummaging through the wardrobe. Mary winced and turned to face the bed.

'Don't be like that. Your children may be brats but tonight is one for fun. Your daughter is getting married. It's not just her day! It's your day as well.'

'My children are not brats,' Rachel snapped. 'This is what's supposed to happen – you grow them in your belly with minimal effort from their father and then you keep them alive for years ... They don't just want to take money from you. They don't even care about destroying your body, even though they eventually do. They don't want to take your life as you knew it, but they take that as well.' Rachel jabbed her chest. 'They want to take a piece of you away from you.'

Mary was silent as she took in the ramifications of her sister's compulsion to breed. It had never occurred to her to try to love someone more than she loved herself, or that she should.

She started laughing.

Rachel knew she should be wounded by the reaction but, as with most things these days, it was too much effort. She joined her sister laughing, leaning over to clutch her heart as her guffaws took over her body.

'You're right: it's my weekend too, none of this would have happened without me, they owe me their lives.' She walked over to the wardrobe. 'Sometimes, Mary, sometimes I dare to think you are jealous of my children for taking me away from you.'

Mary snorted but did not look at Rachel. 'I know you would throw me from a window in a second to stop one of them cutting their big toe.' She pretended not to seethe. 'What are you going to wear?'

Rachel held up a flowing white dress, carefully embroidered with roses. A slip underneath fell to the mid-shins and the overlay had sleeves falling to the elbows. Rachel had spent about 82 per cent of her waking hours over her lifetime ensuring she maintained the weight she was at twenty-five and the dress nipped in to show the years of denial on her waist.

She held the dress to her body, covering the Leicester City jersey she wore to bed. Mary whistled. 'That's beautiful. Is Claudia going to be okay with you in that dress?'

'Why wouldn't she be? It doesn't matter what I wear, I look fifty-two.'

'You're sixty-five.'

'I feel thirty. Sometimes I walk past a mirror and think, "Ma! You're here!" and realise it is my face staring back at me.'

Mary laughed. 'Well, I'll be your mirror, darling, you're beautiful. I'll get us another bottle of champagne.'

∽

Leah rolled off the top of Poppy. 'I'm sorry, I can't.' Poppy groaned and rolled over on the bed, covering her stomach as Leah stood up.

'I can hear your mum giggling downstairs.'

'So?'

'I can't focus on this,' she said, waving her hand over Poppy's body, 'with your mum sounding like she's laughing at us in the room.'

Poppy propped herself up on her elbows. 'She's just going through her special event ritual; she's getting sloshed with my evil aunt. She can't hear anything.'

'But I can hear her!'

Poppy reached across the bed for her Britney Spears T-shirt. Was it ironic or was it just lame? Poppy couldn't decide. But she did like Britney. She pulled it over her head and sat up.

'Fine, we won't have sex to the sound of my mother giggling. I'm out of here in two nights, though, and tomorrow will be all about the wedding.'

Leah cocked her head; she was only wearing her cotton underwear but did not seem to have any of the shame about her body required of women. She had one perfect breast, a perfectly round spongy mango; the other one was a bit lopsided, almost half a cup of water smaller. It wasn't immediately obvious; you had to have spent as much time as Poppy studying them. 'I know, time to bid each other adieu. Maybe I will see you next time?'

Poppy groaned again. 'What about the cliché, Leah? We have been hanging out for five days; lesbian law says we are basically married – we should have a cat by now, grand plans, everything.'

The cliché had become a tired joke already between the pair, but they kept running with it in place of any actual shared history, the kind one needed to build personal jokes, exchange sly glances that sent the other into stitches, true affinity. Leah picked up her jeans and riffled through the pockets, pulling out a piece of paper. 'I actually found the ultimate example of this: the lesbian calling card. I wrote it down to remind you of me. It is almost embarrassing, and a prime example of why everyone thinks lesbians are too emotional. Patricia Highsmith wrote it to the one woman I think she ever had actual feelings for.'

Leah tossed the note on the bed and pulled her jeans on and then her blue singlet.

'Have fun at the dinner tonight, and tomorrow. Call me when you give up and move back here.' She leaned over and kissed Poppy on the mouth and winked. Then she left.

Poppy reached over the side of the bed and picked up her phone, opening her email app hopefully. Groupon, the *New Yorker*, Goop – all the emails she intended to open but never got around to. Nothing from her future employer. They were still out there.

She jumped off the bed and closed the door then picked up the torn piece of paper, examining the back of it. It wasn't from a notepad; Poppy suspected it was the back of a novel. 'Desecrated,' she muttered to herself.

She flipped it over and read it. Pausing. Then read it again. Her shoulders started shaking and soon her giggles were intertwined in the house with her mother's drunken exclamations from downstairs.

'My green and red goddess, my jade and garnet, my moss and hollyberry, my sea and sun, my marrow and my blood, my stop and go baby, I adore you, I worship you, I kiss you, I cherish you, I defend you, I defy you ever not to love me, I caress your nipples with my tongue.'

Chapter 30

George leaned back in the chair he had pilfered from his uncle's house due to his mortality. He pressed the remote and the television flicked on just as the first kick of the game sailed through the air. His timing was a fine art. He poured his mid-strength beer into a glass.

A blissful Friday night, he thought to himself.

Chapter 31

Nora had spent a lot of her time lately lying on the floor listening to Kendrick Lamar. Well, she thought she'd spent a lot of her time lying on the floor listening to Kendrick, but really it was just a lot of time in the past week.

Like Claudia she had the knack of viewing her life from a helicopter perspective – she liked to be melodramatic even when alone, to picture how she looked lying on the floor in her dressing-gown staring at the ceiling and listening to 'Love' by Kendrick Lamar.

Nora muttered to herself 'just love me', then sat straight up. 'Okay, maybe that was a little pathetic,' she said to the room. Speaking out loud to herself was a longstanding habit; it started in the spring of being twenty-five years old when she'd moved in by herself for what she thought would be two years at the most. She fully intended to meet her husband. Her ovaries were aching even back then. She had moved in by herself and begun building her lovely life. Livin' lovely. Then she met Tom and everything was on track and now it was six years later and she had mangled her chance at happiness and was still talking to herself.

She stood up and tightened her robe, pulling her towel from her damp hair and patting it. Dinner was in two and a half hours. She walked over the beige carpet, the exact faded colour of lost hope, and opened the tiny fridge. It was too small for her Tasmanian bubbly to stand up in, so the bottle lay diagonally across a shelf. It was a celebration, right? 'Right!' she answered herself, pouring out a glass. She walked over to the iPod and switched it to 'You've Earned It', her latest favoured podcast. She cycled through various podcasts that were made by and for alcoholics in the forgotten corners of the world. They made her feel better about herself. Smug, almost. This one was the best find by far. It was three women somewhere in the Midwest in America, housewives who had found each other online and rambled to each other every week with barely a nod to structure or form. They spoke about being wine mums and giving up drinking. There was a pornographic quality to it; you heard things you felt you should not be hearing.

This week they were talking about rock bottom. They actually spoke about rock bottom fairly regularly but they usually called it different things: 'realising stuff', 'my turning point', 'when I knew I had a problem', 'when I hated myself the most' – myriad ways of plumbing the depths. They seemed to have had a series of rock bottoms because it was a different story each time.

Nora loved hearing about the wine hidden in laundry baskets, the drunk school runs, the nip of whisky while pretending to brush their teeth. She didn't do any of that. She just liked celebrating. And commiserating. And puncturing boredom.

Nora listened to Margaret telling the story of when she crossed the line. It was when she drove her daughters and their two friends home after a bottle of wine at the school play. She had driven her own daughters after a bottle of wine a few times, but now she was risking other people's children. Nora snorted.

'You were only drink-driving your own daughters so it was fine!' she berated Margaret. She shook her head and took a sip of the sparkling wine. She only ever drank nice stuff; that was the other thing. Of course it was fine. People who have problems don't care what they drink. Nora did.

She pulled out her eye-shadow palette and started smudging her lid with pink the way she had been taught when she was twenty-two on the David Jones floor by a Chanel assistant. Maybe it was time to learn a new technique. She had read somewhere that you can tell at what age a woman was most happy by the way she does her make-up. Women with frosted pink lipstick had a good time in the 1980s and women with brown lipstick felt their most beautiful in the 1990s. Women with black-lined eyelids were watching the Duchess of Cambridge too closely in 2011. Nora had her doubts about the happiness theory. It was more likely it signalled the age when they learned how to do their make-up properly and they had not bothered to update it since. It probably signalled when they were childless and had the most time to think about themselves.

Nora just knew pinks and coppers suited her brown eyes and lipstick would be rubbed off by whatever she ate tonight. And drank. She downed the rest of her glass and poured another one. She rubbed primer on her face. She did not actually know what it did but had been advised to use it by numerous magazine articles and so obeyed.

Margaret's voice floated into the bathroom. 'I would watch the clock at barbecues waiting for a respectable time to pull out the bubbles.'

Nora frowned as Margaret continued. 'Then I couldn't wait to get home so I could drink properly. I should've known then, that's not normal, wanting to leave family and friends so you can drink properly.' Nora smiled and returned to feeling smug.

She thought about picking up her phone for another peek at her email. She didn't really need to look again. She had read it so many times it was memorised ... 'because I cannot give you what you want as you grow (and I try desperately to stay in place).'

'Don't think about Tom,' she told the mirror. Instead, she thought about Claudia.

Would Claudia be doing this for her? Renting a sub-par motel room, buying her cake toppers, trying to get along with her siblings. Of course Claudia would do it for her. But, would she actually end up doing it? Had Nora built her life too much for herself? Her question for the ages. What if she didn't meet someone? Was she okay with that? Intellectually she should be. Intellectually she kind of was. A life of RSVP-ing for one to weddings. Of sleeping on the couch in family holiday houses because it was deemed she did not need her own room. A lifetime of going to events with the faint hope she would meet someone.

She finished dusting her blusher across her cheeks and smiled at her reflection. 'It's not time to be put out to pasture just yet,' she told the mirror. As she spoke, 'The Final Countdown' boomed through her speaker in place of Margaret's confession about putting her daughter in front of the TV in the morning because she was too hungover to deal with her.

Nora walked over to the phone and saw Tom's name on the screen. Tom was calling her. 'Arrrrrrgh,' Nora said to the screen. 'Whhhhhyyyy?' She cleared her throat and mashed the screen to accept the call, raising the phone to her ear.

'Hello?'

'Uh, Nora, hello.' She heard his voice and sat on the edge of the bed, cradling her forehead with one hand. She looked around and spotted her wine glass next to the bathroom sink amongst her make-up brushes. She stayed silent and stood up to fetch it.

She took a slug and finally replied. 'Hey Tom.' She let the silence between them hang in the air. 'What do you want?' she finally said.

'You haven't replied to my email.' Tom stated the fact as if it was a question.

'What am I supposed to say to it?'

'Jesus, Nora, whatever you think. What your response is. Are you just going to be finished with this?'

Nora exhaled and opened the fridge (again) to pour out another glass (again).

'You want to write your way through it, that's fine. I don't see why it has to be a correspondence, though.'

'You finished this, Nora, and that's fine. But you're also the one who rang me asking if you had made the right decision.' Nora winced; she only had the vaguest recollection of that late-night phone call. Tom continued. 'Why can't you show any emotion in a break-up?'

Nora clenched her fist in time with her teeth.

'I don't owe you emotion. I actually don't owe you anything. You can write anything you want; the winner can always write history. Comprehending it is an entirely different thing, and I don't owe you any comprehension.'

Tom snorted. 'Listen to you – you think you sound so poetic in the face of real emotion. The winner may write history but, remember, in some cases the loser ends up sapped, trapped and never moving forward.'

'Did you just call me a loser?'

'You called yourself the loser.'

'Tom, why are you calling me?'

Nora heard his breathing become slightly shallower.

'I just miss you, is all.'

Nora allowed herself an emotion, a safe one, but an emotion nonetheless. Fury.

'You miss me so it's okay to torment me? Do you ever think of anyone but yourself? Do you know what a sad cliché you are? Moping around over the break-up you made ninety times worse with a savage email and then calling me to make you feel better, calling me to demand correspondence?'

'Nora, we're grown up, surely we can talk?'

'Tom, we are grown-ups with no children together, no pets together – we don't even have a lease together. There is no reason we have to talk after we break up.'

She heard Tom wince at the other end of the line.

'I wrote you something else.'

'Jesus Christ, Tom, I have to get ready for a pre-wedding dinner. Remember? The wedding of my best friend? That I'm here at alone? I don't have time for this bullshit.'

Nora hung up. She might be history's loser but she felt the phone call's winner. Satisfied. She hesitated and then opened her email app. 'I am *affronted*,' she yelled at the room.

There was an email from Tom. She couldn't help herself. He obviously couldn't help himself.

From: Tom Tran
To: ANoraAble
Subject: Fury

So yeah, your fury. I can understand it to an extent. I don't know why I feel the need to justify myself but I also think I owe you some kind of response after our last conversation, and all those years.

It's ironic, one of the reasons I always felt kind of uneasy in the relationship was the way you and your friends took on sharing emotions as a kind of group sport. There's no denying there is a huge amount of love in that particular unit. Huge.

But given the amount of people and the demands that this level of affection accorded, it was just as much a force of nature with the power to cause huge rifts as much as forge bonds. It was overwhelming.

I came in and seemingly faked entry to this group WHICH SPENDS SO MUCH ENERGY TRYING TO LOVE OUT THE COLD by remaining in a relationship I don't really know I was into.

And the fact is, I know what I have done, even if I can't face up to the motivations or what stray neurons were bounding through my mind, and it is the worst kind of thing to do to any kind of love between two people. It is. To turn something into a big lie – whether or not it was – is probably the coldest thing I have done. Am doing.

Nora slammed her laptop shut. Arsehole. Arsehole arsehole arsehole. She wanted to write back and she knew that she should not. She would not. She tossed the computer onto the bed and ran her fingers through her hair. 'You won't write back,' she said to the mirror. She looked at the green printed dress she had carefully hung in the bathroom so the steam from her shower would get the creases out. She needed to get out of this motel room.

Chapter 32

Dylan grabbed at the zip at the base of Claudia's spine and pulled it up, leaning over and briefly kissing her on her back as he did. She turned to him with half of her hair curled and the other half still frizzy and kissed him on the mouth.

'Is there still time to run away?' she asked.

Dylan grinned. 'We don't have to get married here if you don't want. We could've stuck with the original plan; I know you just wanted to make your family happy.'

'Wellll, it wasn't just about making my family happy.'

'It was a lot about making your family happy.'

Claudia put her hands on each of Dylan's shoulders – she only came up to his chest when she was in her bare feet – and rested her head on his shirt. He put his hand to the back of her head and smoothed it along her hair.

'You look so pretty, you are so pretty, we're going to have fun, I promise.'

Claudia exhaled.

'I know but I just wish Dad was coming. He would come if it was Poppy's wedding dinner. He just doesn't care enough about me.'

Dylan pulled Claudia closer so it wasn't just her head pressed against his chest.

'That's not true, your dad loves you so much, he's just being a bit strange. Don't let it get to you like that; you can still have a good time.'

Claudia finally stepped back and picked up her curling wand, turning away so she was facing the mirror again and could continue burning her hair in an effort to make it look bouncy. Dylan moved closer to her again and kissed her in the same spot on her back that he had before.

'Don't let it wear you down; it's going to be great. Dad and Yvonne are here, so that will make the dinner easier tonight. You worry so much about the rest of your family – just enjoy it. Have you eaten this afternoon? Do you want me to go make you some toast before you put on your lipstick?'

Claudia looked at Dylan's reflection and smiled guiltily.

'Can I have an apple and slices of cheese?'

'Of course, my love!' Dylan walked out of the room but before he was halfway down the hallway Claudia called out his name again and his head reappeared at the doorway. 'Yes, my love.'

Claudia studied his face for a second, drinking in the details of his slightly crooked nose and deep-set eyes. 'Can you cut up the apple for me?'

Chapter 33

'Things You Should Be Afraid Of', an extensive but not exhaustive list by Poppy Blanche Carter:

That there is hypocrisy in lobbying against victim blaming but refusing to walk home at night by yourself

Susan Miller dying

Gen X becoming like boomers

Nuclear war

A robot taking your job

If the priest has washed his hands before giving communion

Never getting to the stage where you don't mentally add up your grocery basket before going to the checkout

Being homeless in your sixties

The pension not existing when you're in your sixties

The moon – it is not trustworthy

People finding out you secretly think cultural appropriation is not a real problem

That you're inherently unlovable

Your parents getting old. Truly old

Having to move home when home is fifteen hours from anything interesting

Being left behind

Being irrelevant

Never properly understanding political theory

Brioche buns

Things you shouldn't be afraid of:

Looking fat at your sister's wedding

Ruining your sister's wedding

Ruining everything

Poppy looked up from her phone and sighed. She had always been averse to recording her thoughts, but some long-ago article in what would euphemistically be called a 'women's' magazine had suggested lists. At least once a month she found herself typing two fingered, into the notes section of her iPhone, lists that were loosely based on what had distressed her lately. She knew she had come home at a stressful time: her work was in flux, her renting situation was in flux, it would be generous to say that the state of her finances was in flux. And now she had an almost severe allergic reaction to Claudia's wedding. She found herself relegated to the role of sooky youngest child and bizarrely played along accordingly.

The brute force of her changes in mood shocked even her at times. But she also felt helpless in the face of them. If she examined her situation closely she guessed she would find shame at the root of it. The week with Claudia had seemed a parade of everything she was failing at. Poppy wanted to be happy for her sister but felt her faith broken in a queer way by how easy it was for her. She had the partner, she had the job, she had the city life. There was so much Poppy would've done for an ounce of the security and yet Claudia was so blasé about it. She was blasé about it and also seemed further and further from Poppy with each year. When they were teenagers, Claudia would have been more loyal; she would not have brought a friend into what was supposed to be a family week.

Poppy had always had problems with rage, but she had shocked even herself with what had been brought to the fore this week. Before she had only been dimly aware of the fury that was evidently running through her veins. After each outburst she felt guilty, but then Nora would show up, rubbing in their faces her bond with their sister. Or Claudia would appear, apparently manufacturing emotional problems the week before her wedding while Poppy had her own real problems. She was still dismissed as a baby; every suggestion she made was talked down; she couldn't even raise the prospect of doing something different with the daisies without feeling as though she was being derided. She was just an extra at any supposedly important family event, basically ignored at the dress fitting, entire conversations going on as if she didn't exist on the beach day. If that wasn't enough, she'd watched Nora being deferred to the whole week, with Claudia sneaking off to the motel room thinking she was so clever and that nobody would know where she was spending those hours.

Coming home had only confirmed to Poppy how alone she was.

Chapter 34

Claudia was the first to arrive at the restaurant, wearing a sweeping strapless purple dress. It was almost a gown, but her lack of jewellery made it a dress. She was trying to go for Kim K simplicity but her hair was not sleek enough and the dress needed tailoring. The overall effect was one of cluelessness. It would show up well in photos against the restaurant's wall of hanging plants, so, small mercies. She had managed to slip past her exuberant mother and aunt with her dress and shoes and make her way to Dylan's hotel, which he had managed to rent just for the afternoon under the guise of an odd kind of romance. Any excuse to be away from Claudia's family.

Claudia had silently got ready while Dylan played her songs from niche bands in the nineties (Mclusky, Guided by Voices, Pissed Jeans). It was nice but Claudia was gloomy. She walked through the doors of the restaurant reeking of apprehension; it shrouded her as she made her way directly to the long table without bothering to ask the waiter about the reservation. Nobody else was bothering to sit eleven people in the middle of September.

A girl of about nineteen approached her wearing black pants that were slightly too long and leather shoes that she obviously used to wear to school the year before. She smiled widely as she pulled a notebook from the pocket of her white shirt.

'The Carter table?'

Claudia nodded. 'I'm evidently first to arrive.'

'Are you getting married?' the girl asked, holding her pen over her notepad as if interviewing Claudia, not preparing to take her order.

Claudia nodded again but didn't say anything.

'That's so exciting! How long did it take to find your dress?'

Claudia smiled weakly. 'A couple of tries.'

The girl cocked her head and let out a sound, something like a blissful groan and a clucking. 'You're nervous! It's so cute! I can't wait to get married. Is your sister Zoe?'

Claudia looked around the restaurant, willing one of her family members to appear. The country town politeness did not return easily to her when she was home and she hated small talk. She didn't even want to make eye contact when telling someone to get her a wine. Nobody materialised; there was nobody to save her.

'Yes she is; can I have a glass of pinot grigio?'

'I love her flower business!'

'Her flower business?' Claudia finally looked at the girl properly. Her greasy fringe was trying hard to cover a breakout and her eyes were the same colour as the plants behind her.

'Yeah, I follow it on Instagram; it's very cool what she's doing.'

More to add to the list of things Claudia did not know about her sister. She'd been mysterious when she was getting dressed to go to parties when Claudia was thirteen. Back then Zoe seemed like a person who was only fully formed when away from her relations. Everyone suspected there were entire aspects of her hidden from the family and only coming into full view once they were not there to witness it. Claudia remembered being shocked when she saw her sister order a passionfruit juice. They had never known she liked passionfruit. It went further than material tastes. It seemed that, away from her family, Zoe read different books, watched different television shows, had an entire set of political beliefs they were not allowed in on.

She had not only somehow managed to maintain the emotional distance as an adult, but also created a new physical one. The family barely knew what she did for a living and Claudia would bet $500 nobody even knew exactly what her degree was in.

And now Claudia was being told she ran some kind of business. They vaguely knew she was a florist but that was the extent of it. Of course they had asked her about her work, but the family were used to Zoe's easy dismissals. A question about how she was going always seemed to turn into a discussion about what was for dinner that night or some recently released movie. It's easy to get away with in a large family, being deliberately obtuse. When there are so many people vying for a place in the conversation, distraction is a daily occurrence. And that was before the chronic self-obsession was factored in. She was like one of those riddles that gets more complex the closer you look at it, that opens up double the amount of unsolvable aspects once one part has been figured out.

The girl interrupted Claudia's thoughts. 'We don't have any pinot grigio.'

'Of course, I'll just have chardonnay,' Claudia said, pulling out her phone. 'What did you say the Instagram was?' The waitress told her the pun in the hushed tone of someone who was saying a password out loud for the first time.

Claudia had just brought the page up and was scrolling through photos of roses dip-dyed in food colouring to turn the tips shades of blue, green and red when she heard her name shrilly called out across the restaurant. She winced. Without looking up she knew it was her aunt and that her aunt had been drinking.

Claudia had taken a seat in the middle of the table out of a sense of duty, since the dinner was supposed to be for her and Dylan, and from her vantage point had a direct line of sight to the front door of the restaurant, as well as through a window to part of the car park.

Mary made her way across the maroon carpet with Rachel clutching her elbow. They were both wearing high heels they were clearly unused to and Mary had even put on a push-up bra to give the effect of two slightly milky orbs spilling out of a black sleeveless top, which was tucked into a mid-length skirt of the same colour. Next to her, Rachel watched her feet as they took each step; she was wearing bright red patent leather heels that had seemed such a good idea in the shop.

Without hesitating, the two sat down in the middle of the table in the prime position directly across from Claudia. 'Of course,' she whispered to herself.

'Hello darling.' Mary's cheeks were flushed and an unsure hand had applied liner to her lids. 'We're first here!'

'Yes, so far everyone is four minutes late,' Claudia responded as the waitress gently put down her wine in front of her.

'Can we get a bottle of prosecco, sweetie?' Rachel said, looking up at the girl. The girl nodded, carefully writing the order in her notepad and scurrying away.

Over her aunt's head Claudia saw Zoe and Phinn walk in together with Poppy slightly behind them. She looked at her mother as she spoke to her aunt. 'No funny business tonight.'

Claudia enjoyed the spectacle of watching her siblings when they didn't know they were being observed. It was like seeing yourself on film: familiar but not quite like you imagined. Perhaps a bit more clumsy. She saw Zoe squeeze Phinn's upper arm as she turned to say something to Poppy, and from Poppy's reaction she knew it was an inappropriate comment, most likely about Mary. Zoe was making peace with Poppy; she had obviously not been in a good mood in the lead-up to the night and Zoe was trying to diffuse her before the dinner. Claudia could tell all of this from the few steps they had taken, just before Zoe met her eyes and waved enthusiastically. This was the tribe for which she knew all the codes, the secret signals, the language. That you cannot choose your family is such a pathetically obvious statement, but it is often forgotten what else you can't choose. You can't choose to fully and wholly extract yourself – you can sometimes, if you're lucky, choose to learn the language and signals of another group, but you'll never be properly fluent. Not only does the language have to be learned from birth, but you have to help create it as well.

Zoe, Phinn and Poppy formed a line as they arrived at the table, swarming on three seats across from Claudia. 'You can't sit there. It's reserved.'

Zoe raised an eyebrow. 'Reserved for someone more important than the bride's sister? The maid of honour?'

'I don't have a maid of honour,' Claudia said, without having to even form the words in her brain before they were out of her mouth.

'As a matter of fact, yes,' Mary said, ignoring Claudia. 'It's for my plus one.'

Zoe laughed cruelly and nodded to Claudia before moving down a seat, not-so-secretly pleased to be saved from an evening next to Mary.

Claudia narrowed her eyes. 'Are those my earrings?'

Zoe touched the toucans studded in her ears. 'I found them at Mum's.' She turned to Phinn and they began what looked like a serious, hushed conversation that Claudia assumed was just about which drinks to order. She tried to think of the last time she saw her older sister with a bunch of flowers but couldn't come up with anything. She thought, perhaps, maybe it was Zoe who had sanctioned her decision that daisies would be the easiest, prettiest and most understated flower to have at her wedding.

Poppy sat at the end of the trio, fiddling with her phone and whispering, as an aside, that she would drink whatever. Claudia thought just a few years back to being Poppy's age and what it was like: the uncertainty, the hope. The realisation that you don't have all the time in the world, that it does matter if you leave things for a few days or a few months. Every word you don't write, or sing, or film is in fact a backwards step, a black mark against your supposed fate. She remembered it dawning on her that perhaps her life would in fact be ordinary, that maybe she was not destined for specialness. She remembered it was hard letting go of the hypothetical futures with friends: 'when you're a graphic designer for *Vogue* and I'm a famous writer we will ...' 'when I'm in charge of the company and you are based in Los Angeles ...' It was harsh realising some things were irrevocable, that sometimes they had messed up, but she didn't remember being as mean about it as Poppy was. Perhaps because, secretly, in the bowels of her soul, Claudia was not shocked.

'Are you, Claudia?' Mary drew the attention of others at the table back to the bride to be.

'Hmmmm?' she responded noncommittally, trying to convey flippancy.

'Are you changing your name?'

Claudia laughed. 'No, I'm not, I'll still be Claudia Carter.'

'Such a good feminist,' Poppy called sarcastically down the table. 'You're still getting married but it's okay, it's tantamount to the third wave, because you're not changing your name.'

Zoe winced and Claudia's nostrils flared. 'Excuse me?'

'What? I'm just saying, you must be proud you're not changing your name. It must make you feel like a good feminist. Even though you're still getting married.'

'What do you mean "even though"?'

'Well, it's still an oppressive institution, any way you look at it. It's oppressive for women; you can't erase its long history. And you're choosing to take part in something that deliberately excluded queer people for so long, so I don't really find it tenable that you could pretend you're not taking part in something archaic and harmful. But hey, love is a compromise and feminism now is just a series of personal choices that conveniently benefit the individual.'

Zoe tried to intervene. 'Come on now, I don't think Claudia's marriage is a political act.'

'But that would mean the personal isn't political,' Poppy responded, staring at Claudia.

Claudia responded by snorting, 'A lot of people don't have time for the "personal is political" because they're focusing on things that matter, like legislating on reproductive rights and marching for fair conditions for the working class. I know it must feel so nice to think at this point in history your identity is unimpeachable and righteous but, Poppy, let me tell you, some people have real problems and your unblemished soapbox is an illusion.'

Phinn visibly bit the inside of his cheek trying not to laugh as he turned his head from his youngest sister so she couldn't see. But with his eyes he said to Claudia: 'Owned.' Claudia quickly looked down at her hands so as not to provoke her sister further with her satisfaction while Rachel slammed both of her hands on the table.

'Enough!' she yelled, but her children were silenced anyway by the arrival of chinking glasses and a promising bottle. The young waitress looked at Zoe adoringly as she poured red wine that seemed to be within the price range of 'I know I'm not paying for this'. Zoe nodded to her in thanks while Phinn leaned back to allow his glass to be poured and pulled Poppy's next to it. Poppy ducked her head to look at their mother, who still had the secret power of ending arguments when she truly wanted to invoke it – the wedding eve dinner of her daughter being such an occasion.

Before she could launch into a mini-lecture, though, two male hands landed on Rachel's shoulders, causing the entire table to jump in their seats. 'RA-CH-EL,' the voice that belonged to the hands boomed. 'I see nothing has changed.'

Wearing an ill-advised and ill-fitting powder-blue suit with an Akubra on his head, it was their uncle Mick. He leaned down and kissed Rachel on the cheek as she laughed, and then turned to Mary and kissed her on the mouth, as an almost undetectable groan rippled down the table. Mary blushed and pulled her beaten handbag off the table. 'Here's your chair, darling.'

'And here's the beautiful bride!' he responded, leaning across the table to give Claudia a kiss as she patted his back in reply. 'Hello Mick.'

He let out a satisfied sigh as he sat down and bellowed to nobody in particular, 'A schooner of Guinness, please,' then turned to the Carter siblings on his left. 'How the hell are you? I haven't seen you since the official shunning!'

'Well,' Phinn said, breaking the silence, 'I missed the official bit.' The girls, who had suddenly found the patterned walls so fascinating, waited for Mick's permission to laugh before they joined in his chortling.

Claudia relaxed. Maybe the worst was over.

∽

Through a mix of shame and champagne, Mick's presence righted the topsy-turvy balance caused by people at a table who are far too intimate to be polite to each other and have spent

273

enough time together in a week for age-old resentments to be at precise boiling point. The Carter siblings and Rachel were all too embarrassed by their treatment of Mick over the past few years, and shy from the lack of contact, to truly be themselves with him around. Mary was giddy to the point of being sick and did not seem to have the capacity for her usual barbs and varied hypocrisies.

So it was to an unusually subdued group that Dylan's father and stepmother were introduced when they at last entered the restaurant thirty minutes later. Claudia's furious text messages with a running commentary on the time had been studiously avoided by Dylan, and Claudia couldn't even manage a pissed-off glance in front of his parents.

Yvonne and Jerome had arrived in Winston that afternoon and spent a blissful few hours gossiping with their son before the dreaded formal proceedings. They had not been given fair warning on what to expect but the Carter charm could be deployed on a whim and they would not have to face the reality of the family that evening. Instead they got a sparkling and entertaining alternative.

Rachel was the first to rise from her seat and embrace the couple. 'It is so lovely to finally meet you. Claudia talks about you all the time. I am so sorry her father can't be here to see you as well. How was your trip?' she enquired as she squeezed each of them, and Dylan gave Claudia a peck on the forehead. The couple could barely mutter a greeting as the rest of the Carters descended upon them, a rampage of hugs and compliments. Dylan pulled out the two chairs that had been left empty next to his own and ushered his dad and step-mum into them, at which point an expectant silence fell.

Yvonne smiled finally. 'Lovely to be here.'

Mick cleared his throat. 'I was just telling the rest of them, I devote about 35 per cent of my day to not being Catholic, to not blessing myself, to not offering a compromise with God for anything, whether it be for my daughter to survive or for the light to change to green quicker. I want to thank God for everything: for Mary, for my sisters, for my father, for my job, for my city. It takes enormous concentration to remain ambivalent on the subject of religion.'

Jerome smiled weakly. 'My father thinks we might be part Jewish,' he responded.

Mick seized upon it. 'Aha! Then you would understand perfectly the daily battle of the cultural Catholic to steer clear of any actual God.'

Jerome signalled for the waitress and ordered more red wine for the table. He was sitting next to his son and directly across from Zoe, for which Claudia privately thanked God, Allah and Oprah. Zoe could chat at any level: rich boomers loved her, country people loved her, Nationals voters loved her, socialists loved her, teenagers loved her – everyone could chat to her. She leaned across the table and asked Jerome how he and Yvonne had spent the afternoon, securing at least twenty-five minutes of the couple feeling comfortable.

Claudia checked her phone. It was now fifty-seven minutes since the supposed start of dinner and still there were empty chairs. She suddenly grabbed Dylan's wrist underneath the tablecloth and leaned over. She whispered sharply, 'Nora isn't here.' Confused, Dylan looked over at the bar of the restaurant where the waitress was fetching the fifth bottle of wine for the evening and back to Claudia, repeating her statement to her as a question.

'Nora isn't here?'

'Nora isn't here.'

Claudia tried not to sound betrayed and focused more on the alarm. Nora had taken on the role of bridesmaid over the past few months. She had taken Claudia out to a champagne lunch and made her feel excited and special when all she felt was clichéd and put upon. She had picked her shoes and booked facials. She had told her, 'It's one day,' when Claudia had tried on the bridal persona of melodrama, and now Claudia sat facing her mother and wretched aunt and her siblings, with Dylan and his parents on one side but nobody on hers. Nora was supposed to be on her side. Now she was an hour late and counting.

Claudia stood up with her phone. As she excused herself to go and make the call she looked through the windows to the car park and saw Nora. Nora sprinting across gravel in black-and-white heels so high that Claudia could almost hear the crack of her ankle if there was one misstep. She saw her stop outside the door and look down at her gold dress. It was not the green dress for the festivities Nora had showed her earlier and it was not very Nora. It was not very appropriate. From the table it looked like it was made of gold lamé and it scooped down across her chest before joining at the back where it scooped even lower, stopping just above her hips. The dress ended mid-thigh and, beneath, her hastily self-tanned legs glistened. She tugged at the hem and touched her long hair, which in stark contrast to the dress was blown out in understated loose curls. Nora seemed to take a deep breath and pushed the door open, entering with a smile already plastered across her face. Claudia waved mutely from the table and sat back down as Nora picked her way carefully through the tables. She stopped just behind Mary and waved. 'Sorry I'm late, everyone, I have no decent excuse, I must buy a bottle of champagne to apologise.' She leaned down and kissed Rachel. 'You could be the younger sister of the bride!' she offered as penance, and then gave Mary a quick peck and squeezed the Carter siblings' shoulders before making her way round for introductions with Dylan's parents. Finally she sank down next to Claudia. Her lipstick, a deeply uncharacteristic shade of pink, was already smudged around her lips, as if it had been applied by a delighted four year old.

'I'm sorry, I'm sorry, I'm sorry,' she whispered. Claudia leaned in and smelled something sour on her breath: toothpaste from five hours ago and bubbles upon bubbles upon bubbles.

'What are you wearing?' Claudia hissed.

Nora looked down and seemed surprised by what she saw. 'I hated the green dress. I decided it was so boring.' She giggled and ushered the waitress over. 'Have we started on the champagne yet? It is a celebration. Can you bring me a bottle of champagne?'

The waitress's eyes widened and she picked up a menu from the table. 'What kind?'

Nora glanced at the list and giggled again. 'None of this is actually champagne, you know?' Claudia elbowed Nora but she seemed oblivious, studying the list more carefully. 'This is actually quite good, mostly Tasmanian sparkling – hard to find on a decent list actually.' She looked at the waitress and gave her a crooked smile. Claudia noticed her mascara had fallen beneath her eyes and was smudging along with the eyeliner. If Claudia had been in the mood, she would've enjoyed the spectacle of her uptight friend in such disarray. 'We'll have the Arras, thank you,' Nora finally decided. Before Claudia could grab Nora again she had leaned across the table. 'Rachel, you look ravishing. That is exactly your colour.'

And Rachel, easily flattered, was soon deep in conversation about what shoes she would be wearing the next day. Claudia sighed and looked down the table. Mary and Mick had their heads close together, a beast mutated from a family but sharing no actual genes themselves. Poppy was steadfastly ignoring any attempt by Phinn to broker peace for the evening, between Zoe and Poppy or just in general. Claudia watched as she downed a glass and swiftly refilled it. Claudia hated the way her younger sister drank: it was quick and stupid and if anyone dared comment she showed her defiance by aggressively speeding it up. To Claudia's right Dylan was chatting with his mother while Zoe occasionally interjected. It was a moment in the evening when the family was behaving in a way that Claudia assumed almost every other family behaved. Civilly.

The young waitress, a constant presence, hovered at their elbows, eager to take the first order. Claudia counted the bottles on the table and looked at her watch. It was an hour and twenty-seven minutes since their booking had begun, there were seven bottles on the table and they hadn't even ordered dinner. She nodded to the waitress and interrupted the conversations flowing around her. 'Time for dinner?' It was posed as a question but everyone knew it was a command.

The waitress returned from the kitchen with two bottles of Mumm and delivered them to Dylan, who took one and loosened the cork, letting it go off with a *POP* that silenced the chattering table. Claudia raised an eyebrow as Dylan poured her an almost-overflowing glass and handed the bottle to the waitress to finish pouring the rest of the table. He must have arranged for the bottles to be brought to the restaurant earlier in the day; they were not usually served. Her family and his parents looked at him expectantly as he took a long sip.

'I want to say a few words,' he said, wiping his mouth with the back of his hand and looking down at his fiancée. 'Claudia and I agreed there would be no speeches tomorrow, but I couldn't let the occasion go without briefly saying something about Claudia. Mostly, that I love her. I think it's an easy enough thing to say; it's important to show as well. I hope that by marrying her she can see it as my most public declaration and demonstration of what she means to me. When I met Claudia I was a very lonely man. I did not really know that. It was not something I gave much thought to, but having her in my life has revealed so many things to me. How fun life can be; how stupid it is to be too cool. Not that she isn't cool, but she never feels too cool to show how she feels – to be joyous, to be furious, to be sad. It may be clichéd but I did not even know I had the capacity for so much demonstration of love – let alone the love I feel for her – before she showed me how to show it. The joy of saying "I love you" every day; the joy of showing you are excited to see someone just because they're walking through the door at the end of the day. I didn't even know the proper joy – to my great shame – of hugging someone so much.'

Dylan looked down and gently touched Claudia's face.

'We are each other's subtexts. All of my unspoken thoughts and motives, what I really think and believe, it is in you. Life without you would be like walking along without my arm, you are such an essential part of me now.

'I love you.' Dylan glanced around the table before looking at Claudia again. 'Despite everything, I love you.'

The two kept looking at each other, smiling, until Mick finally finished Dylan's speech for him.

'To Dylan and Claudia,' he said, raising his glass. Everyone at the table obediently raised their champagne flutes.

'Cheers,' Claudia said, clinking with Dylan's glass and leaning in to whisper in his ear.

The rest of the table could not hear what she said.

∽

The food came out, stodgy and warm with piping hot plates. Overdone steaks and steamed vegetables were a staple of the venue. But nobody complained and most people seemed to be forcing something into their stomachs without being rude or inappropriate. Dylan and Mick's parents created a stricter atmosphere: whenever there are witnesses, everyone has to be on their best behaviour.

They would've made it through dessert too if Rachel had just eaten her lasagne.

Chapter 35

The Carters had withstood some epic battles over three decades. Rachel had once become so drunk she had screamed at Claudia in front of a restaurant that she should've home-schooled her to make her a better daughter. When they were younger, Zoe and Phinn had a physical fight so brutal it became legendary for the huge tuft of hair that Phinn ripped from Zoe's head and his subsequent broken nose. After one Christmas Zoe and Poppy had not spoken for five months because they had both drunk too much champagne and Zoe had told her younger sister she was spoiled and selfish. Poppy had once left both George and Claudia crying in a pub when she'd told them that she had been emotionally and physically abandoned as a teenager by both of them when everyone had left home. Even Phinn, as a twenty-one year old, had made Zoe cry in a rental car when he said they all couldn't wait for her to leave a holiday so they could finally relax and have a good time. Three years before, Rachel had to put herself between her two youngest daughters when – while still only on the entrées – they had begun punching each other for reasons nobody ever quite untangled. The cruellest lines, the most heartless remarks, the most devoted insults – they had all been said out loud to each other at one point or another, and more often than was believable they had descended into the physical even when they were much, much, much too old for that shit.

But it all paled in comparison to Claudia's wedding.

Rachel had pushed her vegetable lasagne around her plate for most of the meal before declaring she could've made a better version. At the end of the table Poppy smirked. 'When?'

Rachel's eyes flashed. 'What is that supposed to mean?'

Poppy's back straightened. 'Did I stutter? When have you ever made lasagne?'

Phinn made himself smaller in his seat while Zoe tried to stop the iceberg they were heading for. It seemed small now, innocuous even, but there was a hell of a lot going on underneath. A much bigger fight loomed than a casual observer at the table could possibly foresee.

'Mum's made lasagne before – you know her food is good,' Zoe said, trying to catch Rachel's eye. 'My steak was quite good, actually. How was your dinner?' she said desperately to Dylan's stepmother sitting across from her. If she could cut the conversation off at the head then Poppy could simmer by herself for a while longer. But Yvonne didn't see the signals and just nodded.

'Mum,' said Poppy, 'have you ever eaten a meal at a restaurant that you haven't complained about? You have such high and mighty tastes for someone who didn't even make sandwiches for lunch when we were kids.'

Claudia heard someone inhale sharply and realised it was her. Slowly, she exhaled, thinking she should intervene but finding it impossible to raise the energy. Next to her Nora let out a small squeak and Claudia knew she was trying not to laugh. Although, what exactly was funny had not revealed itself.

'Oh, here you go again, I'm just the worst, your father is a saint, never wronged anyone in his life, and as usual I have to be the enemy.' Rachel's voice cracked. 'I don't understand what I have done to you to deserve this. For you to think this was all my fault.'

Poppy finished her glass of wine. She was drunk and petulant. As usual. 'You're so selfish; everything is about you – you're not the victim here.'

Between Rachel and Poppy, Phinn snorted. Beautiful, calm, take-no-sides Phinn. Phinn, who was legendary for vacating the premises so thoroughly during one argument between Rachel and George that they had found him in a garden two houses away, cowering under a bush, hours after the fight was over. Phinn snorted, then laughed.

'Do you ever listen to yourself, Poppy? You have zero capacity for self-reflection. You're the heavyweight fucking champion of self-absorption. What do you mean Mum always has to be the victim? You're the one picking a screaming match at Claudia's wedding dinner after spending the entire thing pouting into your wine glass while you become more obnoxious – if possible – with each passing hour. Grow the fuck up.'

'Hey, hey,' Mick said helplessly. 'It's okay, kids, we can leave it at that.' Mary put a hand on his knee to quieten him. Not only was it hopeless, but also she was delighted, enjoying the spectacle of her sister's children at their most hideous and vulnerable. There was nothing like her sister's perceived parental failings to cheer her so. Having no children herself, she of course didn't know that you don't get to choose how they turn out. Parenting is almost a myth – so many come into the world with their personalities seemingly fully formed, and from there any parenting efforts are constantly interrupted and derailed by friends, shopkeepers, aunts, nanas, even siblings. Particularly siblings. People's precious babies are open and susceptible to corruption from outside sources almost from the minute the midwife hands the baby to the panting and exhausted mother.

Poppy, who had temporarily been stunned into silence by her docile brother's intervention, was standing at the end of the table.

'Finally you speak, after all these years? All these years of being too pathetic to take a side? Do you want Mum to come and hold your hand now? You've always been such a mum's boy. You think it makes up for being the stupidest out of all of us and the most boring. Well, you're still not Mum's favourite and – even if you were – it would not make up for the severe lack of personality.'

Phinn just looked away, while Mick was the only one who made any attempt at remedy. 'Poppy, come on now,' he whispered.

'Just let her ruin dinner; it wouldn't be dinner if she didn't ruin it,' Dylan finally spat. If Phinn was a wild card in the dinner table argument, then a particle microscope would have been needed to pick out the probability of Dylan getting involved. And yet, here he was. Claudia turned to Nora, elbowing her pleadingly in the side. She desperately needed her to do something, to remind the family they were not just around family, to remind them there were reasons to be on their best behaviour, but Nora was nodding along to whichever music was playing dimly over the speakers while the waitress stood three feet away in awe.

Dylan's words had been delivered like a slap. Even Mary didn't seem to get any thrill out of them; instead shame settled on her face, making itself at home with the other Carter siblings.

Dylan stood up. 'Your sister is only here because of you. She's only doing all of this because of you. She never wanted any of this: not the wedding, not to be here, not the party, and certainly not the guilt trips. Can't you just settle down for one weekend? Just looking at you makes her tits itch at the moment, and she's still here.'

Dylan was telling the truth, but aged wounds are not made to withstand the truth. The sneaking suspicion your family is making fun of you behind your back; the nagging feeling that perhaps your father actually thinks you're quite boring as a person; your secret acknowledgement your sister is more entertaining, cleverer than you, doesn't actually need you; the fear that the only people who know you in your guts don't actually like you. All of these conflicts arise from wounds carefully cultivated throughout your childhood. Throwaway remarks nobody remembers. The time when you were thirteen and played kiss, marry, kill with your siblings and each of them chose to kiss or marry each other while one by one saying you would be the one they would kill. It all remains. It's buried deep but always within yourself you carry every eye roll, every whispered criticism, every bit of the fuel for your secret and total belief that you are not good enough.

It never goes away. Usually the only people able to rake over this are the people who were there for the damage in the first place, but occasionally somebody who should know better finds the bit that aches.

Poppy looked from Dylan to Phinn to Zoe, who had managed to escape most of the wrath by refusing to surrender to the desperate pull of her siblings. Poppy threw her glass down and, shaking, turned on her heel and stomped out of the restaurant. Dylan looked down at Claudia who was leaning across her plate, staring at the table, while only the shake of her shoulders gave away her sobs. Torn between the daughter who didn't deserve this and the daughter who was devastated, Rachel chose the latter and pushed her chair out to chase after Poppy.

∽

Dylan's father watched Rachel's retreating figure, a mild look of appreciation across his face. 'I think,' he said finally, 'I think I will have a Scotch on the rocks and perhaps toast the fact I didn't have any daughters.'

Zoe got up slowly, wary of any sudden movements, even after Poppy had left. Nora hiccupped.

'Hey, Zoe's going to leave just as stuff gets too much again.' Nora smiled sunnily in Zoe's direction as Claudia grabbed her leg under the table and squeezed it as violently as she could without being obvious. Nora just brushed the hand from her leg. 'Oh, you're always complaining about your family anyway, Claudia. How many times have you told me you're not coming back here again?'

Zoe paused as she was starting to turn away. She opened her mouth but decided against it and walked towards the doors through which her mother had exited a few minutes earlier. Phinn looked across at his sister with hurt but, returning to form, didn't say anything.

Claudia hesitated, but so briefly it was detectable only to Dylan. Standing up, she put her hand on Nora and Dylan's shoulders. 'Stay here,' she said firmly, while looking directly at Mary. She walked around the table and nodded at Phinn.

'Oh man,' he muttered, throwing his napkin on the table. He stood up and followed his sister through the doors.

∽

Claudia and Phinn heard Poppy before they saw her. Around the corner of the entrance, in the car park, her voice floated back to them. Or rather screeched back to them.

'You've always been selfish; you only ever thought of yourself and then Claudia and then maybe the rest of us. It has always been about you.'

Poppy's words were slightly slurred. Claudia had not realised how much wine she had drunk. Then it occurred to her that the same went for her mother as her voice rushed around the corner too.

'*I'm* selfish! I gave up everything for you! You think I wanted to be in this town, ever? You think I wanted to do the job I did?

You think you know everything that happened to me? You're a selfish little bitch who I spoiled too much.'

Phinn and Claudia sped up their steps and turned the corner to see Zoe rubbing Rachel's arm, almost pleading. 'Come on, Mum, I can take her home, just go back inside.' Rachel snatched her arm away as Poppy started yelling again.

'You have no idea what is going on in my life because you have never thought to ask, and I come home and have to keep being treated as some kind of invalid, as stupider than a baby. I don't need your permission for anything; the only time you ever notice me is when you think I should be asking for permission.'

Rachel pushed Zoe to the side and grabbed her youngest daughter by the shoulders, squeezing them hard as she finally screamed.

'I REGRET EVER HAVING YOU.'

The siblings froze as the words reverberated between them. One can always suspect, or even just half suspect, that perhaps their existence isn't the greatest thing to ever happen to their mother. Perhaps she could have been smarter, richer, prettier, happier if you'd never existed. But the home is designed – for the lucky ones – to quash any of those notions. Popular culture is designed to put motherhood on an impossible pedestal and there is little to no evidence anywhere that women ever regret having children.

But, they must. Sometimes, they must. Something as simple as the law of averages says they must. Children may suspect it, but it is rare as snow on the Great Barrier Reef to actually hear it. Especially from a mother who still loves you.

Phinn looked at Claudia who looked at Zoe, who was the only one who could bear to look at Poppy. Poppy stood defeated in her ill-fitting dress. Her shoulders slumped; she held her head in her hands desperately. Rachel stood panting and staring at her daughter, who finally met her eyes. Poppy's eyes went cold as she screamed and rushed at Rachel with her hands outstretched. For a moment Zoe thought Poppy was going to hug their mother, then she thought she was going to hit her. Poppy rushed at Rachel and with the full force of her body shoved her. Family legend would speculate on the reason for the shove. There could be thirty-four different viable reasons for the shove: she could have been shoving her out of the way to run away, she could have just had a physical reaction, she could have just wanted to touch her mother but hate her at the same time. Poppy never said why she pushed their mother.

All four of Rachel's offspring – the womb-mates, the babies she had nursed in her insides between her bladder and liver, and torn herself open again and again and again and again to bring them into the big wide world – watched in horror as Rachel stumbled backwards and in her stupid shoes lost her footing, her ankle falling away while the rest of her followed backwards. It was likely a combination of shock and hurt and wine that made Rachel fall the way she did, and a combination of wine and hurt and shock that stopped any of her children from reaching out to try to catch her.

She fell slowly and then all at once and the silence was broken by the crack of her head against the corner of the gutter.

Rachel went limp.

Claudia was the first to scream. Then Zoe screamed. Then Phinn screamed. And they were all screaming. Poppy, the drunkest, was also the one who had done a first-aid course as part of the requirements for one of her legion of jobs.

'Don't touch her! Don't touch her!'

'What the fuck, Poppy?' Claudia yelled, kneeling on the ground. '*You* don't touch her!'

'No! I mean it. If she's hurt her neck you shouldn't touch her.'

Claudia rocked back on her heels and sat on the ground, looking to her older sister for guidance. Zoe was still standing with her hands over her mouth, gaping at their mother. She looked at Phinn and then Poppy.

'I don't know but it makes sense – who has their phone? We need an ambulance.'

Phinn touched his back pockets while Poppy patted her sides. They had all left their phones inside. 'I'll get them,' Phinn said, gratefully stepping back.

'No.'

Phinn stopped mid-step and looked back to see who had spoken. His sisters were now crouched around their mother and he saw Rachel's hand grabbing Claudia's.

'No,' she said again, her voice raspy and thin. Phinn stepped off the footpath and stood next to Rachel's shoulder. Her hair was fanned around her head, and her lips – along with the rest of her face – were drained of colour but her eyes were open.

'Ma! What do we do?' he said.

'Water,' she whispered. 'Don't tell anyone.' All of her effort went into the last three words while Claudia stroked her head and rolled her eyes at the command.

'What people think is incredibly important right now.' Zoe couldn't help herself.

Phinn nodded at his mother. 'I won't tell anyone.' And he turned and ran inside.

'Sorry Mum, sorry Mum, sorry Mum,' Poppy was muttering on the other side of Rachel while Zoe and Claudia glared at her. Rachel grabbed her hand and tried to sit up but immediately realised it was too ambitious and lay down again.

'Don't try anything, Mum,' Zoe murmured, 'it's a concussion.'

Claudia kept anxiously stroking Rachel's head. 'How do you know it's a concussion?' she asked her older sister.

Zoe allowed herself a smile. 'It's pretty basic; what else would it be? She can move, she can talk, she's completely out of it, she hit her head – she's concussed.'

Claudia felt her sides for her phone but realised again it wasn't with her.

'Don't google it. It'll say she's going into seizure and has cancer,' Zoe said, trying to sound reassuring. Poppy rocked on her heels and eased back so she was sitting on the other side of Rachel, the movement reasserting her briefly forgotten presence with her sisters.

'You should get out of here. You need to leave. Look what you did to Mum,' Claudia said sharply.

'She's my mum too,' Poppy said, seemingly groping for a way to somehow defend herself.

'Go away,' Claudia said again.

'Don't,' Rachel whispered, 'it's not her fault.'

Zoe snorted. 'It's absolutely her fault.' But she nudged Claudia; her eyes were pleading.

'Be nice to your sister,' Rachel croaked as Phinn reappeared with a bottle of water. He briefly relayed the scene inside, explaining how he'd managed to give the impression they were in some kind of family conference and shouldn't be disturbed. Tenderly, he lifted Rachel's head from the ground and held the water to her mouth so she could drink. She managed a sip and then turned her head away, signalling enough.

Somehow the four of them were going to have to get her home without anyone knowing her youngest daughter had ever so briefly knocked her out. The siblings huddled closer to her and in the shadows of the streetlight attempted to devise a plan. The oldest three did most of the devising, the youngest having been unofficially banned from any attempt at contribution.

'We could borrow Mick's car, or maybe Dylan's parents'.'

'Who here is under the alcohol limit?'

'Nobody.'

'We could let Mick in on this and get him to drive us.'

Rachel grunted in protest.

'We could Uber.'

'Mate, this town has not entered 2003 yet, let alone 2017.'

'We could taxi.'

'Mum knows all the taxi drivers; she won't let us.'

'This is one curly evening.'

'We could ask Leah.'

Poppy had waited until her siblings could see all avenues were exhausted before she broke her self-imposed embargo (silly for her brother and sisters to even entertain the thought they had imposed it). Claudia began to shut it down but was stopped by the fact it was the closest thing to a legitimate course of action any of them had. Phinn looked down at Rachel, who did not register any protest.

'Should we be calling an ambulance instead?' he ventured.

Rachel gingerly shook her head. 'I'm fine. God isn't letting me die tonight – I've said too many prayers,' she whispered.

Claudia sighed from deep in her bones and asked her mother again if there was not a single person inside they could ask to take her home. But Rachel was resolute. And almost everyone inside was drunk. Poppy grabbed Rachel's wrist and examined her watch. 'We've been out here for forty minutes.'

'Everyone was ordering dessert when I got the water,' Phinn offered.

Despite herself, Claudia laughed. Their guests ate dessert while outside they had come to terms with their mother's death and resurrection and then her pride. Standing up, Poppy made the decision for everyone and left them crouched in the gutter while she went to get her phone and call Leah. 'As usual, the only goddamn one who can make a decision,' she said as she walked away. That it was her fault their mother was lying in a car park with a head injury didn't seem to occur to her.

❧

Dylan was trying to decide whether he would make it worse or better if he went outside. On the one hand all of the siblings had been gone forty minutes with their mother; on the other it was Rachel out there with all of her children.

He smiled tightly at his father, trying to pre-warn him against any jokes about in-laws and outlaws. But if Jerome was finding any of the behaviour odd, being on his best behaviour was preventing him from saying anything.

Nora turned to him and smiled lopsidedly. 'Maybe they're all just entranced by Tinder!'

Dylan frowned. 'What?'

Nora, who had already consumed about eight more 'one mores' than she should've, did not quite grasp the enormity of what she had just said. She giggled.

'Well, you know, it can be quite addictive.' She looked around the table at the polite conversations everyone else was trying to immerse themselves in. 'We only had a look the other night and it turned into two hours.'

Dylan's face went stern. 'Who's we?'

Nora's brain finally caught up to her and, after a few seconds' delay, her eyes widened and she clapped her hand over her mouth.

'Nora. Who. Is. We?'

'It was just a lark, me and Claudia, having a lark. It was nothing – I was just showing her the app dating world.'

Dylan looked down at the seat between them. On it sat Claudia's bright green purse, decorated with ostentatious flower brooches in purples and reds. He glanced back at Nora who still sat with her hand over her mouth, but her wide-eyed stare had turned to terror as she clocked Claudia's purse at the same time. Dylan flipped it open and reached in, bringing out Claudia's diamanté-covered phone. He typed in the numbers of Rachel's birthday and flicked across the screens until he realised he didn't actually know what the Tinder icon looked like. He scowled and opened the search bar; the app appeared before he had even typed in the N.

Dylan did not even consider if he wanted to open it: driven by a quiet rage that usually lay dormant, he stumbled through the app until he found the inbox.

Nora was quietly pleading with him, 'Don't open it, it really was nothing, we were just looking at it, there's nothing on there, it doesn't mean anything,' her begging interrupted when she finally saw that Dylan wasn't merely swiping through. He was reading. Reading when there was not supposed to be anything to read. She leaned over for a better look at the screen but Dylan pulled back so that only he could see it.

There were at least seventy messages. Most of them were unopened and were simple one- or two-word introductions from the men, but he could see at least a couple that were more than that.

He opened one from a David. His last message was unanswered from Claudia and simply said, 'I'll show you mine if you show me yours', but before that was a stream of mundane questions, answered loquaciously by Claudia.

The first concert she had ever been to.

The last Coen brothers movie she'd watched.

The best Spice Girl.

It was the dullness of the exchanges that made it even more offensive. Dylan could feel something deep inside him crack open. He had an impulse to do something violent and memorable: he wanted to punch a wall; he wanted to punch someone's face. He felt all that made him happy in the world falling away, an entire future rearranged beyond recognition.

Dylan was brought back to the room by Mary's roar; he looked up to find Mary, Mick, Jerome and Yvonne smiling at him expectantly.

'Sorry, what . . . ?' A long-vanquished stutter almost returning.

'I was just saying, you proved the old proverb right about bad beginnings making good endings – remember when you refused to eat anything but carrots and chocolate eggs for two years?' his father said.

Dylan looked down at Claudia's phone again and locked it, shoving it back into her purse without looking. He took a deep breath and smiled.

'And then I changed so much I had trained myself to eat olives and chillies by the time I was twelve!'

Chapter 36

The most terrifying things in the world mostly revolve around your children and your parents. There's nowhere to hide from your children. If you have them you have to accept you leave yourself completely exposed. Even with a partner you can obscure the most unsavoury aspects of yourself; sometimes the other just won't notice them, or other times they are simply too consumed by their love for you, their luck at finding you, to really care.

But children rarely feel lucky that you are their parent. There are no alternatives to consider. Not only do they see you clear-eyed, but also there is no way you can hide from them. Every hypocrisy, the way you talk to waitresses, how much work you actually do in the home, how often you are angry, how often you repeat the same joke, the fact you use packet mix for gravy, how you choose to spend a spare hour, how long you lay in bed in the morning, the worst smell you leave in the bathroom, how you treat the friends you complain about the most in private, how long you spend on Facebook – your children see it all. You cannot present a more glittering, a more palatable, a more *together* version of yourself to your children.

Alternatively, the most terrifying thing that can happen to you is seeing a parent weakened. Being essential to them. After relying on them for so long, never questioning their existence, having a central tenet of faith that not only will they always be there, but that they will always care.

Zoe and Claudia were both considering this – unbeknownst to each other – as they carried Rachel to Leah's waiting car. Rachel was doing a half imitation of walking, but her stagger relied on a daughter on each side holding her up as they guided her to the red Nissan Pulsar, sitting with its lights dimmed, like a drug dealer waiting for a client, just around the corner from the bright entrance to the restaurant.

Poppy walked ahead of them and leaned through the passenger window to exchange hushed words with Leah. It looked intense but the conversation could be boiled down to: 'Hey. Hey. Thanks for doing this. What happened? Never mind. I will tell you later.'

Poppy opened the back door and her sisters eased their mother into the back seat before each sat on either side of her. 'Hello Leah!' Claudia said brightly. She couldn't help herself; even in times of chaos she tried to put on her best face for strangers.

Poppy hesitated and opened the passenger door, manoeuvring into the front seat. She looked up to see her brother standing at the door, relieved. 'No room for me,' he said. 'I'll go back inside.' The awkwardness of providing an explanation for a tipsy and prying audience was infinitely preferable to a car trip with his concussed mother, angry sisters and a possible lover.

The group sat in silence as Leah put the car into first gear and carefully pulled onto the road. 'Thanks, sweetie,' Rachel muttered, resting her head on Zoe.

They moved through the night past the chicken shop Claudia had once thrown up in when underage and drunk; the café where Phinn had made terrible coffee on Saturdays during high school; the tree they used to sit in smoking on Friday nights.

Claudia thought about her wedding, the next day. She thought about the future mapped out for her; the love of a good man; how exhausting excitement actually was.

Poppy thought about how close Leah was sitting next to her.

Rachel thought about her headache.

Zoe thought she shouldn't have come home.

Their considerations were punctured by Leah delicately turning into Rachel's driveway, her duty done. It took longer to get Rachel out of the car than the entire drive had taken, but finally Zoe and Claudia had their mother balanced between them.

'Should we be putting you to bed?' Claudia asked anxiously as she shuffled forward.

'I told you,' Rachel was barely audible, 'I'm not dying tonight.'

Poppy watched them move towards the front door, and turned to Leah. She leaned over and quickly kissed her.

'Thank you. I'll see you later.'

She opened the door and self-consciously followed her sisters and their mother inside without looking back. Once the door was closed she heard Leah's wheels reverse out of the driveway and the motor fade down the street.

Without speaking, the sisters undressed their mother like a doll, lifting her arms for her while they pulled her dress over her head and rolling her stockings down her legs. Startled, they all noticed her bikini line had been waxed. They had grown up with a mother who had embarrassing dark tufts exploding outside of either side of her swimwear. Maybe we don't know everything about our mothers. But they didn't say anything to each other. They lay Rachel on her back and kissed her forehead. Just as they were turning to leave the room, she beckoned. Claudia, Zoe and Poppy looked at each other and bent over their mother.

'Be nice to your sister,' she whispered.

They weren't completely sure which one she meant.

∽

Later, after the sisters had gone to different rooms with no explanation, too tired to lay any more blame for the night, Poppy crept into her mother's room wearing the same faded pink LCD Soundsystem fan club T-shirt she had worn to bed when she was fifteen. She walked around the bed and climbed under the blanket next to Rachel.

She lay in the dark and listened to her mother breathing.

Chapter 37

Claudia was already asleep when Zoe flung her door open.

'Claudie! Claudia!' she shout-whispered. She took two steps in and saw the lump that was her sister underneath the doona, even her head obscured. She put her hand on the lump and shook it. 'Claudia! You need to wake up.'

Claudia groaned and rustled under the doona, revealing her face but still refusing to open her eyes.

'Claudia, it's Nora.'

Claudia sat bolt upright. 'Nora? What?'

Zoe held up her phone. 'Dylan just rang. Nora is really sick at the restaurant; the others had gone home and he found her vomiting near some bushes.'

'She what?'

'Don't tell anyone but ... her and Tom broke up.'

'Wait, what? Nora is throwing up and Tom and her broke up?'

'She didn't want you to find out during this week but her and Tom broke up just before she came here. Don't tell her I told you that, though – nobody is supposed to know.'

Claudia stood up and grabbed a pair of shorts to put on under her makeshift pyjama top. She pulled her phone from the charger and was greeted with a blank screen, no notifications. She wondered why Nora hadn't tried to call for help.

She did not wonder why Dylan had called Zoe.

Shoving her feet into her Nikes, she grabbed Zoe's arms to steady herself and then stood up properly to meet her eye. Something was not right. She felt the mechanics of an emotional demotion as she grasped the meaning of it being Zoe who had burst into her room and not her ringtone direct from the scene.

'Why did Nora tell you about the break-up and not me?'

Zoe shrugged Claudia's hand off her in irritation. 'Let's stick to things that actually matter.'

The sisters didn't bother to put up a pretence of quietness as they rushed out of the house. Rachel would not be waking up for a while, and neither of them cared if Poppy was disturbed. In fact, it would have given them both an ounce of pleasure to disturb her.

Zoe drove as Claudia texted Dylan to say they were on their way and to ask for a condition update.

'Still breathing. Still vomiting,' came the reply.

As Zoe pulled into the restaurant's street she could see Dylan's shoulders outlined by a streetlight as he bent over, seemingly to pat a petrified dog. Zoe swung the car to the left and then reversed back so they were parked next to the two figures. As

Claudia got out of the car she could hear Dylan muttering in soothing tones.

'You're okay, it's okay, nobody thinks anything.'

His sentences were punctuated by sobs as Nora, on all fours, heaved her shoulders back and retched. Claudia kneeled down beside her and started rubbing her back as she looked up at Dylan, who eased his hand from between her shoulders where he had been patting her.

'She's pretty sick,' he finally said.

Claudia instinctively leaned over and kissed Nora above her ear. 'It's okay, I'm here.'

Nora sobbed again. 'I can't do this.'

'Can't do what?'

Dylan answered for her. 'She's been saying that for half an hour; I think she means she can't keep feeling this sick.'

'Jesus,' Zoe interjected. 'She hasn't stopped vomiting for half an hour? How long was she out here before you found her?'

Nora's gold dress had ridden up at the back, revealing her tummy-tightening underwear, and her hair was matted with vomit. Zoe pulled a hair tie from her own head and clumsily gathered Nora's hair in her hands, pulling it back from her face to secure it. Dylan crouched on his haunches. 'We left pretty soon after you guys had gone. Dad picked up the bill. I think Nora was there at the end; she knocked over a full glass of champagne and then asked for another one.' He hesitated and looked at Nora with pity. 'They wouldn't let her have one.'

Nora heaved again but this time nothing came up and she simply spat. Claudia kept rubbing her back while Zoe tried to objectively assess the situation. 'I don't think we need to take her to the hospital.'

Claudia snorted. 'This is the second time tonight we are considering such action.'

Dylan looked confused but Zoe ignored both of them.

'She's still conscious, the vomiting seems to have slowed, I think we can get her to bed, and if she can keep down water then she can just recover at the hotel.'

Nora attempted to contribute to the plan but could only muster another sob. Claudia leaned forward to look her in the face. Nora's lipstick was smudged across her lips and her eyeliner had almost been wiped away, leaving black splotches from her cheeks to her hairline. She met Claudia's gaze and closed her eyes before hanging her head, conceding that the effort was just too great to keep it upright. Claudia put her lips to her ear again.

'It's okay, I'll look after you.'

$$\sim\!\!\infty\!\!\sim$$

True to her word it was Claudia who stayed in the hotel room with Nora. Dylan was out of the question, and the embarrassment at waking up to Zoe in her space would've been too traumatic for Nora. After Dylan and Zoe had helped her to get Nora into the room and left, Claudia had spent minutes that felt like days tugging at the tight dress, coaxing Nora to keep her arms over her head as she eased it off. She put Nora under the shower and filled up a glass of water for her to drink out of while she sat on the floor, unable even to stand while trying to wash away the night.

Claudia turned off the water and gathered Nora in a towel, helping her to the bed without bothering to find new underwear or a nightgown. Once she was lying down, Claudia pulled up the blanket and sat on the floor to keep watch over her friend. Nora opened her eyes.

'I told Dylan,' she whispered, her throat hoarse and raw from the evening's turn of events.

'Told Dylan what?'

Nora groaned. 'Tinder.'

Then she rolled over and softly began to snore.

'Jesus Christ, between this and telling Zoe about Tom, it's a confidentiality spree,' she said, more to herself than her semi-unconscious friend. Then the panic started to rise. Dylan knew about Tinder. What exactly did he know about Tinder? Just that she'd downloaded it? She had left her phone next to him all night.

Nora would not only be wrought with the hangover of nausea and aches in the morning, she was definitely heading for The Fear. The physical hangover is small time compared to The Fear, a cringe-fest of emotional paralysis as all the actions from the night before are slowly recalled.

Claudia already knew this was not the end of the friendship but the thought would surely be with Nora once she sobered up. If Claudia was going to rage at anyone, it was going to have to be herself. She'd had a lifetime of lessons in forgiving and not-quite-forgetting, courtesy of her sisters.

Chapter 38

Claudia rolled over, raising her arm before it landed with a thud on the empty space next to her. She sat bolt upright. The empty space next to her? In a moment she got her bearings. She wasn't at home. Any of her homes. She was on the floor of a beige motel room with Nora in a bed snoring next to her. She had had no intention of falling asleep. She stood up and walked out of the motel room. It would take her thirty-five minutes to walk to Rachel's house but she needed the time. She was in no rush to break Dylan's heart.

The sky was indigo as light from the imminent sunrise began to creep through the shadows.

'I'm supposed to get married today,' she said to a few tree branches full of leaves as she started down the street. 'All I need is a husband.'

She was still wearing her pyjama T-shirt and shorts from the night before and she could feel her make-up caked on, streaked with the oil from her skin. She rubbed her eyes and inspected the impressive amount of eye shadow that had stayed put through the drama.

She wouldn't have minded if the walk had taken a couple of days. Weeks, months even.

Instead she was at the front door long before she wanted to be.

She felt along the ridge above it and took down the spare key, opening the door just enough that she could sneak in but not so far so that it squeaked. She squeezed through the gap and a sound as familiar as her fingernails greeted her. Dylan's breathing.

In the living room she found him shirtless and still in his trousers from the dinner, sleeping softly in a barely contained position on the couch. Claudia kneeled beside him and rested her forehead on his shoulder, kissing it gently as he stirred awake.

Dylan looked at her groggily and rolled onto his side, reaching his arm out towards her. She winced as he gently started stroking her hair.

'I really wanted to marry you,' he finally said.

'I know.'

Dylan began to quietly weep. Claudia averted her eyes, but beyond the guilt found herself strangely unmoved.

'Don't you kind of want this too? Haven't you felt something missing?' she finally offered.

'No.'

'I'll pay back my half of the money we put in.'

'No you won't.'

'I guess it's a good thing we didn't have enough money to book a honeymoon.'

'For you, yes.'

'You'll be okay.'

'I hope you will be.'

Acknowledgements

Thank you Séamus, Anna and Alice for being born. All characters are fictional.

Thank you to all of my friends who have inspired and motivated me over the years with sparkling and tough conversations, including but not limited to Ricky Morton, Candice Gallimore, Kylie Dunn, Shannon Molloy, Katherine Feeney, Tulsi Combe and Maria Lewis. Thank you in particular to my early readers Georgia Waters and Veronica Foulkes. I also owe a deep gratitude to Australia's premier group chat.

To Christopher and Philomena Jabour – nobody says it enough – you are wonderful parents.

My agent Jeanne Ryckmans seemed to make magic happen, and Angela Meyer took my draft and made it a book. I am also indebted to Clive Hebard and Penny Isaac who were the midwives at the end; and the talented Alissa Dinallo for her striking cover design.

Helen Garner allowed a few of her devastating sentences to be used in this book, for which I am deeply grateful.

And finally, to my husband, who was the first person I gave this book to and still hasn't finished reading it but who makes me cleverer and funnier every day; and to my son, who did absolutely nothing, but whom I feel the need to acknowledge nonetheless.

Want to read
NEW BOOKS
before anyone else?

Like getting
FREE BOOKS?

Enjoy sharing your
OPINIONS?

Discover
READERS FIRST

Read. Love. Share.

Sign up today to win your first free book:
readersfirst.co.uk